My Lovely Daughter

R.P. BOLTON

ONE PLACE. MANY STORIES

HQ
An imprint of HarperCollins*Publishers* Ltd
1 London Bridge Street
London SE1 9GF

www.harpercollins.co.uk

HarperCollins*Publishers*
1st Floor, Watermarque Building, Ringsend Road
Dublin 4, Ireland

This paperback edition 2022

1
First published in Great Britain by
HQ, an imprint of HarperCollins*Publishers* Ltd 2022

ISBN: 9780008503802

Now, Sunday

Annie stopped and stared at the text.

The dog stopped too, ears pricked and sensitive nose twitching on high alert. Then a squirrel broke cover up ahead and Smudge sprang forward in an explosion of leaves.

'Leave the poor thing alone!' Izzy shouted, her jacket a flash of red between the trees. Twigs snapped and popped like tiny gunshots under her thudding trainers.

'Watch where you're going,' Annie called automatically.

The muscles in her legs trembled and she steadied herself against the trunk of a huge, fallen tree, a casualty of the fierce storms that had torn through the woods a few weeks earlier. Its exposed roots, ripped from the ground, hung in a confused, tangled clump.

She picked leafy debris off her sleeve. There had been nothing out of the ordinary about this morning. *Nothing.* Up at seven to let the dog out in the garden. Headlines on the radio with a mug of tea. A stroll through the woods behind the house with Izzy. Casual conversation about school, dog and what to have for breakfast.

And then *ping*.

A mistake. Had to be. Without her glasses, she had misread the message. That was it.

She held the screen close to her nose. The stark black letters didn't change.

Hello, Annabel.
Happy Mother's Day?

A few metres ahead, the terrified squirrel shinned up a pine tree, and Smudge, yelping wildly, scrabbled her front paws against the trunk.

'Bad girl,' Izzy admonished affectionately. 'You're a bad, bad girl.'

A cloud drifted over the sun, and the accompanying chill breeze stirred the trees to whispers. But that wasn't why goose bumps rippled up Annie's arms.

'Is that from Liam?' Izzy said, gesturing at the phone. The dog's lead was slung round her neck like a thin fluorescent scarf. One tug, and it slithered off. There was a click as she clipped it to the collar. 'Mum?'

Annie fiddled with the metal tag on her zip, careful not to let her voice give her away.

'Yes. Liam. Reminding me about dinner on Tuesday. Anyway, come on. I want that breakfast you promised me.'

What she actually wanted was to rewind to the minute before the message pinged. Or to hurl the mobile into the tangled undergrowth and pretend it didn't exist. But what she did was jam the phone deep in her jeans pocket and steady her legs enough to walk.

And while her body dodged grasping branches and hazardous tree roots, her mind split in two. One half dealt appropriately with Izzy chatting about overfishing or the evils of hunting or some pet topic while the other scrabbled to make sense of the text.

Ask anyone and they would say she was Annie Smith. Mother

2

of Isabel. Late forties. Resident of Uppermoss. Veterinary nurse. Excellent mother.

And she *was* Annie Smith.

She hadn't been Annabel for years.

Back at the cottage, Izzy cracked an egg into a pan of boiling water and dropped two slices of bread into the toaster. Annie cut the top off a dog food pouch and Smudge, alerted by the snip of scissors, skittered across the tiles.

'Watch you don't knock that handle, Iz,' Annie said, squeezing the jellied chunks into the dog's bowl.

When she bent to put the food on the floor, the phone jabbed through her jeans. She shoved it behind the fruit bowl on the worktop, half hidden from view.

Warm toast smells filled the kitchen. *Their* kitchen. Its walls decorated with photos of various stages in Izzy's life. A wonky clay bowl made in Year Six on the windowsill. A sack of dog biscuits by the back door. It would never grace the pages of an interior design magazine, but this space overflowing with the flotsam of everyday life was their fortress.

Izzy opened the fridge door, careful not to dislodge the layer of coupons, receipts, photos that covered its surface. Above her, strands of cobweb hung like grey bunting, and a thin crack in the plaster ran down to the worktop where two discarded eggshells glistened in a viscous pool.

Annie nibbled the skin around her thumb, teasing a tattered strip with her teeth. Could the text be a marketing thing? A scam?

No.

She had been Annie Smith for years. The deed poll certificate tucked safely away from prying eyes proved it. And anyway, the only person who had ever called her by her full name was Oliver, and she hadn't heard a peep from him since the divorce.

One last tug, a sharp sting and the paper-thin strip of skin tore away.

The toast popped up. Izzy fished about in the pan with a slotted spoon, pinched a sprig of parsley from the pot on the windowsill and set the plate down with a flourish.

'Mother's Day brunch is served!'

White liquid dribbled from the egg, spilling over the toast in a slobbery trail. Her appetite withered.

'Thanks, love,' she managed to say as she pulled out a chair. 'Looks delicious.'

'And that's not all.' Izzy beamed, oblivious to the tremble in her mum's voice. She held out a shiny silver gift bag that didn't quite contain the square canvas inside. 'Happy Mother's Day!'

The picture instantly transported her back to last summer. Even blown up to A4, the sliver of Norfolk sky retained that improbably perfect blue and, just out of shot, was the crabbing bucket and net that smelled of low tide. More memories crowded in: the slap of water on fibreglass hulls. Salty air. Gulls circling in a cloudless sky.

People had milled around the Wells seafront, clutching ice creams or eating fish and chips, but in the photo it was just the two of them. Mother and daughter, cheeks squashed together. Her arm wrapped around Izzy like a shield. Those beautiful hazel eyes crinkled against the glare while her own were hidden behind huge sunglasses. Their identical dark shiny curls intertwined, blurring where Annie ended and Izzy began.

Just the two of them. Safe.

She'd always been so, so careful. Her expression must have betrayed her unease because the smile dropped from Izzy's face.

'Don't you like it?'

At thirteen, she was already a head taller (how did that happen?) but she could never be too big for a hug. Annie squeezed her tightly, burying her nose in familiar coconut-scented curls.

'I love it,' she said fiercely. 'I love *you*. God, so, so much.'

Gasping, Izzy extricated herself. 'Mum, I can't breathe. Eat it up before Smudge steals it.'

Annie busied herself straightening the faded cushion pad. 'Have you switched the hob off?'

In reply, Izzy pointed at the dial set to zero on the cooker then propped the smiling picture of the two of them next to the fruit bowl, next to the phone. She selected a tangerine, leaned her elbows against the sink and, with extreme concentration, dug her thumbnail into the thick orange peel.

The dog slunk past, side-eyeing Annie as she pierced the poached egg with her fork, and the yolk swelled then bled out in a slow-moving ooze. She swallowed a surge of acid.

Now the initial shock of the text had sunk in, a knot of fear gathered behind her breastbone. The slippery egg sliding down nearly made her gag, but she chewed and swallowed, forcing her body to accept food it didn't want.

How could this have happened?

Well, that was obvious: she hadn't been as careful as she thought.

The vigilance chromosome was deeply embedded in her maternal DNA. Sharp things, hot things … these everyday hazards were easy to control. What weapons did parents have against dangers that lurked a click away? Izzy was growing up fast and already chafing at the armoury of parental controls, the Family Safe app, the social media restrictions. And yet, despite all that pre-emptive worrying, the push-and-pull of tested boundaries, it was *her own phone* that had let danger enter their home. She tore off a piece of kitchen roll, folded it and quickly pressed it to her eyes.

The phone buzzed against the worktop and Izzy, who was dropping bits of peel in the pedal bin, reached for it.

Annie shoved her chair back. The cutlery clattered to the plate. 'Don't touch that!'

'Er, *okaaay.*' Izzy held both palms in the air and slid her back along the worktop edge, eyebrows raised.

But thank god, it was only *Samara Khan* that pulsed on the screen.

An out-of-hours call from her boss usually made Annie's heart sink. Not today.

'Hi, what's up?'

The relief was short-lived. Stress permeated Samara's voice. 'I'm really sorry: I know it's Mother's Day, but can you get the black bag from the office and bring it to the Frasers' farm?'

'Will do,' she said, lowering the volume even though Izzy had stalked into the lounge out of earshot. 'What's happened?'

'Pony caught his foot in a loose drain in the yard. Hope it won't come to that, but it doesn't look good.'

'Shit. On my way,' she said.

After over a decade as office manager and vet nurse, she knew 'bring the black bag' meant the euthanasia kit, which was a nightmare under any circumstances, but Lucy Fraser was Izzy's best friend. And Lucy's pony, Caspar, occupied almost as much space in Izzy's heart as Smudge.

There was a voicemail from one of their farming clients, trying to get hold of Sam. And then another straight after, saying it was okay, he'd spoken to her. Her number doubled as the surgery's second emergency contact, but it was rare to have two call-outs on the same day. Small animals tended to be bundled into their owners' cars and taken to the animal hospital.

Another message icon appeared, triggering a palpitating thump of her heart, but this time the text really *was* from Liam.

Hope you're being spoilt rotten for Mother's Day. Looking forward to Tuesday.

Despite everything, her lip twitched upwards as she replied en route to the lounge.

Me too.

Izzy reclined on their ancient saggy sofa, balancing her laptop across her thighs. On-screen, a swan built a plastic nest. Scraps of carrier bags woven with faded food wrappers into the sad facsimile of a home.

'Sorry,' Annie said. 'Sam has an emergency. Will you be okay on your own?'

Keeping one eye on YouTube, Izzy half-turned towards her. 'Yep.'

'Any problems, ring me straightaway.'

'Okay.'

Smudge curled like a soft black cushion, not even stirring when Izzy fussed her velvety ears. Beautiful girl and four-legged friend in an Instagram-worthy moment. She hesitated. She should tell Samara she couldn't make it after all …

'No, not fair,' she muttered.

'What?' Izzy said, re-glued to the screen.

Annie hooked her fingers under Izzy's headphones and slid them to the back of her neck.

'Nothing. I meant don't answer the door while I'm out. And if you let the dog in the garden, remember to lock up straight after.'

The swan disappeared, replaced by a pack of hounds cornering a fox cub.

'And definitely do not leave the house no matter what.'

'I won't.'

Happy Mother's Day?

That question mark scratched at her brain. Was it a typo?

She lightly touched Izzy's head. 'Say "I promise."'

Izzy twisted around, draping her arms over the back of the tired sofa. Narrowed her eyes.

'Why are you acting so weird? I mean, more weird than usual.'

'I just don't know how long I'll be. Actually, why don't you …'

Forget it. She couldn't take her, not to the Frasers'. Not if Caspar was in a bad way. She'd be traumatised.

'Why don't you keep the volume down so you can hear if I ring?' she finished. 'Any issues, call me.'

The response combined exaggerated patience with rising irritation.

'There won't *be* any issues, Mum, because I am a. nearly fourteen and b. not stupid. We'll be fine, won't we, Smudge?'

The dog's pink tongue flopped out in reply.

'Well, I'll activate the door chimes,' Annie said, opening the security app. 'That way you can hear if anyone comes in.'

The risk assessment followed a well-worn route, honed by daily practice. Window locks. Check. Bolts on back door. Check. Security camera on. Check. Done. And the pinging alert that sounded every time the door opened or closed, because there was nothing 'weird' about home security.

She opened the front door a crack. At the beep, Izzy released an epic teenage sigh. '*Yes*, I hear it.'

'Don't tell any of your friends you're home alone,' she said, lifting a bobbly woollen scarf off the peg in the hallway. 'You never know who they might tell.'

Another frustrated *tch*. Izzy clapped both palms to her face and shook her head, rattling the headphone cable against the keyboard.

'God's sake, Mum. Stop being so paranoid and just *go*.'

Now, Sunday

Spring sunshine warmed the streets of London, but two hundred miles north of her hometown, winter lingered in the spring breeze. Annie buried the fringed ends of the scarf inside her fleece and turned the car's heater on.

At one end of their pot-holed lane, an overgrown farm track led to a barn filled with rusted farm equipment. At the other, the narrow country road that led to Uppermoss Village. She kept flicking her gaze to the house dwindling in the VW's rear-view mirror. By the time she reached the junction, a dark bank of trees swallowed it completely.

Their house sat in a sat nav black hole that infuriated delivery drivers. Tucked between fields in front and woods behind, the secluded former labourer's cottage wouldn't be everyone's ideal home, but it was theirs. Even that first winter when the roof leaked into the nursery and the boiler entered a terminal decline – she had spent a blissful Christmas huddled under blankets drinking hot chocolate while snow piled up in the lane.

Yes, life in the middle of nowhere suited them.

Usually.

Today, the isolation felt oppressive. The further she drove, the more life in the middle of somewhere appealed.

Right now, Izzy could be engrossed in YouTube, headphones on full. Oblivious to the dog barking, the door handle turning, floorboards creaking a warning as a stranger crept in, intent on …

She shook her head and muttered aloud, 'It's fine, it's fine.'

She continued under trees dotted with succulent green buds waiting to unfurl. Birds flitted in and out of the hedgerows. Daffodils bloomed on this picture-perfect Mother's Day.

Happy Mother's Day?

Stop it. Focus on the moment. On work. Hopefully, Caspar could be saved, but there were things Samara might need, either way. Syringes, roll of blue paper towel from the staffroom, bandages, gauze, box of gloves …

The panic subsided. Through the windscreen, nature gave way to the shops lining Uppermoss High Street. The village bustled during the week, but on Sundays only dog walkers and families strolled past the church and the library and the pub with the chalkboard advertising the Mother's Day specials. She flicked her indicator at the sign for Uppermoss Veterinary Clinic. There was only one other vehicle in the car park today.

She stared at the transit van a fraction too long, slamming the brake at the last second. Jerked forward. Back. Knocking her ponytail against the headrest and missing the surgery wall by a hair's breadth.

Heart pounding, she shrank down until her chin was level with the bottom of the window.

The van's paintwork was white, the no-nonsense logo bold and black: *Manor Ltd.* In the driver's seat was a man in a hi-vis jacket. A black hood concealed his features, as did one of those neck warmer things bikers wore hoicked up to his nose. A phone glowed in his hands, the reflection lighting a square of windscreen. Both thumbs danced energetically across the screen.

Oh god. Suppose he was someone she knew, someone from the old days? He could be texting, *She's here now. I've found Annabel.*

Her mouth dried as the panic surged free.

It couldn't be a coincidence. First the text, now this.

Manor.

Then

A stack of drab Lego bricks built by an unimaginative toddler. *Four grey walls and four grey towers overlook a space of ...* well, there weren't any flowers. Only iron railings and stunted saplings guarding a car park built by people who didn't give a toss about other people's lives.

Its official name was Manor Park but to its residents, it was simply the Manor. And as far as Annabel Naughton-Smith was concerned, it was just another block of flats flashing past her train window twice a day.

If she ever *had* spared it a thought, it would have been: Soviet bloc. Four floors of faded women boiling cabbage on one-ring gas stoves. Grey walls, grey skies, grey people.

But she never did give it a thought. Not then.

She certainly never imagined that one day she would call the Manor home.

The young estate agent's expression flitted between professional and gossipy as she swept her mascaraed gaze over what remained of Annabel's designer wardrobe: a Donna Karan dress and expensive ballet flats.

The question hung like a cartoon bubble above her head: *Why would someone like you want to live here?*

A handwritten sign, curling at the edges, announced the lift was *Out of Order*. Annabel followed the agent up two flights of cannabis-scented steps and onto a concrete external walkway. Five doors overlooked the car park.

'Here we are,' the woman said. 'Second floor. Flat Two.'

The swollen door needed a firm shove. Annabel followed the agent into the stale air of a narrow hallway. Ten paces more and she could touch the back wall.

Box bedroom at the front. Main bedroom at the back. Lounge. Bathroom. Kitchen with a car park view.

She took in the rusty sink with its mould-framed splashback, so different from her former kitchen, and experienced a surge of something like mourning for granite worktops and pristine stainless-steel appliances polished by a rota of agency cleaners. She missed her kitchen more than she missed Oliver. A fact that was either desperately funny or desperately sad.

'Fridge and cooker are included,' the agent said. 'You can rent the washing machine for five pounds a week. Prepay meter, so you'll always know where you are with the bills.'

She ushered her past the doors, each with a fist-sized hole in a different panel.

'Lounge with balcony.'

The door slid open to reveal a narrow, tiled strip that continued under the bedroom window, separated from the neighbours by an opaque sheet of corrugated plastic. Diesel and fried chicken thickened the air.

And the *noise*.

Thud-thump-thud of garage music, high-volume TV, angry vocal exchanges. A British Airways plane flew close enough to read the numbers on the side.

The last time Annabel set foot on a balcony had been with Oliver. A chance to 'reconnect' he called it. Too much wine in

13

their Paris hotel room while he listed the ways he was going to change.

Well, he *had* changed. Just not for the better.

The agent lifted her arm to close the door, releasing flowery deodorant with a hint of sweat, saying, 'Outdoor space is such a bonus in the city. Dry your washing. Enjoy the view.'

Poor woman, racking her brains to put a positive spin on this dump. No doubt the men in the office snapped up the big commissions and tossed her the scraps: broken flats for broken people with nowhere left to go. People like Annabel.

And it was cheap.

'I'll take it,' she said. 'And I want to move in as soon as possible.'

The agent stared as though she'd started speaking in tongues.

'Is that a problem?'

Blink, and the woman was back and hardly daring to believe her luck, if the grin was anything to go by.

'No, that's fine. Well, I've got a contract here,' she said, rifling through her faux leather shoulder bag.

Annabel swapped the two sheets of printed A4 for the brown envelope containing almost every penny she had left.

'Here. Deposit and two months' rent as per the advert. Cash.'

The other woman licked her index finger and counted the crisp notes that represented the end of Annabel's marriage. Not much to show for almost a decade.

'Sorry, what was your name again?' the agent said.

Did she read the local papers? Had she seen the photos from outside the court? Annabel had kept her head down and her solicitor had given her a copy of the *Evening Standard* to shield her face, but still.

'My name is Annie Smith.'

She held her breath, watching for a flicker of disbelief, recognition, *something*.

The girl didn't miss a beat.

'Miss or Mrs?'

'Ms.'

The unfamiliar syllable buzzed on her tongue. *Ms Annie Smith*. A stage name for this stage in her life. Not killing Mrs Annabel Naughton-Smith off, exactly. More putting her on gardening leave while she figured out what to do next.

The agent put the signed contract in her bag and checked her watch.

'We'll be in touch by the end of today,' she said, ushering Annie towards the door. 'You should be in by the weekend. Good luck.'

She locked the door behind them. Annabel – no, *Annie* – listened to the woman's heels tap down the stairs and outside to where a group of women gathered round a white transit van, purses at the ready. A man in a green bomber jacket unloaded what looked like a portable freezer from the back. A group of teenagers on bikes circled the car park. One cat-called the agent, and the rest of the pack laughed.

Then a whistle came from within the labyrinth of apartments and, as though obeying a command, the boys dispersed with choreographed synchronicity into the underpass.

Annie lifted her gaze from the scene and stared across the concrete vista. Somewhere beyond the Manor, out among the skyscrapers glittering in the midday sun, Oliver was moving on with his life too.

An argument exploded in the flat behind her and she turned instinctively. Although the words were muffled, the spiralling voices – one male, one female – reverberated with anger. Fists hammered against interior wood or walls, punching through her Citalopram fog to demand decisions.

Ignore, help, ring the police?

A man stormed out before she could decide. He looked like an extra in a Jason Statham film. Late thirties with a shaved head, classically handsome features and despite the setting, an obviously expensive suit cut to accentuate his bulk.

'That's right,' the female voice screeched after him. 'Run off back to Megan.'

Annie scurried in the opposite direction, keeping her gaze locked on the scarred concrete floor. A cloud of woody aftershave mingled with the smells of bacon and car fumes. People shouted. Traffic roared. A door slammed with the finality of a breakup.

She pressed her hands to her temples. Every part of her screamed, *You can't live here!*

But what choice did she have?

She had lost her job, her husband, her home.

She had nowhere left to go.

Now, Sunday

The man in the Manor Ltd van placed his phone on the dashboard and pulled his hood back. Even without her glasses, he was clearly far too young to have known her in London. Whoever he had been texting had nothing to do with her. She unpeeled her fingers from the steering wheel and got out.

Stop being so paranoid. The voice in her head sounded suspiciously like Izzy's.

She flipped through the bunch of surgery keys on her way to the entrance: staffroom, consultation room, store cupboard. The distinctive hexagonal top of the shutter key. Front door mortise and Yale.

She frowned. When she locked up yesterday lunchtime, the daffodils along the path bloomed fit for Wordsworth. Today, their broken stalks bled white; the yellow blooms lay in tatters. *Destroyed.* Every single one.

And – she sucked in a breath – shards of green glass glittered on the concrete. A load of empties, hurled at the surgery wall. Some recognisably bits of bottle, others smashed to grit that scrunched into the tread of her trainers. She scraped the soles against the edge of a paving slab. Imagine the poor dogs booked in tomorrow morning, with the soft pads of their paws negotiating this carpet of glassy splinters.

As for the vandals' identity, that was a no-brainer: the Maguires, who else?

There was no time to clear it up now. Caspar was the priority. Either she'd come back after the farm or ring the cleaning agency. She pulled the metal roller shutter open, picked up a flyer for a pizza place from the doormat.

The red light flashed on the alarm, and she keyed in the code: 0207. Second of July. Izzy's birthday. Scanned the cluttered room. Her desk, the rack of dog toys and treats, the corkboard hidden by grateful clients' Thank You cards – everything was as she left it after the Saturday morning clinic. Good. No break-in.

She unlocked the drug safe. The steel door swung silently open, and Annie's practised fingers found the correct vials. She double-checked the dosage and hurriedly gathered the kit: correct gauge syringe; back-ups in case of breakage; box of blue disposable gloves; a stethoscope; and a small torch for checking pupil reflexes. For the first time since the text arrived that morning, her anxiety faded into the background.

God, what must it say about her that she was soothed by preparations for death?

This time the voice in her head was Samara's: *it says that you can keep your head under pressure.*

The black bag sat next to her like a macabre passenger as she drove to the Frasers' farm. Thick grey clouds shrouded the sky now, snuffing out the blue, and when she wound the window to press the intercom at the farm gates, a chill engulfed her.

The mechanism whirred, the VW's tyres bumped over the cobbled yard. She had been here many times with Izzy over the years but even if she hadn't, Lucy's heart-rending sobs clearly signposted the way to the stable block.

Annie inhaled and exhaled, steeling herself.

A feed sack propped open the entrance to the block, and Caro stood inside, a few feet from Caspar's stall. Her normally immaculate, highlighted hair lay flattened on one side, as though she'd been caught in a gale. Tear tracks streaked her blusher, and wet mascara clumped her eyelashes. Both her arms wrapped tightly around Lucy, alternating kisses and murmurs while her daughter's heartbreak soaked into the soft fabric of her cashmere jumper. Caro glanced up when Annie came in and shook her head slowly in a sad, helpless gesture that snuffed out the last tiny spark of hope.

Poor Lucy. And poor Caro. Losing a pet hammered home the first commandment of motherhood: you will always feel your child's emotions – the good, the bad, the terrifying – more intensely than your own.

'I'm so sorry,' Annie said, pushing the door with her hip, trying to keep the black bag out of Lucy's sightline. The other woman took a few deep breaths, getting her emotions under control and mouthed, 'Thank you.'

The usual scents of fresh hay and saddlery were overlaid with an instantly recognisable stench. Sweat, shit, blood and gone-off meat: the smell of death. She pulled the scarf up as a filter, but it was futile. Death always found a way in.

Inside the stall, the pony lay on the straw, his chestnut coat, usually gleaming from fastidious grooming, matted and clumpy with sweat. A black towel covered the lower portion of his hind leg.

Samara acknowledged her with raised eyebrows. Her plastic apron, daubed with drying blood, rustled as she stroked the horse's neck with one gloved hand.

'It's all right, boy. Good boy, Caspar.'

Without breaking off the soothing murmur, she jerked her head towards the near-hysterical Lucy. *Get her out.*

Annie nodded, snapping on disposable gloves as she stepped back into the main block.

'I think you should go back to the house now,' she said quietly. Lucy's cries climbed a notch and Caro led her away.

When they were out of earshot, Samara said, 'You never get

used to this, do you? Even when you know you're doing the right thing.'

Leaning in to pluck a piece of straw from her boss's fringe, Annie replied, 'You'd be a terrible vet if you took it in your stride.'

'I guess. Even under sedation, the pain must be horrific. Take a look.'

Sodden, crumpled paper piled in the corner indicated Samara's attempts to stem the flow from the wound. Annie gingerly lifted the bloody towel.

'Jesus.'

'I know,' Samara said with an answering grimace. 'Do you agree then? It's a quality-of-life call.'

'Even if you do set it, I can't see how he could recover. He'll be in constant pain ...' She set the black case down on a straw bale. 'The consent form?'

'Signed.'

Samara undid the bag buckle and peered inside.

'You bring everything?'

'All ready.'

A moment later, the needle winked in the light. The barrel glinted with the fatal mix of anaesthetic and barbiturates.

Annie knelt on the stable floor to stroke the pony's fluttering ribs. 'Good boy,' she said. 'Good boy.'

'Right, then,' Samara murmured.

As the lethal liquid entered his bloodstream, Caspar's flanks heaved with several jerky breaths. Only a few hours earlier, his heart had pumped life into organs and muscles, tissues and bone. Now as it slowed, one hoof scraped feebly against the concrete, swishing strands of reddened straw.

'That's it, Caspar love. Just go to sleep. It'll all be over soon,' Annie murmured.

They waited. Somewhere on the farm, a dog barked. A wood pigeon cooed above them and unseen creatures rustled in the straw.

When the pony's ribcage stilled, Samara pressed the stethoscope against the warm body. Adjusted. Listened again. She lightly touched one cornea then the other with a blue gloved finger. No reflex.

'He's gone,' she said, gently closing the lids.

A burr had caught in Caspar's forelock, and Annie gently teased it out, combing his mane with her fingers, then quickly wiped her sleeve across her eyes.

Meanwhile, Samara arched her back and groaned. 'What a waste. Worst part of the job, especially when there's a kid involved.' She got up stiffly, shaking the circulation back into her legs. 'Listen, you head off and I'll go and speak to Caro and see whether she wants me to call a van.'

'I can wait with you,' Annie replied, dropping the discarded vials and syringe into a medical waste bag. She peeled off her gloves.

'No, it's fine. Go home. I bet Iz will be absolutely distraught.'

Izzy, who still slept with a photo of their beloved first dog, Paddy, next to her bed. Who refused to dissect a dead frog in biology. Who cried over roadkill.

'Yep.'

'And pick an afternoon to take as time off in lieu. Helen will be only too happy to come in. She's going stir-crazy on maternity leave.'

Helen, Samara's wife, usually worked part time at the surgery. But after the heartache of four cycles of IVF, she was now eight months pregnant and taking it easy. At least, that was the plan.

'How's everything going?'

'Physically, great. Emotionally ... well, one minute the nursery's green, the next it's yellow. When I get home it'll be bright orange. We've got deliveries turning up every two minutes, boxes everywhere. Our bank account is literally weeping. Anyway, I'm sure you remember all that from when you had Izzy. Anyway,' she brushed hay dust from her jeans, 'time to go.'

21

Annie crouched down and gave Caspar's neck a final pat.

'Good night, boy,' she whispered. 'Sleep well.'

They went out into the silence of the yard. No horses whinnied, no dogs barked, no birds sang. She inhaled beautiful lungfuls of crisp, cleansing air. But knew death would cling to her nostrils for hours. It always did.

Lights blazed from every window of the farmhouse, but the elegantly furnished rooms undoubtedly echoed with the sounds of misery. Henry, the farmyard cat, wound around her ankles, staring with huge green eyes as she took out her phone: three missed calls from Izzy. *Shit.*

'One last thing,' she said, bending down to scratch behind the cat's ears. 'Someone has smashed a load of beer bottles right outside the surgery and I didn't have time to clean it up. I can do it when I drop the bag back.'

Samara rolled her eyes. 'By "someone" I take it we're thinking our friends the Maguires? I'll take the bag back when I'm done here, I feel bad enough for spoiling your Mother's Day. I can check the CCTV, see if it's worth logging with the police.'

Henry sashayed on silent paws towards the farmhouse.

'Right, then,' Samara said, setting her shoulders back. 'Better go and tell them it's all over.'

Izzy answered on the first ring.

'Hi, love.' Annie sat with her legs out of the car, stamping mud and straw from her trainers. She kept her tone neutral. 'I'm on my way home. Everything okay?'

There was a long pause during which she shut the door and turned the key in the ignition. The engine spluttered once, twice. Died.

Izzy responded in a tiny voice. 'Lucy told me about Caspar.'

The car let out a few staccato coughs then, thankfully, fired up.

'I'm so sorry, darling,' Annie said, cautiously dabbing the accelerator. 'We'll talk about it when I get home. I won't be long. Love you.'

On the other end of the line, Izzy let out a long, quivery breath. 'Love you too.'

Only the occasional vehicle joined her on the quiet Sunday roads. People on their way back from their Mother's Day visits.

'I'm sorry for spoiling your Mother's Day,' Samara had said.

But she hadn't. Whoever sent the text had.

It didn't make sense. No one from her current life knew *who* she was. No one from her old life knew *where* she was. Not even Oliver.

As far back as she could remember, her parents, friends, teachers, everyone always called her Bella. But Oliver – never Olly – 'didn't believe in' abbreviating names. From the first time they met, he had called her by her full name and, still reeling from the death of her parents, she didn't have the strength to argue.

She *was* stronger by their last wedding anniversary, but by then she knew there were many things Oliver didn't believe in: Joint financial decisions. Listening. Honesty.

When she turned off the main road, the rain that had been threatening since she arrived at the farm finally began to fall. Fat drops exploded on the windscreen and as she neared home, the wipers' rhythmic tick taunted her.

Anna-bel. Anna-bel.

Half a mile from the cottage, a police van flashed in her rear-view mirror. She swerved onto a grass verge. Fear spiralled from the knot in her chest, embedding its hooks in every part of her until the blue lights passed her. Then she waited, listening to the rain drum on the roof, until her hands stopped shaking.

The text had to be from Oliver. But what did he want after all this time?

And how had he got hold of her number?

Then

'Police,' a gruff voice shouted.

Annie swam up from the depths of sleep, her mind conflating the noise outside with the chaos of the custody suite in the aftermath of her arrest. She had been to court. Paid the money back. It didn't make sense.

The flat on the Manor. Of course. She lived there now. But was it Friday night or Saturday morning?

The voice shouted again. 'Elliot Devlin. We know you're in there.'

Elliot Devlin? So, they were after someone, but not her.

Awake now, she swallowed. Or tried to. The anti-depressants that fogged her brain turned her mouth to dust. She reached for the glass on the bedside table, grimaced at the stale taste. The red digits on her radio alarm clock flipped to 3.03am.

Outside, another, calmer officer said, 'Lauren, open up. We just need to talk to him about a complaint.'

Through the wall came the snap of a bolt being drawn back followed by a muffled reply – young, female, angry. And then, close by, an almost imperceptible creak. Annie clutched the duvet.

Another subdued thud was followed by the scuff of a careful footstep.

Shit! Someone was on her balcony.

A weapon. Pillow? No. Umbrella, hanging on the wardrobe doorknob? She slid out of bed and crept towards the creak, brandishing the umbrella like a club.

A shadow passed across the sliding doors. Annie got down on her knees, holding her breath. A stranger's hand lifted the corrugated plastic separating her flat from the empty one on the other side. Climbed over. Dropped the partition gently into place.

Five seconds later, torchlight probed her balcony. A shout: 'Clear at the back.'

She exhaled. Footsteps scuffled by her front door and the woman – Lauren? – yelled, 'I told you he wasn't here.'

When the police finally left, Annie curled on the sofa, still clutching the furled umbrella, while jeers and shouts from other disturbed neighbours echoed down the concrete walkways. She stared up at the stained ceiling tiles until glimmers of light filtered through the thin curtains, illuminating the unfamiliar lines and shapes of her second-hand furniture. She had tried to create a homely feel with charity shop finds – cushions, a throw, a lonely spray of artificial freesias in a vase – but this felt nothing like home.

When the sun rose to promise another scorching day, she got up, rolled her stiff shoulders, and popped an anti-depressant from the blister pack on the table.

The city had wilted in an unseasonable heatwave all week and traffic belched fumes in a tainted blue ring above tired September streets. When she inhaled, she imagined soot lining her nostrils, trickling into her lungs. A world away from the house she grew up in, the garden redolent with the scent of roses. Thanks to Oliver, she breathed this polluted air while the strangers who bought her home benefited from the trees and flowers her mum had planted.

She made a cup of tea and poured the milk in. Curded white specks floated on the surface.

Great.

*

The overpriced and understocked minimart opened at eight and, alongside milk, she picked wrinkled apples and cereal from shelves loaded with shrink-wrapped and tinned food. The yawning woman at the till took her money without a word of acknowledgement.

She didn't mind. She wanted to be invisible.

After the bright glare reflecting off the pavement, returning to the Manor's dank stairwell was like entering a cave. The huge sunglasses and cap she had pulled down to her eyebrows, were they overkill? Maybe. Even if anyone here followed the press coverage of the trial, Annabel Naughton-Smith's salon-perfect highlights and make-up disappeared months ago.

That was Oliver's fault, too. He'd wrecked everything – her career, her reputation, her identity. And yet *she* had a criminal record. *She* lost her childhood home to pay for his mistakes. *She* was the one who—

A woman hurried down the stairs, rapid footsteps beating a counterpoint to her clicking lanyard. Instinctively, Annie shrank against the banister rail. But the woman blurred past, bristling with anger.

When she turned the corner onto the first floor, two things happened in quick succession. First, someone shouted, 'Fuck you, Donna!' Second, air rushed past her cheek as a mug shattered inches from her head. Warm liquid splattered on the baseball hat, the lenses of her glasses. She'd only just had time to duck.

She straightened. A slight woman – a girl, really – in jersey shorts and a loose vest top came towards her, one hand clutching a tobacco tin, the other clasped over her mouth.

'Oh. My. God,' she whispered. 'Did I get you?'

Had she? Annie brushed her fingertips gingerly across her cheeks, feeling for fragments of ceramic.

'No, I don't think so.'

The girl clapped her hands to her temples, trapping long

strands of blonde hair, and the vest strap slipped, revealing a collection of yellow bruises across her collarbone.

'Did you see her? My sister. She made me so mad that … oh my god. Your face though.' The girl pantomimed open-mouthed terror then let out a laugh that sounded like a rusty seesaw.

Unsure what to do, Annie kicked the biggest shards to the side.

'You just moved in, right?'

Still stunned, she responded automatically. 'Annie. Nice to meet you.'

'Lauren. You got tea?' the stranger said, peering at the bag. 'I threw the last of mine at the wall. I'm gasping.'

Without waiting to be invited, the girl followed her into the kitchen and leaned against the worktop, swishing her flip-flops on the faded lino. Momentarily lost for words, Annie put her sunglasses and hat on top of the microwave. Throwing mugs was one thing. But was strolling into other people's homes uninvited a thing here, too?

'Two sugars,' the girl said. 'Please.'

Sweat tickled the side of Annie's neck. Where was the air? Even with the window open, only the stink of frying bacon from the café on the corner drifted in. Occasional feral cries and whistles broke through the tidal roar of traffic.

Taking the mug Annie held out, the girl went into the lounge and dropped on the sofa. Took a packet of Rizlas from the tin.

'My sister say anything to you?'

'Er, no. No. She seemed in a bit of a hurry to be honest.'

'That sounds about right. She hates coming here. I don't know why she bothers.'

Sprinkling tobacco into the creased paper, she monologued Donna's many failings. Getting her out of bed for no reason. Up herself. She wasn't even her real sister, only her foster sister. And worst of all, she worked for the police.

'Not actually *in* the police. She's a call centre supervisor. That's why she hates my boyfriend.' She mimicked a bossy sister tone. '*I cannot be connected with someone like Elliot Devlin. It will affect my vetting.* Well, I say bollocks to your vetting, Donna. You don't like my boyfriend. Well, I don't like your *job.*'

Meanwhile, the remnants of Annabel Naughton-Smith, former investment banker, wife of Oliver, stirred. *Say something! She barged in to your flat! She's on your sofa! Look, she's actually getting a lighter out!* But the cocktail of anti-depressants and tiredness placed a wall of glass between her indignation and the girl from next door.

Pulling a shred of tobacco from her lip as she exhaled, her new neighbour continued, 'She says it's about association. She thinks he's a criminal, but he's not. He's a legit businessman.'

'Ah. Was that Dev who climbed across my balcony?'

The girl's voice went hard and flat. 'What do you mean?'

'Don't worry,' Annie added. 'I don't want to get involved with the police.'

A smoke ring twisted and uncoiled into the pause while Lauren appraised Annie.

'Sylvia, the bitch downstairs, called them. For no reason,' she said eventually, using the lid of the tobacco tin as a makeshift ashtray. 'You don't sound local. Why are you here?'

What could she say? *Don't tell your sister, but I actually am a criminal.*

Hardly.

She pushed the balcony door fully open. The smoke swirled lazily but didn't leave.

'I lost my house when I split up with my husband,' she said. 'And now I'm broke.'

A thin blue stream curled from one side of Lauren's mouth.

'Welcome to the Manor,' she said and gestured with her flip-flop at the blister pack of anti-depressants on the table. 'You're going to fit right in.'

Now, Sunday

In the short time since leaving Samara at the farm, dusk had arrived, blackening the high wall of conifers that hid the cottage from the road. Gloomy enough for the security light to blaze to life.

Izzy's bedroom window was a black square. So was the lounge underneath.

Why hadn't she turned the lights on?

Annie braked sharply, and a spray of gravel dinged against the ancient VW's wheel arches. Opened the front door, bracing herself for the dog to come hurtling out, tail swishing.

No dog.

And no music. No light. Not even the blue flicker of the TV stirred the gloom.

She pressed the switch and the hall light glinted off the gallery of familiar pictures: Izzy's school photos from nursery to Year Nine, portraits of pets long gone.

'I'm back,' she shouted. 'Izzy? Smudge?'

She wasn't in the lounge. Or the kitchen, where her beautiful face smiled from the Mother's Day gift. Taking the stairs two at a time, Annie barely registering the painful crack of her elbow on the banister. The laptop, abandoned on the rug, played a silent montage of YouTube clips to an empty room.

Where the hell was she?

She tapped the locator app on her phone, but the little Izzy avatar said she was safely home. She hit the dial button and, sure enough, muffled ringing started somewhere under the cushions.

Fear swelled in her chest. What teenager went out without their phone?

Izzy used to be afraid of the dark. She'd clamber into Annie's bed in the middle of the night, sobbing, convinced a monster was hiding in her room. And while the hysterical child burrowed under the duvet, refusing to come out, Annie stumbled across the landing, half asleep. Loudly fling the wardrobe open and inspect under the bed and murmur *the dark is nothing to be afraid of* and *no such thing as monsters*.

'Iz?' she shouted. 'Stop messing about!'

She wasn't in the bathroom. Or Annie's bedroom at the back. There was nowhere else in their tiny cottage to hide.

Happy Mother's Day?

Now the question mark didn't feel like a typo, it felt like a threat.

Black charred the edges of her vision, and she braced her spine against her wardrobe. No, she refused to have a panic attack while her daughter was missing. She bit the inside of her cheek. Salty blood oozed onto her tongue and pain brought her sharply back.

Then, through the bedroom window, she caught a flash of red bobbing among the trees. Something, some*one* in the woods.

She flew down the stairs, threw the back door open.

'Izzy!' she called desperately.

A shape barrelled through the back gate, triggering the security lights that momentarily blinded her. A tail whipped like a riding crop across Annie's legs. Smudge.

'Isabel!'

'Hey, Mum, what's up?' Izzy said, walking across the grass with her hands stuffed in the pockets of her old red jacket. Actually, walking wasn't the word. *Ambling*, that was it. Not a care in the world. No big deal.

Annie clutched the doorframe. Her first instinct was to cry, but anger swept it away.

'What's up' – she breathed in sharply – 'is you wandering about in the dark when I specifically told you to not to leave the house.'

'Smudge kept barking at the gate,' Izzy explained, pulling her wellies off. One of them landed on its side with a *thwock*. 'And it's not that dark, not yet.'

'You could have just let her out in the garden.'

'I did. But she was going mad, jumping at the gate so I opened it and she ran off into the woods after a fox and refused to come back. I couldn't just leave her.'

Annie snatched the boot and slammed it upright on the back step.

'Going into the woods on your own. You're thirteen years old, for god's sake. Do you have any idea how stupid that is? How *dangerous*?'

The door slammed, startling the dog into a volley of barks. Two round pink patches stained Izzy's cheekbones and her reddened eyeballs indicated recent tears. She leaned down to comfort the dog. 'Sh … Sh … it's okay. It's just Mum freaking out over nothing.'

'It's not nothing. Suppose it was a person out there, not a fox? Someone could have abducted you. I could be ringing the police right now to report you missing or be waiting to identify your body.'

There was a pause.

'But you're not, you're here, having a go at me because *you're* paranoid.' The words vibrated with anger, but Izzy trembled on the brink of fresh tears. 'I know it's because you love me, but I'm not a little kid anymore. Trust me, nothing bad is going to happen.'

So many responses leapt to Annie's tongue.

You have no idea of the things that could happen.

The things I've seen.

31

I should have kept you afraid of the dark.

I should have taught you to believe in monsters.

But instead she mentally chanted the demons away. *She's safe. Relax. No one is out there.* Took a deep, steadying breath and said calmly, 'I'm your mum. Worrying is in the job description. But you're right: you are nearly fourteen, and I'm sorry if I forget that sometimes.'

She opened the larder door and, steering them away from the topic, added gently, 'How was Lucy when you spoke to her?'

Izzy caught her lower lip with her teeth. 'Sad.'

'Poor girl.' She tugged the ring pull on a tin of Pedigree Chum. 'Can you pass me a fork?'

Alerted by the smell, Smudge wound anxiously around her legs. The cutlery drawer rattled as Izzy rummaged through it and Annie watched their reflections in the window while she mashed lumps of meat in the dog's bowl. The glass drained the colour from her face. She looked like a stranger. A ghost.

Hello, Annabel.

Izzy tugged the drawstrings on either side of her hood, pulling the fabric tight around her face and let out a juddering, gasping sob.

'It's not fair. He wasn't even old. There should be some treatment, like an operation or something.'

'Come here,' Annie said. 'If there was the slightest chance Samara could have saved him, she would have.'

'It's just hard to believe one minute he was totally fine, and the next he's dead. Lucy's so upset.'

'I know,' Annie said, folding her into a hug. 'But even with an operation, his injuries were too bad to survive. So even though it's hard, you have to focus on the fact he's not suffering.'

Early evening gloom darkened the patio and the garden. Beyond their fence, the woods formed a block of shadow against which her reflection floated, like a ghostly balloon over Izzy's shoulder. According to the window fitter, this safety glass was near impossible to break, but even so she'd seriously considered metal security shutters like the ones at the surgery until the man's startled expression put her off. She should have insisted on a quote.

She broke their embrace to close the blind. The chain rattled as the fabric dropped.

'And just so you know, no matter how it might look, I *do* trust you,' she said. Shadows played across the cheerful botanical print. Blowsy roses morphed into grotesque many-eyed monsters as she added, softly, 'It's other people I don't trust.'

Then

For seven years, Annabel Naughton-Smith swayed and swung on the 6.37am to Euston to be at her desk before eight. Grabbed a sandwich hunched over paperwork. Never left the bank before six. Spent the overcrowded return journey fantasising about a life empty of people and filled with nothing to do, nowhere to be.

Since being reborn as Annie Smith, each day unfurled like a flat, grey carpet stretching to nightfall when she could take the pills the GP prescribed. And yet her eyelids still sprung open at five thirty, and for a few cruel seconds she was Annabel again. Before she had nothing to do, nowhere to be.

Turned out an empty life wasn't so great after all.

In the three weeks since their explosive first meeting, Lauren next door had taken to dropping in most mornings, and Annie had started buying chocolate biscuits, making sure there was enough milk in the fridge, putting an ashtray on the coffee table.

She'd only interacted with one other neighbour: 'that bitch' Sylvia, who lived downstairs with her grandson and who had discreetly dropped a foodbank voucher in her basket at the minimart. Annie hadn't known whether to laugh or cry at this unexpected kindness. How had she gone from donating to foodbanks to needing them?

This morning, Lauren arrived just after eleven with her tobacco tin in her pocket and gossip falling off her lips. Annie made two mugs of tea. Lauren was stirring spoonfuls of sugar into hers while bad-mouthing some old schoolfriend when someone rapped – suddenly and hard – on the front door.

'Who's that?'

Annie shrugged. Journalist? Debt collector?

'Can't be the police,' Lauren added with a sage nod. 'They always shout first.'

Putting a finger to her lips, Annie crept to the kitchen. Through the net-curtained window, she saw a man in a suit looking impatiently at his watch. A tall, dark-haired, utterly familiar man.

'Oh my god,' she whispered.

'Who is he?' Lauren had come out of the lounge on silent socked feet. She leaned against the kitchen doorframe, twiddling the silver ring in her eyebrow.

Annie flapped her hand urgently to convey both *shut up* and *get out of sight*.

The letterbox rattled. Fingertips waggled through the nylon bristles that edged the slot.

'Annabel, we need to talk. Please open the door.'

'*Annabel?*' Lauren mouthed.

'Shhh!'

Annie inched away from the kitchen, keeping her back pressed to the wall.

'Annabel, please. I know you're in there.'

His petulant tone revived a hundred broken promises. She sat carefully on the arm of the sofa, out of the letterbox's narrow field of vision and said under her breath, 'Go away, Oliver.'

Twisting her mouth to one side, Lauren nodded once, briskly. 'I'll sort him.'

She turned back towards the door. Annie snatched at her T-shirt too late. Her fingertips brushed thin cotton.

'No!' she hissed. 'Don't!'

But the chain clinked, the hinges creaked and outdoor air entered.

'What?' Lauren said.

'Oh.' Oliver inhaled audibly. Then, brimming with customary self-importance, adopted the imperious tone he reserved for waiters, cleaners and anyone he considered his inferior. Which essentially meant everyone else on the planet.

'I'm looking for Annabel Naughton-Smith.'

'Wrong flat,' Lauren said, and shut the door in his face.

She turned to Annie, sweeping her palms together. *Done and dusted.*

Oliver Naughton didn't give up that easily. The brass flap lifted.

'I know you're here, Annabel.' His voice was muffled. 'I can see the photo of your parents.'

A spindly finger poked through and waggled at the wall. Her stomach clenched. Just to the left of the letterbox hung the framed picture, taken on the beach at Wells on Mum and Dad's honeymoon. One of the treasured things she'd rescued before she lost the house. Lost because of *him.*

'I understand you're angry,' he continued, his voice like nails scratching her eardrums. 'But you need to be a grown-up. You can't just go to ground like this. You need to sign the paperwork.'

With a clang, the brass flap dropped shut, but Annie remained glued to the sofa with shock. How had he tracked her down to the Manor? They hadn't spoken since the trial. Her solicitor dealt with the correspondence, and she was under strict instructions not to—

'He's off.' Lauren had gone into the kitchen to provide a commentary. 'Into the parking. Hang on … keys out. Black Mercedes.'

So he'd got to keep his car, then.

'And he's gone.'

The words chased themselves through Annie's mind. *He's gone.*

But the truth was he had been gone since the day she was arrested. He hadn't appeared at the police station when she was arrested. At her sentencing, she had scanned the court for him. No sign. Not even a personal phone call. He exited her life so smoothly, it was as though he'd never been there.

'They're all the same,' Lauren said, padding back down the hall. 'Rich or poor. Tell you what to do and smack you about when they're in the mood. Nice car, is he rich, then?'

'He was. For a while, anyway. And despite his many faults, he never laid a finger on me.'

'Why did you leave him then?' Lauren tipped her head to drain the cooling tea.

'I didn't.'

'Sorry to hear that, *Annabel*,' Lauren said, with sarcastic emphasis. 'Oliver and Annabel. That is so posh.'

Annie laughed. 'Not in the slightest. It's a funny story really. My mum was a childminder, and she looked after a little girl who had this doll called Annabel and …'

But she had lost her audience.

Lauren burped unselfconsciously and dropped her cigarette into the empty mug.

'I'm knackered. Might go for a lie-down.'

In the hallway, she paused in front of the photo. Mum's heavy eyeliner and Dad's polo neck were pure Sixties, but there was a timeless quality to the black-and-white portrait. Two people in love, and that's how Annie remembered them. Always together, always smiling.

'Where are your mum and dad now?'

'They died,' Annie replied. 'Dad when I was twenty. Mum when I was twenty-four.'

Lauren lightly touched the glass. 'That's sad. You know, I don't have any photos of my mum and dad. I wouldn't know them if they came round here. Not that they would.'

'When did you last see them?'

She shrugged. 'Never met my dad. My mum when I was …' Her brow furrowed. 'Three? Four? She left and didn't come back.'

'I've never met my biological parents,' Annie said. 'Mum and Dad adopted me when I was six weeks old. But I was really lucky. They always made me feel special because of it. Like they *chose* me because—'

A loud knock halted her mid-sentence. She clutched the neck of her T-shirt. Oliver?

No. Next door.

'That'll be Dev,' Lauren said, taking the door chain off. A quirk of the pierced eyebrow accompanied the final word. 'Bye, *Annabel*.'

From her vantage point in the kitchen doorway, she watched a muscular man with a shaved head catch Lauren by the arm and swing her round.

'I'm in a hurry. I told you to be in,' he said.

The accent was unexpected. Not quite Hampstead, but definitely more leafy suburb than concrete jungle. Putting his hand in the small of Lauren's back, he turned, revealing the classic profile of an action hero. But even a film-star face couldn't mitigate the twisted scowl and the propelling shove.

Action, yes. Hero? Not so much.

As she slotted the knobbly end of the door chain into position, she caught sight of herself in the hall mirror. A woman she barely knew stared back.

Mousy root growth skimmed the top of her ears, like cut-price balayage, streaked here and there with new silver threads. She pulled at the lines fanning from the corners of her eyes. Noted the gaunt hollows under her cheekbones. It didn't matter that Oliver had tracked her down: if she'd answered, he wouldn't have recognised her.

The documents from his solicitor sat read but unsigned in her bedside drawer. Every time she picked up a pen to add her signature under his, her hand refused to comply. She didn't want to be married to him. She hated him. And yet, in the space of ten years, she'd been orphaned, arrested, made homeless and friendless, and now divorced? It was so … final.

She went out to the narrow balcony, slumped to the dusty floor and pressed her forehead against her knees.

Maybe she hated Oliver, but she hated herself more.

Pungent weed smoke drifted over the balcony partition and settled on her clothes drying on the airer. Thuds and scrapes followed, as though the furniture were being rearranged next door. She was about to get up when Lauren's boyfriend came out, rippled and shadowy behind the corrugated plastic, and whistled loudly. Hugging her knees tight, she prayed the hanging clothes provided a degree of cover.

Within thirty seconds, bike wheels scuffed to a halt on the pavement directly under next door's balcony. Dev dropped something over the edge. The unseen cyclist pedalled off. Dev disappeared back inside, sliding the door closed. Start to finish, the whole shady episode lasted under a minute.

So, Lauren's sister had a point. Whatever Lauren believed, a 'legit businessman' didn't throw packages to passing cyclists.

Annie stood, picked a pair of sweatpants from the airer and folded them. Somewhere out there, Oliver drove his shiny Mercedes towards his shiny new life. Away from the Manor. Away from her.

Broke, depressed, fooled into believing the lies of a dishonest man: she had more in common with Lauren than she could ever have imagined.

Now, Sunday

After dinner, and with Izzy safely upstairs on the phone to Lucy, Annie took a bottle of Shiraz from the cupboard and poured a generous glassful. Too generous for a Sunday night, really. But she needed something to soothe the jagged edges of her day.

And prepare for what she had to do next.

Canned laughter erupted from the TV and she scrolled through the channels and curled her feet up on the sagging sofa next to the dog. But the noise was just camouflage.

Delving into Annabel Naughton-Smith's past wasn't something she did lightly. Too many risks. Phones could be hacked, IP addresses traced, search histories scrutinised. Very, very occasionally over the years, when paranoia threatened to overwhelm her, she had used PCs at internet cafés or libraries for reassurance. She hadn't looked Oliver up since she first moved to Uppermoss.

But she needed answers and she needed them now.

Skin prickling with trepidation, she muted the TV and clicked on the browser on her phone. Typed *Oliver Naughton* into Google and scrolled through the many results. Too old, too young, too American.

Her finger hovered. Just right.

Fifteen years had elapsed since she last saw him in the flesh and the familiar grin from the thumbnail image was a jolt. His teeth were better than she remembered. Very white, very straight. He'd lost weight, too. Tanned, in an open-necked shirt that set off the deep denim blue of his eyes, he radiated money. Smug bastard.

A link took her to his LinkedIn profile. CEO of Vinum Bonum, Prestige Wine Importation for seven years? So, after all the false starts, the debt and the sleepless nights, *everything*, he walked out of their marriage and into success. She knocked back a mouthful of wine. Its acidic taste perfectly complemented the rush of resentment.

The multiple glowing recommendations were on brand for Oliver. *Charm the birds out of the trees*, her nan would have said. There was more behind a members-only wall. But whatever the opposite of networking was … anonymising? Fading into the cyber shadows? That was her. No social media presence. And no LinkedIn.

She typed *Vinum Bonum* into Google. The company's homepage featured a predictably perfect montage of scenic mist rolling over vineyards. A hint of ancient stone colonnade. A beautiful couple drinking expensive wine in the sunset. And columns of obsequious spiel: 'Vinum Bonum … kitchen table start-up to multi-million-pound turnover. Hugely successful global brand … remaining true to his roots. Splits his time between his native London and his family home in Milan which he shares with his beautiful wife, Giovanna, and their three wonderful children.'

She flicked her attention from the bright screen to a faded pink splodge on the carpet where Izzy, years before, had knocked over a beaker of Ribena. Despite her endless scrubbing, the stain refused to shift.

The pain of the divorce had been so completely eclipsed by what came after that Oliver rarely crossed her mind. Still, three kids. That stung. She lifted her wineglass in an ironic toast. *Well done, you.*

She imagined a parallel universe where Annabel, Oliver Naughton's first wife, sipped wine in the Milanese sunset. Where Oliver and Annabel reminisced about the late-night kitchen table conversations where Vinum Bonum had been conceived. Where the home she inherited at twenty-four was not sacrificed to pay for the start-up costs. Where they had three children together.

Maybe his conscience had finally begun to trouble him. She drummed her fingers on the arm of the sofa. Did he want to pay her back?

And how the hell had he found her? A private detective?

The rim of the glass clashed against her bottom teeth as she took another slug, the wine acidic in the back of her throat. Whatever. This wasn't Vinum Bonum Chateau de Posh, just bottled courage. She drained the glass, coughed as it burnt its way down, and immediately poured another. Faint throbs, harbingers of an imminent headache, pulsed at her temples.

While a perfect family silently advertised something expensive on TV, their tiny cottage had fallen so quiet she heard the soft click of Izzy's bedside light coming on. A low murmur filtered through the floorboards. She must be consoling Lucy. She heard the shift of the mattress as her daughter lay down. Replacing that old single bed was way overdue, but at night the creaks and twangs reassured her Izzy was there. Safe.

Stop procrastinating.

She clicked on the text and studied the number. Flicked back to Vinum Bonum's contact section to compare.

None of the workplace numbers matched the anonymous message, but that meant nothing. People bought burner handsets or anonymous SIM cards or cloaked their real number using tech she had never heard of. Or, more mundanely, owned both work and personal phones.

She swilled the wine around her glass. Of course it was Oliver. No one else knew her as Annabel. No one living, anyway.

She shuffled straighter against the sofa that had moulded to

42

her shape through use. Cleared her throat and pressed to ring the number on the text.

It went straight to voicemail. Emboldened by wine, her voice stayed firm.

'Oliver, it's Annabel. Whatever you want, either tell me straight or leave me alone. We're both too long in the tooth to be playing games.' She paused. Despite the brave words, it wasn't the no-frills wine that made her stomach churn. 'And what I want to know is how did you get this number?'

She hung up. Closed her eyes, fighting the emotion that was surging through her. That was the problem with reminiscing: once you opened the box, a swarm of unwelcome memories rushed out.

She readied the house and herself for bed. Izzy had fallen asleep with one arm flung above her head, long hair spilling across the pillow like a Renaissance muse. Except for the phone lying on her pillow. Annie shut it in the bedside drawer and gently kissed Izzy's warm forehead.

As she slid under her own duvet, her thoughts pinballed between her ex-husband, the Manor and Uppermoss in a random slide show of mould-covered walls and stained carpets. Loud music and thuds that drifted into her head like cigarette smoke. Oliver, the family man. The businessman. Living the Italian dream. What could he want with her now?

She was catapulted from the fringes of sleep by a text alert.

She blinked and fumbled on the bedside table for her glasses. The sudden illumination when she clicked her phone stung her eyeballs.

Black lines and dots wobbled, then the letters snapped sharply into place:

Who the fuck is Oliver?

Sleep dissolved in a flood of adrenalin. The phone slipped between her fingers, landing on the duvet with a soft thud. Was this his idea of a wind-up?

Her stomach rolled. Water. She needed water. Her trembling fingers struggled to tie her dressing-gown belt and when she tried to stand, spikes of pain skewered her temples.

Water *and* paracetamol.

Instinctively avoiding the creaky floorboards, she crept down the stairs. Opened the kitchen door slowly to appease the hinge that needed oiling. Put her mouth to the tap and gulped a pain-killer down. It stuck in her throat like a stone and she drank again. Straightened. Wiped streams of water from her chin.

Think.

She slumped on the sofa, its sagging upholstery as familiar and taken for granted as her own body felt lumpy and strange. The wedge of warm light from the table lamp only emphasised the surrounding darkness as she read and re-read both texts. Yes, they were definitely sent from the same number.

Come on, *think*.

Make it go away. Press delete and reset life to its ordinary settings. And despite the far-from-ordinary events that preceded it, their lives now *were* unremarkable. Dull, even. She made sure of it. Cooked, cleaned, shopped, walked the dog, worried about money and did everything to maintain the shield of ordinariness that protected them.

Until today.

Delete. Block.

But her finger hovered, then instead of pressing the screen, lifted to massage the creased skin between her eyebrows. It couldn't have been easy to track her down. Someone had put time and money into finding her number. And that meant they were unlikely to give up. If she ignored one message today, two would take its place tomorrow and the day after …

The back of her neck spasmed and she tipped her head from side to side to release the knotted muscles.

She inhaled deeply to marshal her courage. Typed: *Who is this?*

The reply pinged instantly.

An old friend.

Oh god.

Myriad voices clamoured in her brain. Half-forgotten faces swarmed from the labyrinth of memory where her darkest secrets were stored.

She nibbled her lip, tasted the metallic tang of blood. There was no question of block and delete now.

Her finger shook as she typed: *What do you want?*

This time, the seconds stretched into minutes while she waited for an answer. The lines and shapes of the cottage shifted in the gloom to cast unfamiliar shadows and despite the late-night chill, sweat prickled her skin, raising goose bumps as it dried. Silence whooshed in her ears, like distant water.

And when the phone finally pinged and she scanned the reply, all the air escaped from her lungs. The world shrank away until there was nothing left but Annie, the darkness and black letters on a glowing screen.

I want £50k by Friday. Or I will tell the girl everything.

Now, Monday

Izzy sat on the bed, one leg curled under her, and unzipped her rucksack.

Annie stood in the doorway. Her sinuses throbbed with the threat of a cold. She rubbed her eyes, gritty from a night of sleepless chaotic thoughts.

An old friend. Fifty thousand pounds by Friday. Tell the girl everything.

Badges covered the schoolbag's nylon surface with stern warnings: *There is No Planet B. Slow down fashion. Stop the cull.* They clinked lightly as Izzy jammed a fat folder inside.

'Think that's everything,' she said.

Everything.

Acid churned in Annie's stomach, the queasy mingling of last night's wine and this morning's coffee.

There were moments in the past, moments she preferred not to dwell on, that she had recognised as pivotal even as they happened. One split-second decision and her life ricocheted completely off course.

This could be one of those hinge moments. A scenario unfolded: Put the rucksack on the floor. Pat the mattress, saying,

46

'Sit down. There's something I need to tell you.' Open her mouth and let the *everything* tumble out.

She could tell Izzy the truth.

She could lose Izzy forever.

The acid rose up her gullet, burning the back of her throat. She snatched the Uppermoss High blazer from the back of the chair. 'Well, get a move on. It's half seven already.'

Izzy, affronted, widened her eyes and she stood, leisurely, and tugged the thick school tights that had bagged round her ankle. 'Jesus. All right.'

She had grown so much this year that the skirt rose well above her knees. Delicate wrists protruded from the blazer that had swamped her in September. Even with a sulky frown corrugating her brow, Izzy stood with the grace of a principal ballerina. Elegant. Poised. A world away from Annie at that age.

When she was thirteen – George Michael on her Walkman, kids from *Fame* on the telly – she plastered half of Boots over her flawless skin every morning. Clumpy mascara, pink frosted lipstick, blue eyeliner – the works. And her hair, side-parted, blow-dried, crispy with Elnett, could see off tornadoes. No lie, she would sooner have walked through the school gates stark naked than bare-faced.

In contrast, Izzy's make-up-free skin glowed, lit from within, and the soft curls shone like a dark halo as she combed them with her fingers. She was growing up so fast, *too* fast.

'Why are you staring at me like that?' she said suspiciously, taming her fringe with a stretchy black Alice band.

Annie scratched her nose. 'No reason. Just thinking.'

'Have you signed the letter for the Paris trip yet?' Izzy added, fastening the buckle on her bag, faux casually.

'Have you found a spare six hundred pounds?' she snapped again, instantly regretting it. She pinched the bridge of her nose, trying to ward off tears. 'Sorry, love. I didn't sleep well last night.'

Izzy picked up her rucksack, but instead of heading for the door, perched on the edge of the mattress.

'Mum, *please*, I'm begging you. Lucy's gutted about Caspar and she really wants me to go, and she's already been to Paris. She's been everywhere and I haven't even got a passport.'

'I wish you could,' Annie said, rubbing the smooth painted wood with her thumb. 'But you know how things are at the moment. All the work that needs doing on the car and the house. We just don't have the money.'

Money.

Fifty thousand pounds!

Izzy hugged one long leg up to her chest and rested her chin on her knee. 'Well, I can get a job. I can babysit or walk dogs, I'd love that. I could put a sign up in the waiting room at the surgery. Or I could contact that modelling agency …'

The tension ratcheted up a notch.

Last Christmas, on a rare trip to the Trafford Centre, an agency scout handed Izzy her card with an invitation to audition. Ugh. The idea of strangers' eyes assessing her precious child had made Annie's skin crawl.

'You told me you weren't interested. You said it was hypocritical to promote fast fashion in an industry founded on body shaming.' She stepped onto the landing. 'Come on, you're going to be late for school.'

'We'll be going to museums and art galleries and eating snails and practising our Frrrench.' Izzy rolled the r in an attempt to make Annie laugh.

'Enough,' Annie said. 'Let's go.'

But Izzy was fired up now. 'Four days. And Mrs Jackson said if we pay the deposit now, you don't have to pay the last instalment until June. And my birthday is in July so it could be my present. I won't ask for anything else.'

Just what she needed. Sweat sprang to Annie's forehead and

under her arms. She wafted the hem of her uniform tunic, letting cooler air fan up her mutinous body.

'How many times? No.'

'I don't get it. You say it's because of the money, but when I suggest ways to get it, you still say no. So if it isn't the money, why won't you let me go?'

Because I need to keep you with me.

Because I'm scared to apply for a passport.

Because we have been found.

'Because I said so. Now can you please do as you're told and stop behaving like a spoilt brat.'

With a grunt of frustration, Izzy barged past her and thudded downstairs.

Annie ran a flannel under the cold tap. Looked in the mirrored cabinet. Dull skin, soft pouches under thready eyeballs. Feverish cheeks.

The menopause versus teenage hormones had to be one of Mother Nature's shittier tricks.

No time to think about that now. She dashed the damp cloth over her face and the back of her neck. Lifted her arms for inspection, but the black nylon tunic was designed to camouflage stains. Pulled her curls – coarser and threaded with grey – into a ponytail secured with one of Izzy's scrunchies from the cabinet.

Hair. She had an appointment booked with Pauline tomorrow. She should cancel. But it was such a mess and she was seeing Liam … supposed to be, anyway. Maybe she should cancel that—

'I thought you said we were late?' Izzy called up the stairs.

Twenty sullen minutes later, they pulled up by the sign for Uppermoss High School. Izzy unclicked her seatbelt, swung her heavy bag off her knees.

Annie nodded at the furled umbrella in the footwell. 'Looks like rain.'

Izzy snatched the umbrella and swung the door open. 'You know where it's not raining? Paris.'

'Listen, remember you're going to Lucy's after school,' Annie said.

No reply.

'Do you hear me?'

'*Yes.* Okay.'

Izzy fluffed her hair where it had caught under her blazer collar and hoisted the rucksack onto her shoulders, like a turtle slipping on a shell.

'Have a nice day. I love you,' Annie said.

But Izzy was already striding out of earshot.

Inside the car was warm and stuffy, filled with the battling aromas of dog blanket and air freshener. But despite the cosy fug, she shivered.

The school's grey slate roof and redbrick walls peeked between the latticework of oak trees bordering the playground. Inside, Izzy would be consoling Lucy with a hug. They would walk together to the form room, open their planners to Monday, 29 March, and wait to be registered.

Isabel Smith?

Here, Miss.

Ping. She jerked upright, scrabbled for the phone, but it was only the family tracker app reassuring her *Izzy is at school.* Safe – for now. Home and school. The secure, narrow confines of the refuge she had built around them. A fortress.

The radio presenter's cheery voice rose over the idling engine.

'... news headlines at eight-thirty.'

Shit.

Annie pressed the accelerator, almost immediately braking when the lights ahead turned amber. A woman waited on the kerb, tense fingers clutching the handle of a buggy, hair tangled by the wind.

A sudden spatter of rain hit the windscreen. The wipers

screeched, keeping time with the rapid beat of her heart. Five minutes late already. The wind whipped the trees by the war memorial into a frenzied dance. She pressed the accelerator and surged to the bumper of the white transit van in front.

The traffic slowed to a halt. Across the road, a group of parents waiting to go in to the toddler group where Izzy and Lucy met for the first time. The home-to-school-to-work commute was like a PowerPoint presentation of a contented childhood. Memories whirled like dead leaves caught on the breeze: shepherd-Izzy forgetting her lines in the nativity. Dressing as a bee with net-curtain wings for story time at the library. Remembrance Sunday parades in her Brownie uniform. That time she tumbled off the swing in the park, cut her knee and refused to cry.

Drumming her nails on the steering wheel, Annie glanced down at the cupholder where she stashed her phone.

'Who are you?' she said aloud. 'What do you know?'

An old friend.
Everything.

New damp spread under her arms, across her forehead. She wound the window and let the cool air caress her skin while she mentally crossed through the roll call of 'old friends' yet again. Her? Him? Too young, too old, didn't know, wouldn't care.

And the two primary suspects couldn't be sending her messages.

Because one was in prison and the other was dead.

The traffic eventually carried her to the surgery car park. Unlike yesterday, only her reserved space remained free. The wheels of Samara's ancient Land Rover had strayed across the line, forcing Annie to squeeze out of the driver's door and between the two cars.

Boots and coats and on-the-go snacking debris littered the back seat of the jeep. And among the junk and in full view of any passing lowlife was the black vet bag that should never, ever

51

be left unattended. She tutted and tried the door handle. At least it was locked.

The path showed signs of recent sweeping. Good. No trace of yesterday's smashed glass and the daffodils tidied and reduced to stalks. The surgery door was open, the metal security shutter rolled up out of the way, as expected.

But the window shutter remained closed.

For a heart-stopping second, she thought it was blood daubed across the grey ridges. Crimson streaks dripped down in sticky rivulets, pooling in the curled metal lip at the bottom. But she knew the iron tang of blood and this wasn't it. This was chemical, a reek that stung the nostrils.

Not blood, paint.

Thickly sprayed crimson paint spelling out a single, angry word:

Killer.

Then

The 1970s parade of shops that served the Manor was both unfit for purpose and architecturally grim. Every other unit sat empty behind roller shutters graffitied with layers of scribbles. Some joker had sprayed *Keep Out!* across the entrance to the underpass. Litter swirled around bins that never were emptied. Tattered police incident tape clung to a lamppost, a fluttering reminder of a recent stabbing. Weeds colonised the cracked tarmac and, when Annie collected her prescription, only the pharmacy, the minimart and a bookies showed signs of life. She skirted a pile of broken glass, almost bumped into a man pouring cooking fat down a drain. A collarless dog ran up and feverishly licked grease off the grate. Gross. She pressed her fist to her mouth, stomach churning.

The nausea had barely eased by the time she reached the urine-tinged air of the stairwell.

Hesitated.

Shit.

Peering around the corner, she could see Sylvia's grandson, Lindon, stood with his spine flattened against the wall, panic etched on his face. He clutched a shopping bag to his chest. The older boys who always hovered around the block had fenced him in with their bikes.

'You are fucking going to do it,' one said, low and menacing. 'I don't care if you don't want to. And if your grandma calls the police again, you're fucking dead. You get me?'

She froze.

It wasn't her business. What if one of them mugged her? Pulled a knife? They knew where she lived. She clutched the paper pharmacy bag, ready to hurry past, eyes downcast … and saw Lindon's jean-clad legs tremble. Not much, a little tremor. But enough.

Her heart sank. She couldn't walk by. Couldn't abandon this shaking child to his fate. She set her shoulders, injected confidence into her walk and entered the stairwell.

'Hi, Lindon,' she said, breezily. 'Everything okay?'

The one at the front swivelled his handlebars. From a distance, he seemed late teens, but up close, he was too young to shave. Distinctive, too. That greyed-out complexion and bulging pale blue eyes triggered something. Did she know him? A long, thin strand of dishwater hair, trapped by the red baseball cap, stuck to a pimpled cheek.

'He's fine, aren't you, mate?' The old-young boy's grin revealed brownish teeth in red swollen gums. Her emotions shifted to pity. No one made sure this kid brushed twice a day. No one checked he ate three square meals or washed.

Gollum. That's whom he reminded her of.

Lindon nodded mutely.

'Well, I promised your gran I'd help her with something,' Annie lied. 'So you'd better come with me.'

There was a moment of suspended hush. Lindon twitched like a cornered mouse and the boys looked at each other, communicating without words. Her heartbeat quickened.

And then the tinny static of a walkie-talkie entered the stairwell, followed by two uniformed police officers and, like magic, the boys and their bikes disappeared.

She had registered the patrol car on the way in, but that was hardly a rare sight at the Manor. Even though rationally, she knew the police were not here for her, she bent down to fiddle with her shoelace, but they didn't even look at her. When she straightened up, they – and Lindon – had gone.

She continued up the stairs, pausing again when she reached the turn on the landing for their floor. A woman, wearing charcoal work trousers with a white blouse, a single red streak through her neat black plait, rapped her knuckles on Lauren's kitchen window.

Bang. 'Open the door.' *Bang.* 'It's me.'

The male officer, a bearded man in his forties, stuck his arm out. 'Donna—'

She turned on him, the long plait whipping over her shoulder. 'Don't you Donna me. My sister calls, hysterical, saying she's hiding in the bathroom. That he's going to kill her. Why aren't you breaking the door down? She could be dying in there.'

The female officer turned quickly to scan the gangway. Annie shrank back, clutching her bag to her chest. Too late.

'Excuse me,' the policewoman said, coming towards her. 'Do you live here?'

Oh god. Nothing for it. She stepped out of the shadows.

She nodded. 'Next door.'

The male officer reached for his pocketbook. 'Good morning, madam. Your name is …?'

Her mouth went dry. Uniforms. Questions. Black dots swarmed in her peripheral vision.

The man pressed his thumb against the pen, an impatient *click, click, click.*

'Annie Smith.'

He scribbled it down. 'And have you seen anyone here today?'

It was okay. Different name, different hair, different clothes. Different woman. Not a hint he'd seen her before.

She opened her mouth to reply, but before she could speak, hinges creaked and a voice said, 'What's going on?'

Lauren. Strained and pale, but definitely alive.

Relief flashed across Donna's face, followed immediately by anger. Her eyes widened.

'Oh my god.'

Everyone stared at the reddish-purple marks, each the dimensions of a man's fingertip, strung like a morbid necklace around Lauren's throat.

Donna jabbed at the policeman's notebook. 'Elliot Devlin. Make sure you write that down.'

Lauren bunched the dressing gown up to her chin and demanded, 'Why did you call the cops?'

'What was I supposed to do? You said he was trying to kill you.'

'No, I never.'

The policewoman held up both palms. 'Okay, listen, Lauren. Can we come in?'

'No,' she said, and pulled the door as though to close it.

But the other officer was quicker and stuck his boot inside, wiggling his foot to widen the gap.

'Is your boyfriend still in the flat?' he said.

'He's not her boyfriend!'

'Yes, he is!' Lauren shot back, bristling.

Donna barked out a harsh laugh. 'You're young enough to be his daughter! Does he ever take you out? Have you met his friends? His family?'

Lauren's expression hardened to contempt.

Annie slotted her key in the lock, but the female officer gently pressed her forearm down.

'Could you wait a moment, please?'

'He's using you,' Donna said. 'How many times? He lives somewhere nice and leafy over there' – she waved her hand towards the horizon – 'with his nice partner and their nice daughter. And then when he's in the mood to hurt someone, he comes round here. To you. Then you ring me, again. Scared.'

Lauren slammed the door.

The seconds stretched out in silence. Then Donna let out an

exaggerated sigh and shrugged in a *see what I have to deal with* gesture and addressed Annie.

'You *must* have heard something.'

She would have to give a statement. Give evidence. What if it went to court? Anyway, there was nothing to tell. Not really. Just the odd thud. Furniture being shifted. A parcel thrown. A shadow climbing across the balcony.

'Sorry, I never heard a thing,' she said.

Donna's mouth tightened. 'Don't give me that. You could hear a mouse fart through those walls. They're like paper. Didn't you see her bruises? Don't you care?'

The policeman put his notebook away. 'If Lauren doesn't want to press charges, all we can do is note your concerns on file.'

'You could arrest him.'

'We could,' he agreed. 'But you know as well as I do that the CPS won't be interested.'

There was a pause. A garbled burst of static blared from the walkie-talkie.

'Fine,' Donna said eventually, in a tone that said it really wasn't. 'Let's all let him get away with nearly strangling her.'

She spun around, quick enough to make Annie flinch.

'Next time you turn the telly up or put the pillow over your ears or pretend that nothing's wrong, think about Elliot Devlin. He is a psychopath who gets his kicks from hurting women. God only knows what he's capable of. And you could have helped to stop him. Today. So when he finally does kill Lauren,' she said, eyes glazed with furious tears, 'her blood will be on your hands too.'

Now, Monday

Samara emerged from the washroom wiping her hands on a paper towel. Dark bags puffed under her eyes and her hair needed a wash.

'You know when I first saw it, I genuinely thought it was blood, not paint,' she said. 'I am sick to death of the Maguires.'

'Are you sure it was them?'

Annie unzipped her fleece and hung it on a peg in their tiny staffroom.

Samara shot her a quizzical look. 'Red paint. Killer. Who else could it be?'

'Good point,' Annie said lightly. She went behind the reception desk and dumped her own on top of a neat pile of invoices. 'You've left your bag on the back seat, by the way.'

Samara crumpled the paper towel and pressed the pedal on the waste bin. 'See, that's what the Maguires do to me. I cannot wait for this court case to be over. Back in a sec.'

Only once her boss was outside, did Annie let her knees give way.

Killer.

Of course it was them. Of course. The Maguire family comprised mum Carol, dad Dave plus son and daughter who collectively ran a breeding kennels on the outskirts of town. *Had* run.

The chain of events had happened quickly. First one, then two, then five frantic owners had appeared in the waiting room clutching their shivering puppies. Within a fortnight, each one had died from parvovirus and it hadn't taken much digging to discover the common denominator was the Maguires' kennels. The inspector's findings shut the entire operation down the same day.

The door chimed. Samara put the black bag on the desk. 'Can you sort this out while I ring the police?'

'You know, it's probably not worth calling them,' Annie said, casually. She knelt down and pressed the buttons on the safe keypad. 'You'll be on hold forever and then when you get through, you'll just get a crime number. I bet they won't even come round for a bit of graffiti.'

'True.'

'Unless you've got some evidence,' Annie continued slowly, as though the idea was still forming as she verbalised it. 'Is there anything on the CCTV that might connect it to them?'

The safe door opened. Controlled medication lived on the top shelf, and on the bottom, the cash box with a fat envelope on top and the surgery credit card. Although the majority of clients paid by card now, several still settled their bills the old-fashioned way.

'There is, but it's the usual: figure in a baggy hoodie, scarf pulled up. Impossible to tell who it is. Could be male or female. Could be a Maguire, could be anyone. They run up, get the spray can out. Over in a minute. Same with the broken glass yesterday. Caught that on the camera, but it's useless. And they're wearing gloves, so no fingerprints.'

Carefully, Annie slotted vials and pills in the correct spaces. Her pulse beat in her ears.

'No distinguishing features at all? No sign of a car?'

'Not a thing.'

She used the desk to lever herself to standing.

'That's so annoying,' she said with studied casualness. 'I bet the police will just say there's nothing to go on. Maybe I could mention it to Liam instead?'

No way could she mention this to Liam.

'Yeah. You're right, there's no point. I can't deal with it now, anyway. I had a call-out for a pregnant ewe chased by a dog. Eleven o'clock last night. Now a dead ewe, unfortunately, and now I'm knackered.' She scrubbed her hands through her hair until it stood in spikes. 'Two emergency visits back to back, both ending in disaster and now all this with the Maguires. I really am questioning my career choice this morning.'

'Please don't do that. You've built this' – Annie waved around the waiting room – 'up from scratch. We're having to expand because you're so amazing at what you do. The clients love you. No vet can save every animal, but preventing suffering is just as important.'

'Well, the Maguires clearly disagree, which is ironic, considering how that family treated their own animals. But with Helen not working and the baby and every penny going to the loan repayments, we can't afford any bad publicity. Actually … oh.' Samara's hand flew to her mouth. 'The repayments. I was supposed to do that, wasn't I?'

'Don't panic. I've sorted it.'

Steepling her hands in prayer at chest height, Samara said, 'I honestly don't know what I'd do without you. Probably go bankrupt. Definitely go mad.'

Annie laughed. 'Don't be daft. Listen,' she said. 'I noticed the cash box is getting full. Shall I pay it into the bank at lunchtime?'

'You do look like you could do with some fresh air. That'd be great if you don't mind.'

'I don't mind at all,' she said.

The chimes announced the first client of the day.

'Hello, Mrs Shepherd,' Annie said, walking around the desk and into the waiting area. 'How is Ghillie?'

The elderly dog lifted his ears at his name.

'Getting stiff,' Mrs Shepherd said.

Knees clicking as she bent to pat his docile head, Annie said, 'Oof, you and me both, old boy. Come on, let's get you on the scales.'

For the next hour, Annie switched to autopilot. Her mouth held conversations and made phone calls. Greeted clients, lips smiling or sympathetically pursing as appropriate. Her fingers efficiently typed invoices and notes. Sent emails.

The man from KleanupKrew pulled into the car park. The generator juddered noisily on the van and water shot from the *Ghostbusters* contraption he strapped to his back, rattling the shutters with the force of a cannon.

She checked the Family Safe app. *Izzy is at school.* There were no new notifications on her phone. She glanced around the waiting room. When she was sure no one was looking, she opened the message for the hundredth time. The zap of shock hadn't dulled.

I want £50k by Friday. Or I will tell the girl everything.

She worked part time answering phones and weighing dogs. Shopped for food at Aldi. Bought her clothes on eBay. She was a lone parent, for god's sake. If she finished the month in the black, that was a result. Her bank balance was £293.56. The same as when she checked last night. Ditto her savings account, which contained slightly less than five thousand.

Which was a *lot* less than fifty thousand.

Samara poked her head around the door, raising her voice over the thundering water.

'Blimey, it's like a carwash in here. Mr Beck and Juno, please.' Pause. 'Mr Beck?'

A white-haired man and his white-muzzled Jack Russell shuffled into the consultation room.

The clanging of water on metal almost masked the message beep. Annie snatched her phone then fumbled, sending it skittering across the veneered surface of the desk and down to the tiled floor. By some miracle, the screen remained uncracked. She polished it on her trouser leg.

Morning. L xx

The scrubbing brush banged vigorously over the shutters.

She wiped sudden tears away. Why did this have to happen when she'd met someone she actually liked?

The first time Liam walked into the surgery, Annie noticed him right away because he looked a bit like David Tennant. If David Tennant went to the gym, had a grey crewcut and was bricking it over his dog wolfing down a chocolate Santa. Thankfully, Lola the Labrador had a strong stomach and Liam was all smiles as he paid his bill. As was Annie until he asked, 'Which part of London are you from?'

The answer stuck in her throat. She could only stare, chest tight.

'The accent,' he added after a beat. 'I used to live there.'

She typed the case notes into her PC and smiled politely, 'I've been up north for so long, I thought it had disappeared.'

'I'm a detective,' he said. 'Nothing gets past me.'

When he asked her out for a drink last December, she told herself his job didn't matter. And again a few days later when they went for dinner. And the more she saw him, the more she liked him so by the time she figured out he had been a detective in the Metropolitan Police during the two years she lived on the Manor, she pushed it to the back of her mind. Because she believed Annabel Naughton-Smith didn't exist anymore. That the past was past. Dead and buried.

What an idiot.

The jet-wash roar stopped abruptly. The shutter slammed open, triggering an overweight French bulldog into startled yelping. The door chimed once more and the boiler-suited cleaner strolled up to the desk, leaving watery splodges all over the clean tiles.

'Killer.' He chuckled and dropped his sodden gloves on the veneered desk. 'Dear oh dear. Did you bump off some old lady's cat? Do away with a prize parrot?'

Funny. She gave him a long look, tore off a sheet of blue cleaning roll, lifted his gloves and mopped up the puddle. He slapped the invoice on the counter without another word and left.

By now, she'd been at work for almost three hours. Monday was always busy with clients, and she had to wait for a lull before she could tackle the surgery's social media. Although Annie Smith had no online presence, the surgery's numerous platforms fell into her remit. She didn't mind. Usually, it was a two-minute job to post a kitten photo or hamster meme. Slightly longer to write an update on the surgery's expansion plans.

On Friday, she'd posted with advice on how to toilet-train your new puppy. Usually, this generated a few likes.

Not today.

Fifty-plus comments? Had to be a mistake. She scrolled down, felt her eyes widen in disbelief.

This vet murders puppies.

If you love your animal do not go to Uppermoss Vets.

Samara Khan kills dogs.

Killer.

'Fuck!'

The exclamation shot out before she could stop it. But Mr Ross, the only client in the waiting room, remained engrossed in his phone.

The initial shock turned swiftly to anger. How dare they? Anyone who knew Samara's commitment to animal welfare would see through these comments. Sure enough, numerous loyal clients had posted passionate rebuttals. But like all small villages, Uppermoss had its share of spiteful people who loved a troll-fest.

She wanted nothing more than to scrub the lies out of existence. But it was proof of the Maguires' hate campaign. And evidence for the court case. Screenshot first and then:

Delete

Delete

Delete

She'd just reported the last fake profile when a new comment flashed up. Poised to screenshot, she froze.

This comment had nothing to do with puppies, or the Maguires, or the surgery or Samara. This comment was directed at her.

Hello Annabel, the little white box said.

Instinct took over. Desperate to put a physical distance between herself and the screen, she propelled the chair violently backwards. Almost tipping over, she gripped the edge of the desk. It wasn't the comment that horrified her, although that was bad enough.

It was the profile picture.

At first glance, it seemed innocuous enough: young woman, pretty, in a hard way. Bleached hair, thin eyebrows plucked into high arches, a style that had dated quickly. Even after all these years, she recognised that photo. Of course she did, she *took* it.

View profile?

She pressed *Yes.*

The only post on Lauren Taylor's Facebook profile was a larger version of the thumbnail image. Every detail of the messy flat in the background was exactly as Annie remembered it. From the marble-topped coffee table littered with bills and takeout cartons to the knickers festooning the radiator like lacy bunting. Clothes puddled where holiday outfits had been tried and abandoned. A shocking-pink wheelie suitcase stood in the corner, the half-price tag dangling from the handle.

And in the centre, perched on the arm of her tatty sofa, was Lauren. She wore a pink velour tracksuit unzipped partway to reveal an expanse of sunbed tan. A roll-up smouldered between her neon-tipped nails. And her expression …

The chill that shivered through Annie had nothing to do with the temperature. Lauren looked so young, so smiley. So full of life.

She closed her eyes, but the image burnt behind her lids and with it wafted the sickly smell of vodka and Red Bull and the throb of music shaking the walls. And Lauren's excited voice, louder and louder as the evening wore on. In so many ways, she seemed far older than twenty. But on that evening, three days before she flew to Ibiza, she'd been as giddy as a kid on Christmas Eve.

According to Facebook, Lauren Taylor had no friends, no posts, no life events. The creation of Lauren Taylor's profile picture occurred a minute before she typed *Hello Annabel*. Lauren Taylor followed a single page: Uppermoss Veterinary Clinic.

As she returned to the page, someone was typing a new comment.

'Oh god.' The groan surprised her, escaping from her lips before she even knew it was coming.

The new comment came from Lauren Taylor.

See you soon, it said.

Then

'Out of Order'

Annie sighed at the sign Sellotaped to the Manor's lift and stuck her thumb under the strap chafing her shoulder.

Never mind the lift, her *life* was Out of Order.

It was out of order that she no longer had a car. Out of order she had no money, no job, no hope. Out of order she lived in a block of flats no one cared about. She wiggled her shoulders to move the edge of a tin that dug into her shoulder blade. Out of order that the property management company failed to repair the lift.

Slowly, she climbed the stairwell, feet moving in time to a series of bangs bouncing off the concrete walls. On the first landing, a workman hammered plywood over a window frame. Sylvia stood in faded slippers, forehead crumpled with worry, watching.

'Hello,' Annie said. She set two carrier bags down, flexing her fingers to restore the blood flow. 'Is everything okay?'

The older woman turned resigned eyes towards her. 'I got home from work this morning and the window was smashed. Second time this year.'

'Is there anything I can do to help?'

Tired smile. 'No. But thank you.'

Aggressive shouts squeezed into a gap between hammer blows. A woman's voice from the floor above. Lauren.

'I'm going to kill you!'

A faintly Essex accent responded, 'Is that right?'

Sylvia's fingers strayed to the gold cross at her neck.

'Excuse me. I need to get some sleep,' she said quietly and disappeared inside, leaving Annie staring at the peeling red paint of a closed door.

'Catfight,' the man said, rolling his eyes.

Ignoring him, she gathered up her bags and hurried towards the spiralling shouts.

'I'm warning you, Megan. Back off.'

'You don't scare me.'

Shoes scrabbled on concrete. A metal rail rattled. More shouts.

'Get your hands off me.'

'Or else?'

An anonymous dog barked close by and a neighbour yelled to *keep it down!*

Annie, panting now, reached the second floor. Momentum plus the heavy rucksack sent her staggering onto the concrete walkway towards two figures.

Lauren clenched her fists, her face contorted in a snarl. The woman, presumably Megan, gestured along the walkway with a set of car keys. Mid-twenties, tall and gym fit in black top and grey tailored trousers. Professionally highlighted hair and a spray tan. Clear, glowing skin.

And a rounded pregnant belly.

Cowering behind her was a gorgeous little girl of about five or six, hair in long ringleted bunches.

Annie put the bags down. 'Is everything okay?'

Megan's head whipped around.

'It won't be if she doesn't stay away from Elliot. Lauren Taylor, you are a lying little *whore*.'

On the final word, Lauren grunted, launching herself at her

67

glamorous rival. The little girl backed against the wall, mouth open in a long wail.

Annie hastily stepped between them, holding a palm in front of their respective panting chests.

'Lauren, you can't go attacking pregnant women.' She turned to the other woman. 'Megan, is it? You are not doing your baby any favours. Or your daughter. I suggest you get home and have a lie-down before—'

Fury distorted Megan's pretty face. She grabbed Annie's wrist, her long nails digging into the thin skin.

'Who the hell are you?' Her tone matched the aggression of her actions.

The little girl howled. For a moment, the woman's shoulders sagged, revealing her aggression for what it really was: an act of desperation from a mum-to-be. Scared of losing her boyfriend. Scared of being left alone with two children.

'I just want to help,' Annie said, rubbing the five crescent moons indented on her wrist.

Ignoring her, Megan snapped her fingers. 'Jessica – now.'

At the command, the girl peeled herself away from the wall and, twisting her fingers together, trailed behind her mother towards the cluster of teenagers attracted by the shouting.

'Don't you dare laugh at me!' Megan shouted.

The boys smirked. One turned his baseball cap so the peak touched his collar and widened his eyes in a mocking *who me?* And poor little Jessica's eyes grew huge in her tear-stained face, clearly afraid to walk past them.

'I said now!' Megan shouted, jerking the girl along so she stumbled in her mum's angry wake.

Lauren watched their retreating backs. 'Crazy *bitch*.'

Ketchup-smeared plates and coffee-stained mugs sat in the sink, half-submerged under a scum of oily globs and bits of food. A tangle of wet washing spilled from the open machine. Everything smelled of stale smoke and earthy damp.

Lauren leaned against her kitchen worktop and lit a cigarette. Her knees and feet aligned perfectly, her back poker-straight; her prim posture was at odds with the flaked mascara and the ring of liner clinging to her chapped lips.

Annie set her bags down on the dingy lino. She lifted the kettle, checked the water level and pressed the switch.

'You and Megan could be sisters. You're so alike.'

Lauren picked dried skin from her lower lip. 'She wishes.'

'And the little girl – Jessica, is it? Is she Dev's daughter?'

'According to Megan.'

The tone said *so what*? But the roll-up trembled between her fingers.

'Don't take this the wrong way,' Annie said, washing two mugs. 'But if his girlfriend is pregnant, then he really should be with them.'

The cigarette paper burnt with a faint hiss.

'Yeah, well.' She pulled the hem of her T-shirt taut over a small but unmistakable bump. 'What if she's not the only one?'

God, what was she – nineteen?

'You're having a baby?'

She smiled, half-shy, half-defiant. 'Ten weeks. That's why Megan's mad.'

'Okay. Well,' Annie said, processing this information. 'Congratulations. Does Donna know?'

'She thinks I should get rid of it. Says I can't even look after myself, let alone a baby. That I'm too young, but I'm not.' She stroked her belly and smiled, broadly this time. 'I can't wait to be a mum.'

Now, Monday

'Are you okay?'

Annie jumped. She hadn't heard Samara come into reception. Mr Beck held his wallet while Juno slurped noisily from the water bowl. She quickly closed the browser and Lauren Taylor's smiling face vanished.

'You've gone white as a sheet,' her boss continued.

'Just a headache. I didn't sleep very well. I'll be fine.'

Lauren's grin hung in the air, the afterimage branded on her retinas.

See you soon.

Samara screwed up her nose. 'And that paint thinner gets you right' – she mimed throttling herself and stuck her tongue to one side – 'there. Why don't you take a long lunch after you've been to the bank? I'll manage.'

Samara addressed Mr Beck. 'Call us if the knee seizes up or there are any issues with the boosters. Mr Ross, shall we take Pablo in?'

'So …' Annie pointed at the card reader on the desk. 'Fifty-five for the boosters today, please. Cash or card?'

'Card, love.' His ancient wallet creaked open. 'I was just saying to Samara it's a terrible business, what's happened.'

'Yes.'

She crouched down to open the safe. Petty cash. The money from last night in an envelope. Surgery chequebook.

'People profiting from suffering. I know some people think that animals don't have feelings, not like people, but you've only got to take one look at my Juno to know that's not the case.'

'Oh, absolutely.' She looked up. 'Contactless?'

Too late. He'd inserted the card.

'Pin, please,' she said, pulling herself up by the edge of the desk. 'Let me get …'

He withdrew his glasses case from his top pocket. Eased it open. Slid the glasses up to the bridge of his nose and peered at the keypad. With glacial slowness, he pressed the buttons. Paused. Pressed delete. Tried again.

Annie stuffed the cash in her bag, zipped it up, slung the strap over her shoulder.

'I don't know how they sleep at night, those Magees—'

'Maguires.' She tore off the receipt.

He folded the scrap of paper and slowly scored the crease with his thumbnail.

'Maguires. And I read in the paper that they didn't even get help when they knew the animals were dying. Is that true?'

'Uh huh.' Annie strode around the desk.

Why wouldn't he just *go*?

'Like I said to Samara,' he continued. 'Chances are, it'll be a slap on the wrists and they'll be free to set up all over again. They want stringing up, people like that. I remember when I went to the rescue to get Juno—'

'Thanks for coming, Mr Beck.'

She yanked the door open, wincing at the confusion in the old man's eyes. But she had to get to the bank. Now.

Get the money and she could breathe. Get the money and this would go away.

'I won't keep you,' he said, buttoning his coat. 'All I wanted to say is, don't worry. They think they can get away with murder, people like that, but what goes around comes around. Even if it takes years, life has a way of making sure you get what you deserve.'

Juno cocked his leg on the flattened daffodils while Mr Beck nodded an acknowledgement to Annie's wave. She'd make it up to him next time. Definitely. A brew and a chat. Just not today.

Fifteen minutes later, the automatic door swung open and she stepped into air-conditioned hush. The cashier wore a neat grey suit and a red cravat. She had matching red nails and the gold badge on her lapel said 'Mandy'.

Wiping her palms down the front of her trousers, Annie leaned into the Perspex screen.

'Hi, can I make a deposit, please?'

She dropped the envelope of cash and printed paying-in slip into the hole in the wooden counter. Mandy put the money in the counting machine.

'That's three hundred and fifty-six,' she said. The printer whirred and she twisted around to tear off the paper. 'And here's your receipt.'

£79, 673. The loan for the building work had cleared.

'Can I help with anything else today?'

'Actually, yes.' Annie folded the receipt. 'I need to speak to someone about a loan. Personal, not business. For me.'

'Of course. Let me book you an appointment with our loans adviser. When can you come in?'

Annie spread her fingers flat on the counter, the wood cool against her palms. 'It's kind of an emergency. It'll only take a couple of minutes, I don't mind waiting.'

'She doesn't work on Mondays, I'm afraid.'

'Well, could you do it?' Annie rapped her debit card against the security screen. 'I want to borrow using the equity on my house. You should be able to see my account on the computer.'

Mandy's smile grew fixed. 'I'm sorry, but I don't have anything to do with mortgages or loans. And there are no appointments for at least a fortnight.' She tapped the keyboard. 'No, I tell a lie. There's a cancellation.'

'When?'

'Next Tuesday, at half past nine,' Mandy said, triumphantly. 'Shall I book—?'

'No,' Annie said, sufficiently vehemently for the cashier in the next booth to lift her head.

She hadn't been aware of the queue forming behind her. Feet shuffled, someone coughed, their interest no doubt well piqued now.

Calm down. Don't be memorable.

'Sorry.' She forced a smile and tucked a stray spiral of hair behind her ear. 'It's just … important.'

Mandy bared perfect teeth in a smile. 'I do understand. But I'm sorry, I don't have the authority to help you and even if you had an appointment today, any loan or mortgage would take at least two weeks to arrange.'

Two weeks?

'Please. I can't wait that long, I need the money today. Tomorrow at the latest. If you go on the computer, you can see I've got plenty of equity and that's all I want: a loan against the house.'

A man coughed. Someone whispered.

'There simply isn't anything I can do.' Mandy's attention wandered to the queue. 'Even if the adviser could see you today, the paperwork takes time. We have to follow protocol. Money laundering safeguards and so on. Is there anything else I can help you with?'

Anything *else*? Was she having a laugh?

Tell me how I'm supposed to find fifty thousand pounds by Friday.

And if you can't, tell me what to do when my world implodes.

Chin down, gaze fixed to the fake wood floor, she headed for the exit.

What must these strangers – oh god, please let them all be strangers – think of a woman begging for money in the bank? Pity, from the kinder hearts. A few, consumed by their own worries, wouldn't care. That left contempt. Her spine sagged under the weight of judgemental stares. Like she was nobody. Nothing.

Tut tut. Bitter people whose fingertips spread poison over the internet. Middle-aged woman humiliates herself in bank. Gambling debts? Loan shark? Secret opiate addiction?

The automatic doors opened. She stepped outside, dazed and blinking in the sudden light. A cold wind sent shivers down her neck.

Whatever theories they came up with, they couldn't be worse than the truth.

Then

'It's me,' Annie said, rapping lightly on Lauren's kitchen window.

Cold wind snuck in behind her, rifling through a dusty pile of brown envelopes on the hall lino. Lauren pulled her dressing gown around her bump and said, 'Did you get the stuff?' She sniffed, her nose red and flaky. A cluster of spots nestled at the corner of her colourless lips.

'In here,' Annie said, shaking the plastic bag. 'Food. Tissues, Lemsip, cough medicine.'

Right on cue, Lauren buried her mouth in the crook of her elbow and coughed until tears streamed down her cheeks.

Winter on the Manor was cold, wet and long. Frost glittered on the aluminium window frames. Condensation fogged the glass, freezing to a thin glaze when the temperatures dipped below zero. Patches of mould bloomed in forgotten corners and icy draughts stole in through cracked ceiling tiles and loose skirting boards. If she hadn't had to buy groceries for Lauren, she wouldn't have ventured into the bitter morning.

She put the shopping bag on the kitchen worktop. 'Oh dear, you do sound rough.'

Lauren winced and clasped the small of her back, arching forwards so her rounded belly stuck out.

'Every time I cough, it kicks me. I can't sleep and I'm so fucking itchy. It's doing my head in.'

She lifted her top, scratched the taut skin. The red nail marks ran parallel to the marbled blue veins.

Annie twisted the cap off the calamine lotion. 'Go sit down and put some of this on. I'll make us both a drink.'

Conscious the prepayments meter would be running on fumes, she filled the kettle to the '2 cup' line. While it boiled, she watched the hooded boys hunched over their handlebars, slowly patrolling the perimeter of the Manor forecourt. Did no one care that they never went to school? A huge four-by-four roared into the car park, narrowly missing ploughing into the teenagers, who scattered like pigeons, then parked diagonally across two spaces. Idiot.

Still stirring the Lemsip granules, she went into the lounge.

'Here, this should help.'

Lauren lay on the sofa rubbing lotion onto her belly. An empty toilet roll, a few scraps of white clinging to the cardboard tube, sat next to a mountain of crumpled tissues on the coffee table. Barely an inch of the marble surface showed through the clutter of takeaway flyers and overflowing ashtrays.

'Looks disgusting,' she said, wrapping her fingers around the proffered mug. She blew on the steaming lemon, wrinkled her nose. 'And it smells wei—'

A key turned in the lock. The door slammed against the wall, and the air shook.

'Fuck.' Lauren startled upright, spilling Lemsip on the cushion. 'Fuck.'

Dev filled the lounge doorway. He wore a black knitted beanie and a padded coat that accentuated the breadth of his shoulders. Neatly groomed stubble covered his jaw. Unlike Lauren, he looked tanned, healthy and fit.

He inspected Annie, head to foot. Braced his hands against the doorframe and began to rock very lightly, very slowly back and forth.

'Who's this, Lauren?' he said.

'No one. She's just going.'

'What have I told you about having people round here when I'm coming?'

'You said don't do it.'

Lips pursed in evident disgust, he scanned the room. 'Look at the state of you. And this place. You live here for nothing and keep it like a pigsty.'

Annie prepared the first syllables of protest, but Lauren's raised eyebrows sent her an urgent warning: *do not say anything.* She picked a cushion off the floor and set it neatly on the sofa.

Dev's jaw muscles twitched, working hard on a piece of gum. 'Why is she here?'

A little cylinder of ash dropped on Lauren's dressing gown, and she licked the tip of her finger and dabbed at the grey smudge.

'You can come to mine if you like,' Annie said quietly.

Eyes downcast, Lauren shook her head.

'She's not going anywhere,' Dev said. 'You are. Fuck off. Now.'

The conversational tone jarred with the rough words. A contradiction, like him. The suburb-dwelling bad boy with a posh boy accent.

'Look at this mess,' he said, flipping a pizza box off the chair. 'How am I supposed to have people here? It's embarrassing.'

Lauren's knees jigged and she looked at the partition wall that divided their two flats. Her gaze slid upwards and landed on a ceiling tile that had slipped out of position, exposing the cavity between this flat and the one above. It was about a foot deep and very, very dark.

Annie instinctively tracked Lauren's gaze. As did Dev. A bubble of silence held for one … two … three seconds while the three of them stared at the black square that stood out like a missing front tooth.

Then Dev moved so quickly, she had no time to react. His grip on her upper arm felt like steel.

Lauren slumped on the sofa, hugging a cushion to her belly.

He jerked Annie towards the hall. She yelped, stumbled, barely managing to right herself before his fingernails dug painfully into her flesh, forcing her upright and against his muscled body as he half-dragged her into the hall.

'Fuck off,' he shouted directly into her ear and she let out a pained cry.

He slapped her shoulder blades, kept his hand there and shoved. Hard. She stumbled onto the frozen walkway.

'I'm warning you,' he said. 'Stay out of my business.'

The metal door chain slipped from her fingers twice before she was able to secure it. Not that the flimsy links would offer much resistance. Fighting the urge to throw up, she dropped on the sofa and exhaled slowly. Her eardrum ached. Her back hurt. The impression of his grip smarted on the soft flesh of her upper arm. She sat, silent and still, waiting for the first shout, the first cry. This time she would ring the police. This time, she would make a statement and link it with Donna's earlier complaint. And Sylvia's.

But nothing happened. No yells, no smashing crockery, no cries for help. Only a knock at the door from Dev's business associate and the low murmur of voices. Thuds, bangs, the furniture bumping over the carpet she had heard before.

With extreme care, she placed her single dining chair adjacent to the partition wall, climbed up and put her ear to the painted plaster. A sliding, scraping sound, from … where? She tilted her head. Almost directly above.

More voices, indistinguishable. And a burst of laughter. *Lauren's* laughter. The voices moved into the hall and a moment later, both men were on the walkway.

She crouched down, eyes level with the windowsill, watching their retreating backs. Dev pulled his black hat on. The other man, shorter with thin, grey collar-length hair, zipped up his green bomber jacket.

She waited until both men had driven away then tentatively tapped on Lauren's kitchen window.

Knocked on the door. No reply. But she heard loud coughing.

Annie flipped the letterbox open.

'Lauren, can you let me in?'

Nothing.

'Don't worry, I watched him drive off.'

There was a pause. Then, 'I'm too tired.'

'Well, can I at least get my shopping?'

The excuse worked. A few seconds later, the door opened a crack and the bags appeared on the doorstep.

'Have you had any lunch?'

'Not hungry,' Lauren said and went to close the door.

'Listen,' Annie said. 'You don't need to stay here. I bet Donna would have you in a heartbeat.'

Lauren's eyes narrowed. 'Why would I want to do that?'

'To start over. You and the baby. Get away from this.' Annie swept her arm to include the flat and the teenagers in the car park. She lowered her voice. 'I don't care what Dev is using this place for, but you must see it's not the best environment for a child and I'm worried you haven't thought what it's going to be like when you've got a baby to consider as well. Men like Dev just don't change. Not for girlfriends or for babies.'

A tense pause followed. Annie shifted her weight from one foot to the other. Surely Lauren understood that?

'Well, that's good because I don't want Dev to change,' Lauren said eventually. Her nostrils flared, lips pinched. 'I like him the way he is. He lets me live in this flat. He gives me money. He loves me.'

How could anyone be so blind? Torn between pity and frustration, Annie couldn't help clicking her tongue in disagreement.

'I'm sorry, but he really doesn't. If he did—'

'You don't know the first thing about Dev or me.' A sharp poke at Annie's collarbone punctuated the end of the sentence.

79

She held her palms up defensively. 'Look, I'm not saying this to upset you.'

'My life has got fuck' – Lauren kicked one shopping bag – 'all' – she kicked the other – 'to do with you.'

'I'm only trying to look out for you. As a friend.'

'Don't be stupid, we're not *friends*.' Lauren spat the final word out. 'You're nobody. You're nothing.'

The slamming door sheared off the conversation, left her standing alone on the freezing walkway. Seconds later, dance music shuddered through the wall, the volume cranked up until the speakers crackled. The insistent beats stabbed rhythmically at Annie's sore ear and she pressed her fingertips to her temples, massaging the thin skin.

Back in her kitchen, the outdoor chill persisted. She lifted the bags of shopping onto the worktop to unpack. Stared. Every one of the eggs was broken, the viscous gloop slopping over the apples in their paper bag. The apples could be washed, but nothing could save the eggs. A whole week's worth, smashed.

She tilted her head back, blinking rapidly. On the other side of the gauzy curtain, a movement caught her eye. Sylvia. Her small body bent determinedly, as though fighting against a stiff wind. She hammered on Lauren's kitchen window. In the brief gap before one thumping bass track segued into the next, she shouted: 'I work nights, you know!' The music continued. Sylvia wrapped her cardigan tightly around her thin body and, in her own unexpected act of frustration, kicked Lauren's door.

Annie poured a glass of tap water. Pain pulsed up her back into her head. Her collarbone stung, reddened from Lauren's bony jab. Paracetamol. Bedside drawer?

In the hall, Dad had one arm tight around Mum's shoulders, fingers entwined. Young and hopeful, their honeymoon faces blissful with optimism and love. How different her life would be if they were still here.

Was it weird that she'd kind of enjoyed Mum's funeral? Or,

more accurately, the pub afterwards, hearing endless anecdotes about Mum's kindness, her enviable marriage, her sense of humour, her knack of making everyone feel special.

After the wake, life went on. Kids played in the street. Birds sang. Neighbours said hello. She worked, she spoke, she ate, she sleepwalked through the empty, lonely house. She didn't wake up until she met Oliver. The perfect man. The answer to her prayers.

Well, look where *that* got her: an empty, lonely flat.

She opened the bedside drawer. The paracetamol packet nestled next to the neat stack of anti-depressants and the bottle of sleeping pills.

Even on this drab winter's day, the Manor pulsed with life. Music played. TVs blared. A child skipped past her door, chatting excitedly. Cars drove past. There were people everywhere. People who, whatever circumstance had brought them there, had someone to talk to. Someone to love.

Mum said it was love from the moment the social worker called about a six-month-old baby girl. The details were sketchy: a young mum out of her depth and no family support, giving up her daughter for a better life. Annie felt nothing but gratitude. In gifting her to Mum and Dad, her birth mother gifted her a life overflowing with love and opportunity.

She chased two paracetamols down with water. Felt the pent-up tears finally wash down her cheeks and drip unchecked off her chin and nose.

At least they never knew what she had become.

Like Lauren said: she was nothing. She was nobody.

Now, Monday

She couldn't, just *couldn't* go back to work yet. For a start, she thought she might be sick. Or start crying. Or break down in front of Samara and spill everything in an uncontrollable torrent. Cathartic for a few seconds. But then, what?

The sky had darkened, threatening rain. Outside the bank, miniature daffodils rippled and waved in municipal tubs, their thin stalks close to breaking. She wandered down the bustling high street, listening to bursts of laughter coming out of Costa. Stepping aside to let a family holding gift bags, children chattering excitedly, enter the Pizza Express she and Izzy went to on special occasions.

Rain began to fall. Up ahead, a bus juddered away from a stop and she sat in the empty shelter. *Think.*

If not from the bank, where?

Annie took out the bank receipt, folded it flat and slipped it behind the surgery credit card in her phone case. Not Samara. Even if she screwed up the courage to ask for a loan, the down payment was due to the builder by Friday.

She shuffled straighter, the wooden slats of the bench digging into her spine. Flicked the phone screen to life and typed 'get money quick' into the browser. Instantly, the screen filled with exploitative loans at punitive rates. All capped at two or three thousand. Nothing like the amount she needed.

A bee batted angrily against the transparent side of the shelter, trying to get to the daffodils behind the invisible wall.

She sat under a banner advertising an artisan market and Easter activities and stared across the road at the regional police headquarters. Not that the building deserved anyone's attention. Like the Manor, the concrete-and-glazed façade epitomised no-frills functionality. And if the architect's brief had included phrases like 'people's mental health is not your concern' and 'cheap but not cheerful', then they had one hundred per cent nailed it.

People entered and left the revolving door. Some quickly with purpose evident in their determined strides. Others, on more reluctant feet.

She took her phone out and stared at the text.

£50k by Friday. Or I will tell the girl everything.

'Annie?'

She actually jumped. She smacked her elbow on the unforgiving wood of the armrest, sending skewers of pain shooting in both directions, shoulder to fingertips. The pain shocked her back to the present and the man in a black zip-up jacket and dark trousers. He had a black rucksack hung over one shoulder and a paper bag in his left hand.

'Hey, sorry,' the familiar voice said, full of concern. 'I didn't mean to make you jump.'

'Liam, hi,' she said, slipping her phone into her pocket. She forced a smile and smoothed her hair down.

'This is a nice surprise. I just got a sandwich to take back to work.' He waved the paper bag in the direction of the station. 'And I saw this woman sitting on this bench, miles away, and I thought, she looks like Annie. And here you are.'

'Here I am,' she said. 'I've just been to the bank. Not for me, for Samara. At work. And now I'm going back. To work. Glad I bumped into you, though. Are we still okay for Wednesday?

Around eight if that's okay? I could cook something. Or get a takeaway or something or—'

With her cheeks flaming and her phone burning a hole in her pocket, it was a miracle she didn't spontaneously combust right in front of him.

'All of the above,' he said with a smile when she eventually ran out of words. 'I'm easy.'

He leaned in to kiss her on the cheek, and if he noticed the sheen of sweat dampening her forehead, he didn't show it.

She stood up and buttoned her coat against the chill. It was turning into one of those beautiful spring mornings where the sky was blue but the air retained the memory of cooler days.

He paused at the top of the stone steps to wave, then disappeared through the automatic doors into the vestibule of the police station.

Although Liam didn't wear a uniform, a memory flashed into Annie's mind. She must have been four or five in her hand-knitted cardigan, giggling in the lounge back home. She was trying on Dad's helmet. She remembered the weight of it in her small hands. The soft darkness over her eyes. The thick chinstrap tickling her collarbone. Breathing in the comforting echo of Dad's shampoo. And over the whirring as she wound the camera on, Mum's laughter.

The next time a police officer stood in that house, her parents were both dead and no one was laughing.

A police van, blue lights flashing, shot out of the station car park. She should cross the road, walk into the station. She pictured herself asking the desk sergeant to speak to Liam. The measured words coming out of her mouth. *I'm being blackmailed and I can't pay. Please help me.*

No, I don't know who.

What are they threatening me with?

What do they know?

She dragged her hands down her face. It was ridiculous to

imagine she could share her secret with anyone, let alone a police officer. And one with connections to the Met, at that. One tug on the thread that linked her to London would unravel everything. If the blackmailer had tracked her down, a detective wouldn't have any issues following the trail back to the start. From Uppermoss, to leaving the Manor, to her arrest.

People passed by with dogs, children, shopping bags. Snatches of strangers' conversations merged with the constant rumble of traffic. The juddering hiss of a bus lowering to the kerb. Ordinary things. Ordinary lives.

Telling Liam was the last thing she could do.

Beep.

She fumbled, only just stopping the phone dropping to the pavement.

Can you get some coffee? Thanks, Samara.

Will do. She texted back. *Sorry, big queue at bank. Won't be long.*

When she stood up, a flash of white snagged her gaze. Rows of windows looked down from the police station, all blinkered by vertical blinds. Except one.

The blind had been pushed fully back in the window directly above the entrance. The white strip at the edge still swayed slightly next to a figure. From this distance, it was impossible to make out any details. But whoever it was, they were looking directly at her.

Then

After the row with Lauren, Annie didn't leave the flat for two days. The winter sun rose and set unnoticed behind her closed curtains. She ate cereal standing over the sink at three o'clock in the morning. Didn't bother to shower. Lay on the lumpy mattress staring at the ceiling, listening to the lives of others through the paper-thin walls. Forty-eight shapeless hours felt more like forty-eight days, punctuated only by medication.

Even when she slept, she woke up crying. Curled on her side, she sobbed for her mum and dad, for her marriage, for her home. Cried until her eye sockets ached and her chest hurt. And when she stopped, she took the bottle of sleeping tablets and the packs of Citalopram from the side of her bed and put them on top of the wardrobe, out of reach. Because they crept into her mind too often. Because if she didn't, she might take too many.

Because if she did, who would miss her?

She had nothing. She had nobody.

She was dozing on the sofa when a soft knocking woke her. Lauren stood on the doorstep.

'Quick. Come on!' she said.

Her trainers thud thudded to the ground. She clutched Annie's arm for support then wiggled her feet inside.

Annie cleared her rusty throat. 'What do you want?'

The sky was blue, but it was still cold. Lauren's panting breath came out in misty clouds. The reddened tip of her nose twitched, then she sneezed. She sniffed.

'Aw, don't be like that. Get your purse.' Scraping her hair up in her hands, she peered over the wall at a small crowd gathered around a white transit van. Blonde hairs bristled from her hasty topknot; underneath, the roots were almost black.

Annie folded her arms and didn't respond.

'Or have you got something better to do?' Lauren said, slyly.

And that was it. She didn't. And Lauren knew it.

'I didn't mean what I said the other day,' she continued, fiddling with the zip on her tracksuit. 'Sometimes I just say what comes in my head, you know? I've got anger management issues. That's why I got kicked out of school.'

Annie hesitated. Lauren struggled on with the poor hand of cards she had been dealt. No family, no school, no guidance. Whereas Annie had only herself to blame for ending up alone on the Manor.

'Come on. We're going to miss him.'

Relenting, she grabbed her bag and her keys. 'Miss who, exactly?'

But Lauren, halfway to the stairwell, shouted over her shoulder, 'Ray.'

'Ray?' Annie echoed, grabbing her keys.

The answer was a man in dirty sportswear surrounded by a small crowd. Somewhere between thirty and fifty, he had a boxer's nose, flattened from the bridge down and tilted to the left. Where had she seen him before? That hair. Thin and grey. In need of a cut. Ah. He was Dev's 'business associate'.

He pulled the rear doors of the van open and the crowd shuffled forward.

'Is he taking the tags off?' Lauren said to the woman next to her. 'Quid each.'

87

'Keep my place, Annie,' Lauren said and hurried in the direction of the stairs.

Ray lifted out several big nylon bags, the striped ones with zips that reminded Annie of helping her nan take washing to the launderette.

Maybe as a result of his flattened nose, his voice was a nasal rasp. 'Girls, I've got soap, toothpaste, spray, perfume, cleaning stuff, clothes …' He nodded in the direction of a cool box. 'Meat. Don't be shy.'

Already unzipping her purse, the woman next to Annie jostled past her and peered inside the van.

Lindon, Sylvia's grandson, crossed the car park at a brisk pace followed by a boy on a bike. He broke into a jog, then a run as he disappeared into the entrance to the stairs. The others leaned on their handlebars, watching from the edge of the car park. A door slammed and their comrade returned, adjusting his course to let Lauren through. She had returned with a heap of fabric in her arms.

'Five,' she said breathlessly to Ray and handed him a crumpled five-pound note.

Ray palmed the note like a magician. Lauren rubbed the material of the top item, a sequinned dress, tags still attached. The man rifled through and the grey security discs vanished, one by one.

'Thanks, Ray,' she said, stepping aside. A tiny, older lady carrying a bundle of bras immediately took her place.

Lauren flicked through the shiny and short dress draped over her arm. 'Sell. Sell. Sell. Sell. Definitely keep.' She held up a pink velour tracksuit with 'Juicy' printed across the bottom. 'What about you, Annie? Fiver each.'

'When would I wear a dress? I never go anywhere.'

Despite only having weeks to go, the baby bump was barely evident under the black-and-red dress Lauren held over herself. 'What do you reckon … keep?'

'You've certainly got the figure for it.'

Lauren grinned. 'Dev isn't going to be able to keep his eyes off me, is he?'

At the entrance to their block, a woman came towards them, wheeling an ancient pram. A huge shrink-wrapped chicken nestled inside, like a macabre baby.

The graffitied stairwell echoed with a harsh burst of laughter that descended into a coughing fit.,

'Your face! Trust me, there's nothing Ray can't get. Dresses, cigs, chickens. Fake ID.'

'Does he work for Dev?'

Lauren snorted. 'Don't be stupid. Ray could smile in your face while he's stabbing you in the back. Sometimes Dev sells him stuff, that's all.'

In the flat, Lauren lay the dresses over the back of the sofa next to a plastic bag overflowing with baby clothes.

'How cute is that?' she said wistfully, picking out a blue jumper with 'Daddy's Best Boy' printed on it.

'You can't know the baby's sex already, surely?'

'I know I'm having a boy. I mean, not officially, but … Oh shit …' She grabbed the tag on a camouflage-print jumper and tutted. 'I missed that one. I'll have to get Ray to do it next time.'

She felt dungarees, a multipack of onesies, a soft hat, checking for more missed security tags.

'Have you told anyone about the baby?' Annie said. 'Friends, family?'

Another abrupt mood change. There was nothing wistful in the way Lauren stuffed the clothes back in the bag.

'Only my friend Alannah.'

'What about Donna?'

Lauren ripped the plastic open on a packet of chocolate digestives. Such a slim girl, and yet she could certainly pack food away.

'She's still annoyed about me not getting rid of it. You've never had kids, have you?' Lauren said. ''Cos you need to get a move on if you want babies, before you're too old.'

Babies.

A series of images popped unbidden into her mind. Three positive pregnancy tests. Three twelve-week appointments. Three variations of 'I'm afraid I can't detect a heartbeat'.

It took effort to keep her tone light. 'Hey, I'm only thirty-five. My biological clock is in perfect order.'

Lauren levered two biscuits out of the packet with her thumb. 'No offence but you look loads older.'

'None taken.'

'Why don't I give you a makeover? Sort your clothes and your make-up and that.'

'That sounds really lovely,' Annie lied quickly. 'Another time, though. Listen, you know if you ever need help, you've only got to ask.'

Through a mouthful of crumbs, Lauren said, 'You could lend me a couple of quid for the electric.'

'I actually meant once the baby is born,' Annie said, opening her purse. 'Babysitting, shopping, that kind of thing.'

Lauren wiped her fingers on her tracksuit bottoms and took the proffered coins. She pulled a fluffy white bear from the plastic bag.

'Cheers. I'll pay you back. Promise. I won't need Donna or Alannah or you to help me then. I won't need anyone's help apart from Dev's,' she said, stroking the bear against her cheek. 'Me, Dev and the baby. Everything is going to be perfect.'

Now, Monday

'What are you doing sitting in the dark?'

Izzy stood on the threshold of the lounge, silhouetted by the glow of headlights as Caro's Range Rover did a three-point turn in the lane. She flicked the light switch and Annie winced in the sudden glare.

'Sorry, I didn't hear you come in.' Her fingers, curled around the phone, had stiffened into claws. She opened them, releasing tiny darts of pain. 'Did you have a nice time at Lucy's?'

Slinging her rucksack on the armchair, Izzy replied, 'Yeah, it was good, thanks. What about you?'

She remembered seeing Liam. Going back to work after the bank. Leaving the surgery. Letting Smudge out. Sinking onto the sofa.

'Oh, nothing special. What time is it?'

'Half six,' Izzy replied, with an ostentatious shiver. 'It's freezing in here.'

She'd been sat here over an hour? No wonder her neck ached. She levered herself from the saggy cushioned seat. Pins and needles shot through her stiff calves.

'I'll stick the heating on for a bit. And make us a snack.'

She pressed the button and the boiler shuddered, triggering the radiators into spasmodic groans.

Amazing really, how little instruction her body needed. Her hands functioned on autopilot, crumpling sheets of newspaper to stuff in the grate. Eyes noticed the fireside basket needed topping up. Vocal cords asked Izzy to pop out to the shed for more logs. Ears listened to an account of Lucy's guilt over Caspar's death. Facial muscles adopted the appropriate positions to indicate concern.

Anyone looking in through the window would see an ordinary mum whisking hot milk in a pan. Handing her teenaged daughter a plate of hot buttered toast. Spooning hot chocolate into two mugs.

No one but her would notice the painstaking creation of this scene. The invisible stitching of patchwork stories and scraps of history into a solid, tangible whole. Knots and tangles carefully hidden on the reverse. The side she thought no one else knew existed.

Until yesterday.

'Anyway.' Izzy's tongue darted out to catch a dribble of butter. 'Caro was talking again about the Paris trip and how much Lucy wanted me to go, and she suggested maybe she could pay?'

Paris again.

'That's very kind of her, but no. Absolutely not.'

'How about if she lent me the money for the trip and I could pay her back?'

'I said no.'

For a moment, the only sound was the wind rattling the extractor fan and the faint hiss of a log catching on the fire. Izzy wiped her chin with the back of her hand. Licked butter off her fingers.

'Maybe,' she said slyly, 'it could be an agreement between me and Caro. Nothing to do with you.'

Annie itched intensely like hundreds of biting ants were trapped inside her skin. Something weird was going on with her heart, too. Instead of the customary unobtrusive rhythm, it sped up, kicking every few beats. A tiny foot behind her ribs.

She wanted to snatch the mug from Izzy's grasp and hurl it to the floor, shattering the faded quarry tiles. She wanted to scream.

Instead, she ran the dishcloth under the hot tap.

'Eat properly, you're making a mess down your uniform. And look at these crumbs,' she said, vigorously wiping the table. 'And how many times do I have to tell you to use a coaster?'

Without a word, Izzy reached for the small pile of mats in the centre of the table and slid one under her mug. She glared. *Happy now?*

Annie dropped the cloth in the sink. She tugged the blind cord, shutting out the darkness.

'I was thinking,' she said slowly over the sound of running water. 'Maybe it's time we moved.'

She hadn't been thinking that at all. At least, not until her subconscious presented the idea, fully formed. It surprised her. But not as much as it surprised Izzy.

'As in move house?'

'There's nothing keeping us in Uppermoss, really,' Annie said, warming to the idea. 'We could go this week. Tomorrow. Rent somewhere until this place sold. We could find a new school. You're good at making friends, you'd settle in no time.'

'What for?'

Aiming for nonchalant, she shrugged. 'Change of scene?'

The empty milk pan knocked against the bottom of the sink. Washing-up liquid billowed into a cloud of froth.

'Aren't you bored of the same old things, day in, day out?'

'If you mean same old things like my friends and my school, then no. I like my life. I don't want a change of scene.'

Still waiting to be hung on the wall, the canvas picture remained propped against the fruit bowl. Two peas, happy in their seaside pod.

'We could rent a cottage near Wells,' she said. 'You love it down there. Think about it. Why on earth are we stuck here in boring

Uppermoss when we could be living by the sea? Walking Smudge on the beach every day. You and me, starting again.'

A shard of memory cut in. The Army surplus rucksack stuffed with what she could carry. Red-cheeked baby snot and tears mingling in a sticky stream. A cold train platform in the dark.

Her eyes brimmed and she busied herself rooting about for a fresh tea towel until the threat past.

Izzy fiddled with her school tie. 'Mum, has something happened that you're not telling me?'

'No, of course not,' she said. 'Take no notice. I'm just a bit fed up, I guess.'

'I come home and you're sitting in the dark and now you're talking about moving. You're not ...' Sharp intake of breath. The rest of the sentence tumbled out at high speed. 'You're not dying, are you? Because you can tell me. I would rather know than be kept in the dark.'

'Oh love, I'm sorry, I didn't mean to frighten you. I promise I'm definitely not dying.'

It was Izzy's eyes that glistened now. 'The house, then. Have you not been paying the mortgage? Is that why we have to move? Are we in debt? Is that why you're being so weird about money?'

'Not dying. House is fine. And I'm always weird about money.'

The joke fell flat.

'I don't get it then. We're happy here. I've got my friends and you've got work and Samara.' She frowned. 'Liam hasn't done anything to upset you, has he?'

'Of course not. He's lovely.'

But Izzy looked sceptical. 'Stop treating me like I'm six. You're not telling me everything.'

Tell the girl everything.

Fear swelled and popped like a toxic bubble rising to the surface of a swamp. The messages. The money. The threat of exposure. Izzy's suspicion. And Lauren's Facebook account, posting messages *to her workplace.*

Click. Izzy snapped her fingers inches from her nose.

'Tell me.'

Annie mopped her forehead with the tea towel in a way that wasn't entirely for effect. 'There's nothing to tell except crazy hormones sending me loopy. I think I need to book an appointment at the doctor's and ask them about HRT.'

Convincing? The way Izzy twisted her mouth to chew the inside of her cheek suggested not.

'Okay,' she said, eventually. 'I get that you want to protect me, Mum. But if there was something big, you would tell me, wouldn't you?'

'Of course.' Annie gave her a wide, reassuring smile. 'I tell you everything.'

When Izzy had gone upstairs, Annie poured a glass of wine and picked up the remote control. TV was normal. She needed to do normal. Something that wouldn't fuel Izzy's suspicions. There was a series on Netflix she'd invested hours in about two Manchester detectives. One gutsy and glamorous, the other harassed but wise and both, in the spirit of TV police dramas, with abundant skeletons of their own. Tonight's episode centred on the murder of a young woman. *Every* episode centred on the murder of a young woman.

She clinked the glass with her nail, feeling the wine buzz through her bloodstream. Dead women. *That's showbiz.*

The images flickered, the dialogue floated past her ears, meaningless.

Her phone sat on the coffee table. She picked it up. Twisted it round in her hands a few times. She shouldn't look.

The surgery page loaded. The trolls hadn't returned, thank goodness. And Lauren Taylor was still there.

On-screen, the two detectives kicked open the door of a rundown flat. Lying on the sofa was a young woman, surrounded by drug paraphernalia. A needle hung from the inside of her elbow. She had a mobile phone in her hand. Blood soaked the upholstery and darkened the long, blonde hair. The porcelain skin was drained of life. Sightless eyes stared blankly at the ceiling.

Annie stabbed the off button, and the remote skittered across the table. The screen went black and instead of the dead woman, she saw herself. The empty wineglass, legs curled up, body hunched into a ball. Her ghostly, floating face. Eyes two black holes staring at nothing.

Smudge yapped, demanding to be let out.

'Bloody hell, dog,' she said. 'Do you want me to have a heart attack?'

The wind caught the back door and flung it open. Smudge zoomed around the perimeter of the lawn. Slowing, she traced her nose along the wall to the bins by the side gate then sprinted over the grass, past the shed. Spent a long time investigating the base of the back gate with her nose before selecting a place to pee.

Beyond the reaches of the security light, the woods writhed and rustled in the darkness.

When they first arrived in Uppermoss, she rented a bedsit on a weekly let. It was above a newsagent in the centre of the village. Sometimes late at night, she would hear footsteps pass then backtrack, pausing outside the shop entrance. Or hear the rumble of voices in the courtyard at the back. And while the nocturnal traffic and sirens and pubgoers had nothing on the Manor, the noise transported her to nights she needed to forget. When she first visited the cottage, she fell in love with the location before the house.

But tonight, unease kept her close to the back door. If Lauren Taylor had tracked down her workplace, how safe was home?

'Smudge,' she called.

The dog stiffened, a low growl vibrating in her throat, sensing something in the darkness beyond the high fence. Unease swelled to dread. She peered at the gate. Why were the bolts undone?

'Hey,' she shouted. 'Now.'

The dog obeyed. Gave the gate a final sniff and bounded back into the kitchen. Annie strode across the lawn and slammed them shut. Top. Bottom.

It was nothing. Nobody.

She rubbed under Smudge's greying muzzle, letting the long tongue feverishly lick her fingers. That was the way with rescues. No matter how secure you made them feel, fear of abandonment underpinned every display of affection.

'Good girl, come on, let's go inside.'

The dog shadowed her on the nightly ritual of checking the windows and doors before heading up the stairs for the final check. Izzy, curled up under a heap of blankets, didn't even stir when Smudge jumped on the foot of the bed.

The pipes gurgled as Annie brushed her teeth with a supermarket-branded toothpaste. She dried her face on a towel stained with old black hair dye. Scooped a fingerful of budget moisturiser from a pot and rubbed it into the deep creases between her eyes.

With an exaggerated haunted house whine, the door closed behind her and she crept across the landing and got under the covers. She wriggled straight against the headboard, opened the security app.

Pin? The screen said.

0-2-0-7. She jabbed Izzy's birthdate in.

Arm alarm?

Yes.

With another tap, she opened Live View. Car on the drive. Front garden fine. Side gate closed. Shed closed. Back lawn empty. The trees a dark mass behind the fence.

She put the phone on the bedside table and switched the light off. Shadows washed across the ceiling as the house fell silent.

Moving to Wells had been a stupid idea. Friends, school, Izzy's roots were here. She had never known any other life. Not one she could remember, anyway.

And they'd been found once. They'd be found again.

Despite the warm fleece pyjamas and thick duvet, cold shivered deep within her bones. When sleep finally took her, it was fragmented and filled with jumbled snatches of nights on the Manor. Boys on bikes. Figures in black hoodies. Arguments and babies crying.

Then

The swing doors buzzed and the nurse beckoned her inside. The pink helium balloon trailed alongside Annie's head as she entered an overheated ward redolent with cleaning products and hard-working human bodies.

After the hush of the corridor, it was as though someone had turned up the volume: wailing babies, bleeping machinery, conversations, a phone in the nurse's station ringing non-stop. Extended families chatted loudly around exhausted-but-proud women tucked under stiff hospital sheets.

Every curtained cubicle contained at least one older woman fussily placing flowers in a vase or making room for yet another congratulations card.

Every cubicle except the one by the window overlooking the car park.

Lauren lay on top of the covers, flipping through a tattered magazine. Attached to the bed rail was a bassinet. There were no visitors. No flowers. A sole card on the bedside table.

'Congratulations!' Annie said, brightly. 'How are you feeling?'

'All right, I suppose. Sore. Can you believe there's no smoking room here? You have to go outside.'

'Well, I guess it is a hospital.' Annie peeled back the corner of the cellular blanket. 'Oh my goodness. Look at this little one.'

Lauren's baby was tiny. Her eyes were swollen, and her ears bent at the top. She wore a little knit cap and her miniature boxer's fists curled at the side of her head. Her fingernails were tiny translucent grains. The plastic bracelet around her wrist said: *Baby Taylor 28 March 7.32am.*

She couldn't see much of Lauren in her, and there was even less of Dev in the peaceful innocent who barely formed a hump under the blanket. The baby was entirely herself, from the perfect whorls of her ears to the tiny button of a nose.

'She is gorgeous,' Annie murmured, stroking the impossibly soft cheek. 'What's her name?'

'Keziah Devlin,' Lauren said proudly.

'And has Dev been in to visit you both yet?'

Lauren picked at a loose thread in the blanket. 'He doesn't like hospitals.'

'Well, remind him he needs to be there when you register the birth,' Annie said. 'That's the important thing. Otherwise, she'll stay Keziah Taylor.'

'She is cute, isn't she?' Lauren's tired eyes shone. 'And healthy, even though she's small. They said we should be able to come home tomorrow. They're keeping me in an extra night because of my blood pressure, but I want to go. It's doing my fucking head in being here.'

The woman in the next bed tutted.

'What?' Lauren said, swinging her bare legs over the side of the bed.

The dividing curtain swished closed.

'Bitch snores like a pig, all night.'

'Sssh. You'll wake the baby.'

But the warning came too late. The baby gave a little cry, then a slightly louder one.

'Hey, Keziah,' Lauren crooned. She leaned over and scooped the baby up and held her awkwardly to her chest.

'Support her head.' Annie quickly took Lauren's hand and cupped it on the delicate skull. 'Like this.'

Lauren looked down at the baby buzzing wet lips across her T-shirt.

'Maybe I should ask for a bottle. They tried to get me to … you know.' She mimed putting her breast to the baby's mouth.

'That is what they're for.'

Lauren shuddered. 'No chance. It's disgusting.'

'What are you doing about nappies and food and things like that?'

'I've got a grant from the council. Anyway, Dev will give me money. Here—'

She thrust the baby at Annie. Took her tobacco tin off the bedside table, slipped it in her dressing-gown pocket and stuffed her feet into grubby white trainers.

'Right,' she said. 'Keep an eye on her, will you? I'm off to find a bottle. Won't be long.'

Taken aback, Annie cradled the baby against her chest. 'Are you sure you should be up and about?'

She shrugged. 'I'm all right. Listen, while you're here, I might as well nip off for a smoke. Have you got any money you can lend me?'

Using the length of her forearm to support the baby's spine, she reached for her purse.

'Thanks,' Lauren said. 'I'll pay you back.'

No one paid any attention to the slim woman in the faded dressing gown slowly walking through the busy ward. Annie's heart clenched with pity. Being a new mum must be totally overwhelming even with family support. She put the balloon weight on the bedside cupboard next to a card signed Alannah. She was the old schoolfriend Lauren had mentioned a few times, but there was nothing from Donna. Nothing from Dev.

The baby fitted perfectly against Annie's shoulder, the small, warm body nestled against her chest. Annie smiled and reached out a tentative finger to stroke the gentle curve of the baby's cheek. The translucent eyelids fluttered and closed.

'Beautiful girl,' Annie whispered into the soft, unfused bones of the silken. Hardly daring to move, she slowly lowered herself into the uncomfortable plastic chair at the side of the bed. The baby didn't stir. And for the next ten minutes, Annie felt almost happy.

'Shall I wake her up?'

Lauren had returned, waving a bottle of formula.

'Oh,' Annie said, wriggling up in the chair. 'I was almost dozing off there myself. You sit down and' – she gently lifted the baby off her chest – 'you go back to your mummy.'

As soon as Keziah left her arms, she began to whimper and as Lauren cradled her, head resting in the crook of her elbow, she began to cry in earnest.

'All right,' Lauren said. 'Calm down.'

'Gently, like this.' Annie mimed rocking a sleepy baby.

'There's a lot to learn, isn't there? Took me half an hour to change her nappy.'

'You can ask in here, they'll show you,' Annie said. 'And I bet Sylvia will be able to tell you about parenting classes at the community centre.'

Lauren's curled lip conveyed perfectly well what she thought of *that* idea.

'Maybe Donna then.'

Lauren opened her mouth and Annie added quickly, 'I know you're annoyed with her. But she knows what she's doing and you're going to need all the help you can get. Speaking of which, do you want me to get some shopping in for when you come home?'

Lauren smiled sleepily. 'It's okay, thanks. Dev will be doing all that.'

'End of visiting time, ladies and gents,' one of the nurses called.

'Shall I take a quick photo before I go?' Annie said, fishing in her coat pocket. 'I brought my camera. I can print them off at Boots.'

The baby stirred a little and let out a small mew, like a kitten, as Lauren turned her towards the lens.

'Say cheese,' Annie said and pressed the button. 'Right, I'd better go. Do you need me to pick you up tomorrow?'

'No, thanks,' Lauren said through a yawn. 'Dev will take care of all that.'

'Okay, well, I'll see you both back at the Manor then.'

'Yeah,' Lauren said. 'See you soon.'

The hospital forecourt was busy, cars pulling into pick-up bays. People coming in and out. Drizzle landed on the long queue of visitors waiting for the next bus to town. In front, a woman pulled the pram hood over a baby snugly packed in a nest of blankets. A headband with a felt sunflower attached held back near-transparent wisps of hair. When she yawned, revealing smooth, red gums and a milk-streaked tongue, her dot of a nose crinkled and Annie couldn't help but smile.

A sibilant hiss of brakes announced the arrival of the bus. The queue shuffled, people picking up bags or hunting for passes.

Did Lauren need a car seat? She'd bought a pram from Ray weeks ago, but what about a car seat? She frowned and looked back at the hospital. Maybe she should go back in to check.

At that moment, a muscular man with a shaved head emerged. He was carefully carrying a pink-flowered carrycot. Annie froze.

No, it couldn't be.

Pulling her hood down to her eyebrows, she risked another look.

Dev?

It was. The slim woman next to him, paler than that day she confronted Lauren but equally groomed, was Megan. And that little girl in the pink sparkly dress pulling a suitcase was … what was her name? Jessica. That was it.

The doors whooshed open and the queue began to move slowly forward. Through the scratched Perspex wall of the shelter, she watched Dev put his free arm around Megan's shoulders and tenderly kiss the top of her head, guiding her to the nearest bench. Cupping her elbow, he helped her to sit and then, as though it were made of glass, lowered the carrycot onto the wooden slatted seat. Jessica leaned in to peer at the baby, still clutching the handle of the suitcase. Dev crouched down, steadying himself on the bench until he was at her level.

From this distance, it was impossible to read his lips.

Look after your mum while I get the car? I love you? Take care of your baby sister?

Whatever it was, Jessica nodded solemnly in reply. In one fluid movement, Dev straightened and swept her up into his arms, their faces touching, his hands stroking her long hair. He planted a long kiss on her cheek and she buried her head in his shoulder.

Annie's heart clenched. Poor Lauren.

'Are you getting on or what?'

Sour breath blasted her ear from behind.

'Sorry,' she said, hurrying towards the woman who was lifting the front wheels of the pram onto the bus.

'Would you like some help?' she said.

'I got it, thanks,' the woman replied, grunting slightly as she manoeuvred the back wheels on. She fished around her pockets, then unzipped her bag and rummaged in there.

'I've got … my pass … somewhere …' she said, keeping her head down. The man with the bad breath tutted loudly.

Inside the pram, the baby stirred. Her thick black eyelashes fluttered. Her mouth formed a tiny 'o' and her fingers flexed and curled, reaching for Annie.

The emotions she'd kept tightly parcelled inside for the last hour burst out. A wave of loss closed Annie's throat, forcing her to gaze to the pavement. After her last miscarriage, the hope that dimmed a little with each previous pregnancy finally extinguished, and she packed her dreams away alongside the teddies and stretchy sleepsuits.

She became aware of the mother staring at her, an expression of curiosity tinged with concern.

'What a gorgeous little girl,' Annie said, forcing a bright smile and went upstairs, where there would be no babies.

From up here, she had a bird's-eye view of the entrance. The revolving door fed a constant stream of people with flowers and balloons in and out. Prams, carrycots, car seats all containing miraculous new lives. And among them Dev, Megan and their two lovely girls. The perfect family.

While behind the bank of rain-spattered windows, Lauren and daughter waited.

Now, Tuesday

'Morning.' Izzy yawned. 'Did you sleep okay?'

Even bleary with sleep and wrapped in a dressing gown two years too small, she possessed an elegance Annie couldn't remember having. Long-limbed, graceful, like a principal ballerina. Her healthy, glowing complexion a world away from the putty-coloured mess awaiting Annie in the bathroom mirror.

'I said did you sleep okay?'

'Sorry, love. Not bad. Do you want porridge?'

'Please. Can I make you a cup of tea?'

Annie shook her head and held up the coffee mug to signal *I'm sorted* then drank the last of the contents. She righted a bowl from the draining rack, tipped oats inside.

'Why don't you sit down?' Izzy said, taking it. 'I'll make my own breakfast.'

Annie returned the milk to the fridge. The bare fridge. Supermarket, then, after she'd seen Pauline. They needed—

She put her hands over her face and breathed out heavily. 'Shit.'

'What's up?'

The microwave pinged. Izzy picked up the hot bowl, put it down quickly, fanning her hands.

Liam. Round for dinner tonight. She couldn't cancel. Had

to keep on being normal thanks to Izzy's *something's up* spidey senses.

'Careful,' she said automatically and slid the honey jar along the worktop. 'Nothing, I'm just tired. Sorry for swearing.'

Usually, Annie had to remind Izzy not to drag the chair legs across the tiles. Not today. And a place mat appeared on the scarred wooden table. Even the honey spoon, instead of languishing in an irritating sticky puddle, rested neatly on the lid of the jar.

'Well, at least it's your day off,' Izzy said. 'Got anything nice planned or are you just chilling at home?'

'Nothing exciting. Hair appointment this morning.'

'What time?'

'After I drop you off.'

'Hope you enjoy it. Say hi to Pauline from me.' Izzy dug her spoon in. 'Shall I feed Smudge after I've washed up?'

Hmmm. Spontaneous offers of help? It was Annie's spidey senses' turn to twitch.

The dog sniffed enthusiastically around the top of the garden. Familiar smells? New ones?

In the daylight, she could make out the bolts firmly in place on the gate. Solid. Secure.

'Iz, you left the back gate open on Sunday night, you know.'

'Did I? I'm really sorry. I didn't mean to.'

'Just don't go in the woods again, please.'

'I promise. Oh, and Mum?' The spoon rang against the side of the bowl like a bell. Izzy's tone went from contrite to faux casual. 'Mrs Jackson asked if you could pop into her office after school today.'

Ah.

Mrs Jackson had been the pastoral lead at Uppermoss High since dinosaurs roamed the earth. In the three years since Iz started, Annie had met her on a handful of occasions and had been impressed by the respect the pupils had for her, as well as the genuine care she demonstrated for her charges' wellbeing.

This was the first casual 'pop into her office' invite.

'Why? What's happened?'

'Nothing,' Izzy said hastily. 'Everything's fine. I think it's, well, it's about the Paris trip.'

God, she was like a dog with a bone.

Annie grabbed the bowl and clattered it into the sink.

'I thought you were feeding Smudge?'

The chair legs scraped across the tiles as Izzy stood up. 'Please, Mum. At least talk to her.'

'Don't open another tin. There's some left in the fridge,' Annie said, rinsing wet oats down the plughole. 'And wash the fork afterwards.'

She sounded snappy. She sounded grumpy. See, she *could* do normal.

Izzy remained glued to her phone until they pulled up on the yellow zigzags outside the school. Those swift moving thumbs no doubt complaining about how she did all the chores at home and still her over-protective mum never listened and never let her have any freedom.

Completely unaware that by Friday, missing out on a school trip would be the least of her worries.

'Don't get the bus and don't move one inch away from the gates until I get here,' Annie said. 'Have you got that?'

'Please come and speak to Mrs J,' Izzy said. 'If you're picking me up anyway. It'll only take a few minutes.'

Annie had already mentally bullet-pointed her speech. Something along the lines of *Can't afford it. Mrs Jackson is a busy woman. Not fair to waste her time. End of discussion.*

But the naked hope in those wide eyes. The pleading, clasped hands covering lips that murmured, 'Please, please, please.'

The paradox at the heart of everything: Izzy would understand if she knew the truth. But Izzy must never know the truth.

'I'll use all my birthday money,' she continued. 'And don't buy me any Christmas presents. I'll never ask for anything again. Please let me go.'

And then there was the danger of going too far. At what point did protection cross the line to imprisonment? Acceptance to resentment?

A short-haired woman with a 'Staff' lanyard and carrying a Cath Kidston shopper paused by the gate. She glared pointedly at their idling car and then at the 'It's against the law to park here' banner tied to the railings. And, in case the message was too ambiguous, a cartoon police officer wagged his finger.

Annie puffed her cheeks then blew the air out noisily.

'Okay then, Iz, but I can't promise anything.'

The teacher approached the car. Holding up her index finger in a *won't be a sec* gesture, Annie revved the engine.

'Seriously?' A smile transformed Izzy's anxious face. 'Thanks, Mum!'

'Remember, no promises. Go. Quick before that teacher has my guts for garters.'

Hugging her rucksack to her chest, Izzy jumped out.

'See you tonight!' she sing-songed.

The teacher reached the car, thin lips pursed in disapproval.

'You're breaking the law,' she said, loud enough to be heard through the window.

'Sorry,' Annie mouthed and pressed her foot on the accelerator.

Now, Tuesday

The problem with commuter stations was that the commuters stole all the spaces. Annie navigated her tiny VW between four-by-fours parked like rows of tanks. After two full circuits, she nipped into a just-vacated space. As she pulled the handbrake, her phone pinged with an email notification. Another of the quick loans she'd applied for had been approved. Three thousand pounds this time. Apparently, it would clear into her account within twenty-four hours. That only left …

She rested her forehead against the steering wheel, let the seed of despair she'd been so desperately suppressing bloom inside her chest.

… thirty-two thousand pounds. In, what was left, four days? She didn't make that in a year.

Something made her look up. A warning, raising the hairs on the back of her neck. *Over there, by the payment machine*, it said. *There's a man.*

Was it? She squinted. Pushed her glasses to the bridge of her nose. Probably. Hard to discern gender under the baggy black joggers and jacket. Ethnicity, age – everything was hidden in the deep shadow of the pulled-down hood and the pulled-up scarf.

She made a show of unclicking her seatbelt and opening the

door. *Act confident. Don't let them catch you looking.* She closed her fist around the keys, leaving the sharp tip of a Yale protruding. The car door slammed harder than intended. Noisy. She risked a glance.

There was no one there.

Relief rolled through her, tailed by irritation. What good would jumping at shadows do? She pressed the lock button on the fob, then tried the handle to double-check. Better safe than sorry.

A train thundered past, rattling the overhead cables and shaking through the trees that separated the car park from the station. She buttoned her jacket and joined the pavement that ran parallel to Platform One.

The station had hardly changed since the night Annie arrived with tiny Izzy in tow.

Apart from a few half-barrels of ivy and pansies, the station had been empty. No one around to help the woman with the baby and the pram and the massive rucksack. But that suited her fine. They were there to hide from people, not befriend them.

She passed the taxi rank, recalling that night. A single cab had idled by the kerb and the driver had folded his newspaper at their approach. He popped the boot, lifted out a baby seat.

'Do you want this for your little one?' he said.

They'd been travelling for hours, zigzagging their way up the country, and both of them could barely keep their eyes open.

The driver fitted the baby seat, folded the pram into the boot and put the rucksack on top.

'Thank you,' Annie said, tears prickling at his kindness. 'Yes, please.'

Well, the planters and hanging baskets hadn't changed much, but the terrified woman who fled London with her baby daughter had. Annie put her keys in her pocket and entered the alleyway at the edge of the car park that was the quickest route to Hair by Pauline.

Brambles and ivy hung over the top of the high fence panels

and self-seeded buddleia poked up from cracks in the tarmac. She had read somewhere that narrow places had a negative impact on the human psyche. Something about being funnelled from entrance to exit spooked the primeval brain. Involved the holy trinity of survival passed down via ancestral DNA: Freeze. Fight. Flight.

Things were always easier when you had a way out.

She could smell cigarette smoke. Not the faint, distant whiff, but close enough to tickle her throat. A warning bell rang in her head. They weren't her footsteps bouncing off the fence panels, were they?

Clutching her bag tight to her chest, she picked up the pace. Don't turn. Don't run. The town centre bustle was simultaneously reassuringly close and alarmingly distant from the narrow alley that felt much, much longer than the last time she used it.

And then the exit appeared. Too late to stop, she slammed into the side of the metal bike barrier, but at least she was safe here on the pavement. She pressed her palm to her hip and waited for her sprinting heart to get the message that everything was okay. Jesus, never mind finding the money by Friday. She wouldn't survive till Friday at this rate.

Keep it normal. Okay. Go.

She walked past a couple who stepped off the kerb in unison to allow her to pass. A Cavapoo on an extendable lead sniffed her boot. She smiled at an elderly lady pulling a shopping trolley. Continued past a forlorn giftshop with a dusty display of teddies clutching hearts and saccharine leftover.

She stopped by a steamed-up window. Black vinyl letters announced this was Hair by Pauline. The old-fashioned bell jangled when Annie pushed the door open and a wall of heat and ammonia stung her nose. Older ladies in curlers chatted over tatty copies of *Good Housekeeping* and *The People's Friend*. A brown-and-white Papillon ambled over and she scratched behind the silky ears. 'Hello, Lola old girl.'

'I won't be a minute,' Pauline shouted over the roar of the dryer. 'Have a seat.'

Thankful for the noise and heat to hide her rapid breathing and explain her flushed cheeks, she shrugged off her coat. A strand of hair had glued itself to her cheek and she tucked it behind her ear, wiped her foggy glasses with the hem of her jumper. Then slumped back, eyes closed, and let herself sink into the pink velour sofa.

The junior offered her a drink and then disappeared through the vinyl curtain that separated the back room from the crowded salon.

Annie bunched her sleeve over a fist and rubbed a peephole in the condensation. Peered out. No sign of any hooded figure.

Women chatted, read magazines or scrolled through their phones. The junior brought tea in a pink mug, and she sipped gratefully and took out her own phone.

Good news: she had been approved for three more loans. Bad news: the total only amounted to just over nine thousand pounds.

'Sorry to keep you waiting,' Pauline said, rubbing her hands on her apron. 'Do you want to come and sit down?'

She freed Annie's hair from the scrunchie, bunched the tangled frizz in her hands. 'Same as usual?'

Two hours and two cups of builder-strength tea later, Annie stood at the old-fashioned cash register as Pauline rang up the bill.

'So that's forty for the perm, ten for the colourwash and fifteen for the cut and blow.'

'Looks great,' Annie said, fluffing out her newly curled and darkened hair. She lifted a section to reveal the small pink patches where the hair refused to grow.

'If you keep your parting central, it will hide the smooth spots,' Pauline said, clipping the notes inside the till. 'I don't do many perms on the under-seventies nowadays. If you ever fancy going back to natural, I can cut it so the blonde wouldn't look strange growing out.'

The revived curls bounced as Annie shook her head. 'I think I'm more grey than blonde these days. And I've looked this way for so long, I don't think I'd recognise myself.'

She tipped the junior, said goodbye and went out into the cool air.

Away from the drowsy heat and easy small talk, she found it didn't take long for the weight of her worry to press down on her. It pushed her neck forward, hunched her spine, furrowed her brow. She scanned the road, left, right. Good. No hooded strangers to be seen. Head down, she stuffed her hands in her pockets and began to walk.

It was true, what she had said to Pauline: she didn't recognise herself. Not at first, anyway. For months after she left the Manor, an unexpected glimpse of her reflection could halt her in her tracks. The brunette curly-haired woman in the bus window or the shop mirror didn't tally with the version who lived in her head. Annie Smith, née Annabel Naughton-Smith, had long, highlighted hair that hung as straight as tap water to the middle of her back.

Her reflection never took her by surprise anymore. After over a decade of quietly living in Uppermoss, Annie on the inside and Annie on the outside were the same person. She glanced in the dingy giftshop window. A handwritten notice was Blu-tacked to the glass: 'Mother's Day Sale: *Two for the price of one!*'

She combed her fingers through the shoulder-length spirals and scrutinised her reflection.

If she didn't recognise herself as the woman who fled the Manor years ago, how would anyone else?

Then

Lauren was barely recognisable as the girl Annie had met on her first day at the Manor. Faded leggings under a T-shirt with milk or spit-up crusted down the front. Hair lank with grease. Dark shadows hollowed her eye sockets and a sore-looking crack split her bottom lip.

Annie had spent the last half an hour hunched on the sofa of her own flat, listening to cries like approaching sirens and berating herself for being too scared to offer her assistance.

And now, she hung back on the threshold and whispered, 'Are you expecting Dev?'

The reply was half-laugh, half-cough. 'I've given up expecting Dev to come round,' she said.

The flat smelled of dirty nappies and clothes that hadn't dried properly. Smoke hung in the air. A box of congealed chicken bones nestled next to a half-empty bottle of milk. On the changing mat in front of the radiator, the baby bicycled her legs. Cheeks the colour of overripe plums, mouth a deep red cave filled with raw, rasping screams.

The sofa groaned, and she dropped her forehead to her knees, fingers probing the tendons in her neck.

'What is it?' Annie said, alarmed. 'What's happened?'

'Doesn't matter what I do, she just keeps on and on and on,' came the muffled reply. 'Crying. All night. I haven't slept and I can't even think straight. I want to do it right, but nothing works. Alannah was supposed to be helping me, but she's got this new DJ boyfriend and disappeared. And Dev has only been round once, and even then, it wasn't to see me, it was for …' She hesitated, licked her chapped lips with the pointed tip of her tongue. 'To get something he left here. A work thing.'

She lifted her head, stared bleakly at the squalling child. 'She's doing it on purpose to piss me off. That's why she hates me, just like her dad.'

'Of course she doesn't hate you,' Annie said, shifting a pile of laundry from the arm of the sofa. She put her hand on Lauren's shoulder. 'You're just exhausted. Why don't you go and have a lie-down and I'll sort out madam?'

Thud. Thud. Thud.

Three deliberate bangs punctuated her offer.

'And her downstairs. That bitch, I swear, I'm gonna …' Red-faced and with the tendons on her neck pulsing, Lauren flung Annie's comforting arm off and sprang to her feet, slamming her shin against the edge of the fake marble coffee table in the process.

'Fuck!' She grabbed her leg and hopped on the spot. '*Fuck.*'

A polystyrene takeout box wobbled, then slithered off the table's cluttered surface, glancing off the baby's cheekbone. Fresh howls escalated to a volume that belied her tiny lungs.

Meanwhile, her mother had flung the balcony door open. Leaning against the railing, she yelled towards Sylvia's flat, 'Babies cry, you miserable old bitch.'

Changing a nappy was a skill that never went. Ditto making up a bottle. Within half an hour, the baby wore a clean nappy, and Annie rolled up her cardigan sleeve to squirt a drop of warm formula on her inner wrist.

Perfect.

'Here you go, hungry girl,' she said and Keziah, nestled in the crook of her arm, grunted as her mouth found the teat.

And relaxed.

While Keziah drank contentedly, Annie took the bag of oven chips back to the freezer. Condensation formed where the bag had rested against Lauren's grazed shins, but at least the make-shift icepack calmed her down enough to persuade her to have a lie-down.

Feeding Keziah took her back to the many babies her mum cared for. 'Care' was the right word too. She nudged the freezer compartment closed. For Mum, being a childminder was a vocation, not a job, and some of Annie's happiest memories were of the two of them singing nursery rhymes to the babies in the garden after school.

When the rhythmic sucking slowed to a milky dribble, Annie shifted position and, careful to support the delicate neck, held the baby, who moulded herself like a warm beanbag to her chest.

'Time for your nap, little one,' she whispered into the velvet fuzzed skull.

The tiny second bedroom had a cot in it, made up with stained and musty sheets. With the baby clasped to her chest, she hunted for a clean set, eventually finding them, tangled and soaking wet, in the washing machine.

There was, however, the state-of-the-art pram that had fallen off the back of Ray's transit van. She laid the dozing baby in the pram and surveyed the room.

Smoke out, fresh air in. She opened the windows and hung the washing to dry on the balcony, letting the breeze sweep the lingering smells of ashtray, soiled nappy and old food away. She gathered the piles of dirty laundry and set the washing machine on a hot cycle. Bagged the rubbish. Scrubbed crusty plates and mugs.

When the flat was tidy, she found a pen in the kitchen drawer and wrote a list on the back of a brown envelope: nappies, milk, wipes and teabags.

And throughout all this, Lauren lay flat on her back with one arm across her eyes, slumbering as peacefully as her daughter.

'I'm just taking the baby to the shop,' she whispered, but Lauren showed no sign that she had heard.

The breeze held a promise of spring and even here, in the roaring heart of the city, there were signs of nature. Birds, trees coming into leaf, white clouds in a perfect blue sky.

'Good morning, Annie!' Sylvia's cheerful voice echoed across the courtyard. She had a trowel in her hand and was kneeling over a stone trough filled with weeds and broken glass.

'You look busy,' Annie said, halting the pram.

Sylvia stood and placed her hands in the small of her back. 'If we wait for the leaseholders to do anything, we'll be waiting forever. Thought I'd plant some seeds. And this must be the little one I hear crying and crying.'

'This is Keziah,' Annie said, peeling back the blanket to reveal the sweet sleeping face. 'Not crying now. Isn't she lovely?'

'She is. She's a beautiful baby and I'm glad Lauren has you to help her. I've tried, you know, but she won't answer if she knows it's me. That little baby, sometimes she leaves her to cry until my heart breaks.'

There was something in Sylvia's tone she couldn't quite pinpoint. A sadness.

'How is Lindon getting on?' Annie said.

A shadow crossed the other woman's face. She paused, as if the right words needed to be weighed and considered before they be allowed out.

'Lindon is a good boy,' she said slowly. 'He works hard at school, wants to be a doctor. You know he got a scholarship? Two buses, right across town, but he's thriving. And he's got a kind heart. Anywhere else, those things would mean a lot. But

118

here, he's a worry. This is no place for him. Some of the kids around here ...'

Leaving the sentence unfinished, she tapped soil from her trowel and for a moment, seemed lost in thought.

Annie smiled, a little awkwardly. She opened her mouth to speak, but then Sylvia raised her gaze in the direction of Lauren's flat.

'That man finds these kids no one cares about,' she said. 'Flatters them. He's their big, friendly brother with his flashy car and Armani this and Gucci that. Gives them a bit of money, gets them doing his dirty work selling his drugs and they think it's glamorous, you know? They think they're gangsters. They don't even realise they're victims. And now he wants Lindon to be part of it because he wants a way into his school because there are pupils with a lot of disposable income.'

The boys in the stairwell. Lindon's trembling legs.

'I'm sorry to hear that,' Annie said into the pause. 'Would you like me to talk to Lauren?'

Sylvia snorted softly. 'She's in it as deep as he is. Although I shouldn't be too hard on her: she's as much a victim as the rest of them. No, what I need is to take him away. Raise him somewhere he doesn't have to be looking over his shoulder all the time.'

'Are you thinking of moving away?'

'Isn't everyone?' Sylvia said, and this time there was no mistaking the hopelessness in her voice.

Now, Tuesday

'We're sorry to inform you that your application for a loan of five thousand pounds has been declined.'

Shit. Another email, another knockback.

Thirty-two minus the nine pending. She still needed twenty-three, but the rejections were coming thick and fast now. It had to be connected to her credit score. Fifteen, no, sixteen applications in the space of a few hours clearly waved a big red flag. And the price she'd been offered for the car was a joke.

And what was this on the Family Safe app? Izzy's smiling avatar claimed she was at home, but she'd been dropped off right at the gate in front of a teacher. According to the history, the app showed the last known location because it had been offline since 10.07pm last night.

'Excuse me,' a weary voice said behind her. 'You're blocking the pavement.'

The rest of the world rushed back at her. Traffic, chatter, the early lunchtime crowd.

'Sorry,' Annie said, putting her phone down, and stepped into the gutter.

The woman pushed a double buggy past along the recently vacated pavement. The two children inside writhed and screamed, trying to wriggle out of the straps. Their mother's lips were set in a grim, determined line and she had the faraway stare of the zombie mum. Instantly, Annie was back there, Izzy's terrible twos. Peppa Pig wellies stamping because she was too small for the big slide. Flinging herself to the floor in the supermarket. Clinging to the banister to avoid a bath. Weird how time could expand and contract. Sometimes, those early years felt like a different life. Sometimes, they felt like yesterday. She wouldn't change a moment of it.

And now, in the blink of an eye, Izzy was thirteen. Fourteen in July.

Would Annie look back on the terrible teens so fondly?

Fear flickered. Would she even get the chance?

She stepped back on the pavement, weaving past a tub of daffodils and crocuses. There were more people here, closer to the station, pushing suitcases or wearing rucksacks.

She passed a jeweller's. 'Sell your unwanted watches, jewellery, gold, silver here,' it said. 'Top prices paid.' And underneath, in big letters: 'Loans.'

Do it, Mum would have said without hesitation. *Family comes first. Whatever it takes.*

And the last time she'd needed money, *really* needed it, she bundled Mum's rings and the diamond hoops from their twenty-year anniversary into one of Izzy's tiny socks and pawned the lot.

The memory of going back to retrieve them induced an onslaught of involuntary reactions. Sweat along her jawline, ringing in her ears, a rush of vertigo. She steadied herself against the jewellery shop wall. Pushed the memory away.

She thought about the bits of jewellery, safely hidden in the cottage and earmarked for Izzy's twenty-first. There had to be another way.

Hurrying back to the car, she let her mind chew over ways of raising a lot of money in a short space of time.

The upshot was, there weren't any.

She stood on the kerb by the car park and waited for a people carrier to turn right. The mum was shouting at the kids in the back. A departing train roared past, followed by the quieter rumble of suitcase wheels coming down the ramp.

By the time she got back to the car, she had made her mind up.

She slid into the driver's seat, took her phone out of her pocket. Opened the last text. Clicked to reply.

I've got 23 and that's it. I can't get any more.

She had just turned the key in the ignition when the phone alerted her to a new message. Except it wasn't a message, it was a link. She switched the engine off.

The pain rushed at her, as fresh as if it happened yesterday, not fifteen years ago.

Woman found guilty of stealing thousands from employer
Annabel Naughton-Smith, 35, formerly of Highfield Mews, has been found guilty of siphoning off almost £50,000 from the investment brokers where she worked.

Naughton-Smith admitted fraud by abuse of position while employed at McKee, Hamlyn and Webb Asset Management Ltd between February and April last year when she created a series of false invoices which she then paid into her own bank account.

Judge Sofia Mohammed said she understood Naughton-Smith used the money to pay off loans secured against her own home and had already repaid some of the funds when internal auditors discovered her fraud. She also said that Naughton-Smith's previous good character, her cooperation with the investigation and voluntary repayment of the stolen cash were factors in deciding to award a suspended rather than custodial sentence.

When asked by this paper for a comment, a spokesperson for McKee, Hamlyn and Webb said: 'Annabel Naughton-Smith was a trusted employee for over a decade. An internal investigation revealed she had stolen company funds and the police were duly informed and Mrs Naughton-Smith sacked for gross misconduct. We are pleased to see justice has been served today.'

She hadn't been naked when the police led her to the patrol car parked outside, but that's how it felt. Stripped naked and paraded before twitching net curtains the length of the street.

And Oliver in the porch, staring at her with such unadulterated disgust even though – she clenched her fists – even though he owned a share of the blame. If he hadn't treated the equity in the house like his private piggy bank, then the bank wouldn't have threatened to repossess. He left her out of options. Desperate.

Everyone knew she was a thief. But the absolute worst part had been her colleagues' reactions. These were people she'd worked with day in, day out. People she'd considered to be friends.

And credit to them, a significant proportion had been sympathetic and made attempts to stay in touch. But she couldn't. She was too ashamed.

And yet, while the weight of people knowing and judging was crushing, it was nothing compared to her self-disgust.

Her phone, treacherous as a rattlesnake, buzzed again.

This time, the message said, *try not to get caught.*

Learning her mum was a convicted criminal would throw Izzy's principles and morality into absolute chaos, creating fissures in their relationship that would take years to heal. If they ever *could* be healed. A future unspooled before her, in which every time she nudged her rebellious teen back on the straight and narrow, she'd be accused of hypocrisy. And how could she deny that?

But that wasn't what triggered the panic that rolled from the pit of Annie's stomach. She pressed her fingers against her forehead, thumbs digging into the soft flesh under her cheekbones.

Being a convicted thief was bad enough.

But it was nothing compared with what she'd got away with.

Then

Lauren stood outside the flat when Annie returned, discomfited by her conversation with Sylvia. Even from the top of the steps, she could read the barely controlled rage in Lauren's expression. She'd seen it before. The pretty features twisted in a scowl, a deep red flush staining her neck poised to leap the boundaries of normal self-control.

Dressing gown flapping behind her, she ran towards Annie like an avenging angel.

'Where have you been?' White streaks of spit flew from her lips.

'The shop,' Annie said, calmly. She nodded at the plastic bag stashed under the pram. 'I got you a few bits and bobs. Look.'

The ubiquitous teens wheeled their bikes in lazy circles in the car park below, craning their necks at the spectacle.

Lauren wrenched the pram handle, scaring Keziah. She plucked the baby out, tucked the blanket around.

'Sssh, Mummy's here,' she said, vigorously rocking her and going back into the flat. 'You can stop crying.'

Annie parked the pram outside and followed her in.

The too-vigorous motion only triggered an escalating cascade of howls.

Thump, thump, thump, went the upstairs neighbour.

Wah wah wah, went the baby.

A light went out in Lauren's eyes.

'Here,' she said, flatly, and thrust the flailing bundle at Annie, like she was passing her a bag of potatoes.

Annie slid her palms around the baby, feet resting in the crook of her arm, fragile head moving side to side, leaving dribble spots soaking through the thin cardigan. Lauren tapped a cigarette from the packet, lit it and inhaled sharply.

'Sssh,' Annie said, gently shifting her weight from one foot to the other. 'Everything's all right, little one.'

The cries subsided to wet lip smacks. Her little limbs relaxed.

'That's it. You're okay now.'

Lauren sagged onto the sofa like all the air had gone out of her. A huge bruise was beginning to appear where she'd banged it on the coffee table. She pointed the glowing, orange tip of her cigarette at the drowsy baby.

'See,' she said. 'I told you she hates me.'

Now, Tuesday

The sharp blast of an umpire's whistle joined the shouting from the after-school netball practice. A teacher trudged past the office window pulling a trolley crate piled high with exercise books.

And if looks could kill, Izzy's white-hot glare could slay on the spot. Annie had a fleeting vision of herself, collapsing on the beige carpet tiles while Mrs Jackson calmly dialled 999.

'I'm sorry,' she said again, adding, 'I've already told you, Iz, Paris is out of the question.'

Unlike Izzy, Mrs Jackson's eyes conveyed steady kindness. Deep lines fanned out from the corners as she smiled sympathetically, shoving aside a stack of papers on her desk and perching on the edge, peering down.

Annie shuffled her bum back in the chair. Tried to. But the seat cushion sank, releasing dust motes into the air. A memory of telling her adoring three-year-old that the sparkling flecks dancing in the sun were fairies.

Ten years on, and teenage Izzy swapped fairies for fury. Waves of it radiated from her tense body. Those fluid limbs, so suited to dance and gymnastics, bristled with the realisation that her mum wasn't about to change her mind.

'You see, the plan is to cancel all lessons for the four days while the class are away, but if Isabel is the only one remaining, it's difficult to know what we're going to do with her. It's a problem.'

Call that a problem? her mind screamed. *If I don't find fifty thousand pounds by Friday, going to Paris is going to be the least of our problems. Because Izzy's cosy life, the one she is kicking off against now, is about to explode like a fucking truth bomb. And the only part of me not involved in preventing that, is the part dedicated to ensuring she never, ever finds out. So, while I understand YOU think it's a problem, I cannot fucking deal with this pointless conversation a second longer.*

'I see.' She pursed her lips thoughtfully. 'Can't she just stay at home?'

'Unfortunately, that would be classed as unauthorised absence. The only feasible solution would be to put her in the isolation unit for self-study.'

Izzy shook her head vigorously.

'Now I know Isabel herself is very keen to go and she mentioned to me that the problem may be financial. So, what I propose is …'

In a professionally delicate and confidential tone, Mrs Jackson explained that several parents had arranged 'payment plans' and the school could look at 'minimising parental contribution'.

She shifted slightly, dislodging a pile of folders and moving quickly to prevent them cascading to the floor.

'How about if she goes in with another class for a few days? Maybe Year Eight,' Annie said. 'Her teachers could set the work and she could just get on with it quietly.'

Izzy's mouth dropped open.

'What are you on about, Mum? She's just said it's okay about the money.'

'It's not just about the money. It's—'

'You told me it was because we couldn't afford it!'

Annie put both hands on the arms of the chair and with some awkwardness levered herself out of its sagging embrace. Her arms stayed crossed over her chest, gripping her bag strap.

'The money is still an issue, and I'm very grateful for your offer, Mrs Jackson. But it's also a question of safety. Izzy hasn't travelled away from home before.'

'That's even more reason for me to go! I'll be fourteen in July and I've never been anywhere.'

She didn't show it often, but the stubborn gene was deeply embedded in her genetic code. Flashback to another version of that three-year-old. Red-faced, screaming and stamping her little foot at being denied another Percy Pig.

'That's not true,' Annie said mildly. 'We've been to lots of places.'

'Wells doesn't count. I've never been anywhere *on my own*.'

Mrs Jackson got up from the desk, smoothing her palms down the front of her thighs where her trousers had ridden up.

'Please let me assure you, Mrs Smith, that pupil safety is our number one priority. The staff are all fully trained and experienced, and we undertake externally verified risk assessments, which stipulate the pupils are not left unsupervised at any time …'

As she went on, reeling off all the trip protocols, Annie briefly weakened. It wasn't the school that had failed to protect Izzy. But it wasn't until July and she needed solutions by this Friday.

'And of course, the lead teacher will keep hold of Izzy's passport …'

The passport. The messages had briefly overtaken that particular worry, but now it squeezed Annie's chest. How much stress could one human heart take in a single day?

Time to play the trump card. She cut in.

'I completely appreciate that. But there are certain circumstances that make the situation different for Izzy and I'm sure you understand, I have to be cautious.'

At the mention of 'circumstances', Mrs Jackson's expression morphed into professional understanding.

Over the years, change always triggered a resurgence of her fears. Fate had a habit of throwing obstacles her way and the toughest had been the move from nursery to primary. Back then, she was still regularly plagued by nightmares, and the terrifying legalities – producing official documents, registering their home address, filling in online forms – tumbled her down a familiar black hole. Thank god for the council clerk who had appended Annie's carefully curated version of their 'circumstances' to the file that had accompanied Izzy to Uppermoss High.

When Year Seven arrived, Annie knew exactly what to do. Tick the right boxes on the GDPR forms. *I DO NOT give permission for my child to be photographed, filmed or recorded in school.* Book an appointment with the safeguarding lead. Don't admit, don't deny. Let a few tears fall and leave a blank space for speculation to fill. Troubled background? Abusive partner? Witness protection?

Mrs Jackson's sympathetic murmuring proved the strategy was still working.

'Of course, I appreciate your situation. But I'm still sure we could accommodate—'

Annie cut her off. 'Maybe in the next couple of years, but unfortunately, it's out of the question for now, I'm afraid. Thank you, Mrs Jackson.'

She walked to the door, signalling the end of the meeting.

But Izzy didn't move. She gripped the arms of the chair, mutiny in her narrowed eyes. 'Is that it?' she said flatly. 'You're not even going to think about it?'

'I'm sorry, but I've made up my mind.'

Despite being seated, Izzy was gearing for a standoff. 'Stop saying you're sorry when you're not. Just because *you're* paranoid, doesn't mean I can't have a life.'

'That's enough,' Annie said, anxiety flashing through her. *Shut up, Izzy. Shut up.*

Mrs Jackson held her hand out to guide them from the room.

'I'm afraid we're going to have to finish here,' she said, softening the dismissal with a kind smile. 'I've got another meeting now. Please don't worry, Mrs Smith, I do understand. We'll sort something out that suits everyone.'

Annie could have hugged her. Or cried. She wanted to lay her cheek on that M&S-clad shoulder and unburden herself of all her secrets. To purge the appalling truth in a blissful cathartic rush. Not the sanitised, redacted Frankentruth. The *everything* truth.

But she just smiled and shook the teacher's hand.

Out in the car park, Izzy trailed behind her, thumbs hooked under the straps of her rucksack.

'I get that you're disappointed,' Annie said. 'I really do. And if there was any way you could go on this trip, then you would be booked on it now, I promise.'

'Yeah, right,' Izzy said and fiddled with the bag buckles.

'I mean it, it's just …' She shrugged and finished off lamely, 'Things are difficult at the moment. I'm trying my best.'

Still walking, Izzy snorted sharply, two little puffs down her neat nostrils. She shook her head dismissively and something implicit in the gestures, *you're not worth my time* or *your best isn't good enough*, played on Annie's already frayed nerves. She caught Izzy's arm, looked directly into her sulky face.

'Why is the Family Safe app switched off?'

'It drains the battery.'

'But it's important! I need to know where you are.'

Izzy laughed sarcastically. 'Home or school. You don't need an app for that. You never let me go anywhere else. I'm a prisoner.'

A passing trio of ponytailed girls carrying hockey sticks burst into giggles.

'I'm a prisoner!' drifted back in a silly falsetto.

Izzy flushed crimson. Her shoulders sagged. She stared at her feet.

'I do not have time for your drama,' Annie said. She pressed the fob and the car beeped. 'You're only thirteen and while you're my responsibility, you'll do as you're told.'

'Nearly fourteen. And I'm not a kid anymore.'

Annie opened the car door. 'I know.'

Izzy got in the passenger side and fastened her seatbelt. In, tug, click. Every stage conveyed wounded anger.

Annie started the engine. A movement in the very edges of her vision caught her attention.

'Everyone already laughs at me because I'm not allowed Snapchat or TikTok or whatever,' Izzy continued, warming to the injustice of it all. 'And now I'm the only person not going to Paris, and I'll have to sit in with Year Eights and look like even more of a pathetic outcast than I already do. I must be the only Year Nine in the country who has never stayed away from home overnight. In Year Six, every other person went to Robinwood but me. And not one school trip.'

'That's not true! We go to Wells, and you stay over at Lucy's all the time!'

'You know what I mean. Properly away, without you. Even Smudge gets to go off the lead sometimes.'

She stared fixedly at her bag, anger radiating from her tense shoulders, her lowered eyebrows.

Who was that by the gate? Someone in generic sportswear lifted a cigarette to their lips. He – or possibly she – hadn't been leaning against the school railings less than a minute earlier when she and Izzy walked past. She would have noticed.

A billow of pale blue smoke exuded from deep within the hood.

'And I don't even know why,' Izzy was saying. 'Most kids in my year vape or smoke weed or drink and no one even cares. I don't do anything bad and I get locked up like I'm some sort of criminal.'

Keeping her gaze fixed on the figure by the school, Annie took out her phone. The school took safeguarding very seriously. Some parents were already parked in the side streets, waiting for the four o'clock pick-up. But what about the netball and hockey players on public transport or walking home? She should ring. Let the secretary alert one of the staff. Mrs Jackson or a PE teacher, perhaps. She clicked on contacts, scrolled down: *Uppermoss High*. Heard a gasp of indignation.

'You're not even listening!' Izzy said, aghast. 'You're on your fucking phone!'

Annie stopped. Felt her jaw literally drop.

'*Isabel!* What did you just say?'

'Don't even, Mum.' Izzy's voice thickened. She folded her arms and leaned as far away from Annie as she could without actually exiting the car.

'And I don't believe you just said that.'

Izzy, scrunched up against the window, body all spiky, defensive angles, didn't reply.

And when they got back to the cottage, she didn't need to tell Izzy to go upstairs. She stomped off by herself, pausing briefly to entice the dog to side with her. Slammed her bedroom door.

There were two texts on her phone. One from Liam about tonight.

Shall I bring wine or beer? X

She'd done a quick supermarket shop before she picked Izzy up and got lucky. A yellow-sticker ready-made curry and a couple of naans and she'd only spent a fiver.

Whatever you prefer xx, she texted back.

The second was from Samara. *Hi, have I got the surgery bank card or have you?! Stressing I've lost it.*

Did she? Yes, there, behind the folded-up receipt from paying in the money yesterday. She took the receipt out and laid it on the table. Smoothed it with the palm of her hand.

Balance: £79, 637.

She took out the card and set it by the side. Tapped the plastic a couple of times with her fingernail. Looked at them both.

Loud music started up in Izzy's bedroom, the bass notes shaking the kitchen ceiling. A vocalist rapped, railing against the myriad injustices of life. Well, she could write an entire album on that theme. Maybe she'd name it *Motherhood*.

She couldn't put a name to the sensation swirling in her gut. Nausea, certainly, mixed in with fear, anxiety, grief, anger. But right now, mainly guilt. A whole choppy, rolling ocean of it.

She picked up her phone and replied to Samara's text.

Hi, don't panic! I've got it here.

Then

'Ta dah!' Lauren smoothed one hand over her flat belly.

'Very glamorous,' Annie answered, taking in the clingy leopard-print dress, fringed leather bag and skyscraper heels. 'Also, very tall.'

Wobbling slightly, Lauren pushed the pram into the hall and peered in the mirror. Her newly bleached hair was almost white, and her eyebrows pencilled into two thin, dark arches.

She blinked rapidly, pressed her little finger to the corner of her eye. 'Is my eyelash coming off?'

Annie inspected the feathery strip. 'I don't think so. Where are you going?'

Sliding the long leather fringe on her bag between her fingers, Lauren spoke slowly, 'We-e-e-lll, Alannah's been seeing the DJ at this club who's got us tickets for a big thing tonight. And Alannah's auntie was supposed to babysit but now she says I've got to give her twenty quid and if I give her that, I can't go out anyway so I was hoping …'

There was an expectant pause.

Keziah's dimpled fists curled by her chin, like a prizefighter. It had been T-shirt weather all day, and the rounded cheeks were tinged pink.

'Not got plans, have you?'

Did channel-hopping and a bar of Dairy Milk count? Probably not.

Lauren brushed a stray fleck of mascara from under her eye. 'Come on. Please. I've been trapped inside like a prisoner for weeks. And Keziah wants Auntie *Annabel* to give her cuddles, don't you, baby?'

Flattening herself against the wall, Annie let Lauren squeeze past, negotiating the narrow hallway and parking the too-big pram next to the coffee table.

Annie put the back of her hand to the baby's forehead. Too warm. She removed the fleece blanket and the baby's socks and wheeled the pram to where the light breeze rippled the curtains.

'What time will you be back?'

Lauren pumped the air. 'I knew you'd do it! Twelve.'

'Should I feed her?'

'I suppose so. If she's hungry.' Wiggling her toes, she added, 'Do these go with the dress?'

'These' were beige vertiginous open-toed boots. The graze where she'd fallen against the table had scabbed over, but the bruise remained a deep grey smudge.

'Yes. Your leg still looks sore. What about nappies and formula?'

'In the bottom of the pram. You won't need to do anything, she'll just sleep anyway. Can you really see it?'

She lifted her leg and instantly wobbled on a single spindly heel. '*Shit!*'

'Careful.' Annie steadied one windmilling arm.

Lauren pressed both feet firmly to the ground.

'Always bruised like a peach. It'll be dark in the club, no one will see.' She waggled her fingers. 'See ya. Don't wait up.'

Keziah was a little angel. No trouble, no drama. Unlike her mum.

Twelve o'clock came and went with no word from Lauren. At half past she rang and left a voicemail. At one, she sent a text.

Nothing. She parked the pram next to the bed and lay on top of the covers.

She must have nodded off, because she woke to the acrid smell of a freshly lit cigarette and the muffled thud of a door closing. The alarm clock by the bed read 3.23am. Very much on the -ish side of twelve-ish. She slid her feet into flip-flops and pulled a hoodie over her leggings and T-shirt.

Careful not to wake Keziah, she crept into the lounge. A series of muted thumps came from next door. She smiled. Those heels, plus a night drinking had obviously taken their toll.

The lights were off. She knocked gently. Waited. Rattled the door handle, but it was firmly closed. She lifted the letterbox flap. 'Lauren? It's me, Annie. Are you okay?'

Darkness. Silence.

'Hello?'

Still nothing. She must have gone straight to bed. Annie crept back to the flat and slid back under the covers.

The next thing she knew, early morning sun was filtering through the windows and the baby was crying.

She stumbled, half asleep, to the pram.

'Morning, lovely. Nappy or food?' she said.

The baby cried again.

'Both, is it?' She scooped her up, peppering her downy scalp with kisses. Felt the cold weight of the saggy nappy. 'Let's get you ready for the day.'

While a freshly cleaned Keziah guzzled formula, Annie checked her phone. Lauren hadn't replied to any of her texts and there were no missed calls. Odd.

She was about to hang up when a sleepy voice answered.

'Yeah?'

'There you are!' Annie said. 'Where have you been? Do you want me to bring the baby round now or—'

The phone went dead. Annie immediately redialled.

Hiya, this is Lauren. Leave a message …

'It's me. I'm bringing Keziah round now.'

'Come on, little miss,' she said, cradling the baby in the crook of her arm. 'Let's go and find Mummy.'

But there was no reply to her knock. Peering through the windows revealed no sign of life.

The baby looked up at her and starfished her tiny hands. She was so beautiful, so trusting.

'It's all right, baby,' Annie murmured, turning back. 'Mummy will come for you soon.'

But she didn't.

The sun rose higher, and the Saturday noises rose with it. Kids on bikes, cars revving their engines, music.

'Let's get some fresh air,' Annie said, putting her in the pram.

And as she pushed her along, feeling the warm sun on her skin, she felt something close to contentment.

A woman walked past with a toddler and paused to peer at Keziah.

'She looks just like you, doesn't she?'

'Oh no,' Annie said, 'she's—'

But the toddler had made a run for it.

'Charlie, wait!' she shouted, sprinting after him.

Lauren still hadn't arrived home when they returned. Annie ate her lunch while Keziah took a nap. Changed her when she woke up and finally, when they were down to the last scoop of formula, there was a clatter and a string of loud expletives outside.

'Don't start,' Lauren said, brushing tangled hair out of her eyes. She knelt on the walkway, bare feet filthy. Her handbag lay flat, contents scattered on the walkway. A tube of lip-gloss rolled to Annie's flip-flops.

'I wasn't planning on it.' She passed the tube over. 'Are you okay?'

'No, I'm not. Where the fuck is—?' Lauren finally plucked out her key. Once inside, she dropped her shoes on the floor, went in the kitchen, put her mouth under the tap and drank thirstily.

Following, Annie said, 'I've left Keziah napping. Shall I bring her round now?'

Water trickled down Lauren's chin. She used the neckline of her dress as a towel to wipe it away. 'No, I need to go to bed now.'

The soles of her feet, black with grime, streaked dirt across the fitted sheet. She clutched the pillow. 'Aren't you going to ask me where I've been?'

'Dev's?'

Opening one red eye to throw her a look of disdain, Lauren said, 'What, getting cosy with Megan and the kids? No, I stayed over at Omar's.'

'Who?'

Tch. 'Don't you listen? DJ from the club. Oh my god, his apartment is amazing. Massive. Views across town. Everything is like brand new. Nothing like this shithole.'

'So, you didn't come home at all last night?' Annie frowned, trying to square this with being woken by someone in the flat.

'I just told you. I stayed at Omar's all night.'

'Hang on, isn't he Alannah's boyfriend?'

'Jesus, what are you, my mum? They weren't ser—'

A thin wail cut off the rest.

Lauren groaned. 'Can you look after her a bit longer? I need to sleep.'

'Listen. This is important.' Annie perched on the very edge of the mattress. 'Someone was definitely in here last night. Moving things. You need to check nothing has been taken. I came round and shouted through the letterbox, but no one answered.'

Lauren had tensed while Annie spoke, and now she propped herself up on one elbow. Strands of hair draped over her face and she shoved them back, impatiently.

'*You* listen,' she said, low and precise. 'It might be my name on the lease, but this is Dev's flat and he can come round himself, send someone in, whatever, I don't get involved. Not your flat. Not your business. Got that? You have no idea what you're dealing with. Next time you hear or see something going on here, be like everyone else and look the other way, fast, or I swear you'll regret it. Dev's already on to you and he's got spies all over the place. Including the police. You'd be surprised how many Met officers he goes out drinking with. He's got a lot of good friends in the police.'

She thumped the centre of the pillow, settled her head into the fist-shaped indent. 'I'm warning you, Annie: be careful.'

Now, Tuesday

'Earth to Annie,' Liam said, lowering his fork to the plate. 'You're miles away.'

He had been chatting non-stop ever since he had arrived at the cottage bearing a six pack of Beck's. And she thought she'd been doing a good job of acting like she was listening.

She plastered on a tired smile. 'Maybe I'm coming down with the same bug as Izzy.'

There'd been no point asking Izzy to join them for dinner. When she went up and knocked on the door, there was no response. And when Liam arrived, she'd made up a story about a virus going round school to explain the empty chair at the table.

'And I'm tired. You know? The whole thing with the Maguires is very stressful and we're really busy at the surgery with the plans for the new building and everything. And I haven't been sleeping too well.'

'Guilty conscience, eh?'

There was nothing malicious in his grin.

'Something like that,' she said, scooping up the last of the sauce with some naan bread. 'I've just got a lot on my mind at the moment.'

'Try me,' he said, lining his knife and fork together on the plate. 'I'm a good listener.'

'I'm fine. Honestly.'

He leaned down to pat Smudge, who had come to sniff at the table. She tore off a piece of naan and gobbled it in one, swirling her tongue over his fingers.

'Atta girl,' he said, scuffing her under the muzzle.

He gestured at the dirty crockery on the table. Smears of tandoori sauce congealed on the plates in bloody swirls.

'Shall we wash these up?'

'I'll do it. You sit on the sofa with a beer, I won't be a minute.'

'Don't be daft,' Liam said, getting to his feet. 'Pass me a tea towel and I'll dry.'

She turned away so he couldn't see her eyes fill with tears. He was just so *nice*. It wasn't fair.

But she couldn't shake the nagging anxiety. How well did she really know him? She knew he had two daughters – Zoe and Carly – who lived with their mum down in Essex. He preferred curry to Chinese and beer to wine. He had *House of Games* on series link and played five-a-side on Sunday afternoons. And, most telling of all, he genuinely adored his dog, Lola.

Samara had a theory that everyone subconsciously chose a pet that shared their core values. According to her, hamster owners were hyperactive and hard to pin down. If you had a fish, you were enigmatic. Possibly boring. Parrot owners were wild. Cat fanciers did everything on their own terms. And if you plumped for a Labrador, that showed intelligence and trustworthiness.

Like Liam.

She was just being paranoid.

'You didn't seem yourself yesterday,' he said. 'When I saw you outside the station.'

Annie rinsed suds from a plate and handed it to him. 'I had a bad day on Sunday. We had to euthanise a pony belonging to Izzy's best friend, which was pretty awful.'

'I can imagine,' he said, grimacing. 'Sounds rough.'

There was a silence, not quite awkward, but not exactly unawkward either. Liam broke it first.

'This is such a lovely place to live, out in the woods,' he said, scanning the kitchen. 'You told me you moved here when Izzy was a baby, right?'

'Yeah,' she said, pulling the plug out of the sink. The pipes gurgled as the water drained.

'And you lived in London before?'

'That's right. Do you fancy a coffee?'

'Please.' He passed her the tea towel and she dried her hands then switched the kettle on. 'What made you move?'

What was with the questions?

'Oh, change of circumstances.' She shook the tea towel and hung it on the cooker door. 'Caff? Decaf? I've got tea if you like, peppermint, normal. Some stuff of Izzy's that smells like the dog's bed.'

He laughed. 'Normal coffee please. Milk, no sugar.'

She spooned granules into two mugs. 'What about your ex? How are the alternate weekends working out now you've moved up here?'

'No different from before, really. We meet halfway at the service station on the motorway and do the handover there. I guess it helps that when we broke up, there was no big drama, we just drifted apart. It made it easier to keep things amicable. We still get on fine, me and Lauren.'

Drops of boiling water missed their target and splashed the worktop, but he didn't seem to notice.

'Your ex is called Lauren?' Annie said faintly, getting the milk.

'Laur-a,' he said. 'With an a.'

He continued talking. Something about his parents still living in the same house he grew up in and how close it was to where his ex lived and how much his girls loved their cousins.

'Why did you leave the Met?' she blurted out.

His mouth stopped mid-word. He scratched his chin, the stubble made a rasping sound. 'Well, I'd been there for a long time. Did my training at Hendon in 2000, stayed until last year when I transferred to Greater Manchester. I suppose the answer is I thought it must be a very different pace of life. A lot quieter. But even somewhere as sleepy as this, there's a lot going on behind closed doors that you'd never believe.' He took a sip of coffee. 'Were you living in London then? Hey, maybe we bumped in to each other.'

She pulled out a chair. One of the ties on the seat cushion had come slightly loose and she carefully re-tied it in a neat bow.

'Maybe. What do your daughters think of Uppermoss?'

'They like it,' he said, leaning against the worktop so she had to tilt her chin to see his face. 'I don't think I know where you lived in London. Have you got family there still? What about Izzy's dad?'

'Do you mind if we don't talk about it?'

Liam blinked, taken aback. 'Of course' – he held his palms up in an apology – 'no problem. Sorry, I wasn't being nosy.'

A sip of coffee moistened her mouth enough to offer a weak smile and add, 'No, I'm sorry. I didn't mean it like that. It's just I had a few difficult years in London and as for family, well, I'm an only child and I lost both my parents when I was in my early twenties. Izzy doesn't have any contact with her dad.'

'Ah,' he said on a long exhale. 'I'm sorry to hear that and for all the questions. I don't mean to pry, it's something I've picked up from work. Laura always used to complain that I turned a conversation into an interrogation.'

There was another gap. Longer this time.

Liam put his hand on her forearm. 'I can tell you're not really in the mood for this. Shall we save it for another day?'

She opened her mouth to protest. Closed it and nodded. What was the point?

'I'm sorry,' she said weakly. 'I've got a few things going on at the moment.'

'Listen, it's fine. Honestly.' He got up and put his coat on. 'I'm well under the limit to drive home.'

He kissed Annie on the cheek. 'See you soon, definitely.'

'Thanks for coming,' she said, grabbing Smudge's collar to stop her running away with him.

Outside, the security light reflected on the wet stones, turning the path into a strip of white. The rain had stopped, but it was cold.

'Nothing to be sorry about,' Liam said, pulling his hood up. 'I mean it. If there's anything I can do to help, you've just got to ask.'

Can you lend me twenty-three thousand pounds?

She put her arms around him and hugged him fiercely. 'You might regret saying that. But thank you and I'm sorry about tonight.'

'Hey,' he said, kissing the top of her head. 'Don't apologise. How about if I give you some space for a few days? Then, when you're feeling up to it, give me a call. Does that sound good?'

'That sounds,' she said into the rough cotton of his coat, 'absolutely perfect.'

A minute later, headlights shone through the window and the engine faded away.

She went in the kitchen to put the plates away, moving very slowly, as though fighting against a strong current. Perhaps she was coming down with something. Or maybe she couldn't cope anymore.

She tipped the cold remains of the half-drunk coffee down the sink. Watched it swirl away. Everything built up inside her, like a pressure cooker. The messages. The blackmail. The threats. Lauren Taylor's Facebook page.

She put her hands to her temples. Every part of her screamed, *Do something!*

But she'd tried. What else could she do?

She was going to lose her boyfriend, her job, her home.

And she was going to lose Izzy.

Then

'You're early,' Annie said.

Stale nightclub air wafted into the hall, carried on Lauren's clothes.

'Omar dropped me off round the corner. Get us a water, will you?' she said. She dropped her handbag by the kitchen door, kicked off her sandals and rubbed her blistered little toe. 'Please. I'm gasping.'

Annie turned the tap on. 'Keziah is still in the cot. Do you want me to get her?'

Over the past six weeks, the baby had begun to stay so often at Annie's, it had made sense to convert the tiny box bedroom into a nursery. She'd scrubbed the mould off with bleach, then painted the walls a cheerful yellow and hung a 'Keziah' nameplate on the back of a cereal packet for the door. The second-hand cot came courtesy of Sylvia's foodbank, the sheets from a supermarket sale.

'Let her sleep.' Lauren took the glass from Annie's outstretched hand and waved her cigarettes. 'Do you mind if I …?'

'Oh. On the balcony, please,' Annie said, surprised. Not like Lauren to ask first.

The door juddered along the track. Although it was only just after five, the windows of distant skyscrapers burnt gold against the pastel blue sky.

'Omar doesn't like me smoking. Or drinking. I've had to pretend I've given up.'

'You don't have to do what he tells you,' Annie said mildly. 'But, you know, quitting wouldn't do you any harm.'

Lauren's cheekbones hollowed as she sucked hard. She let out a groan of satisfaction on the exhale that turned into a cough.

'I started when I was twelve. It's hard, but I am going to try.'

Instead of hanging on her slim frame, the leopard dress clung to healthier curves. Her face had changed subtly too during the six weeks she'd been seeing Omar. Less angular, and a new sheen to her complexion. Her fine bone structure was emphasised by a new sharp shoulder-length bob that she'd twisted into a high topknot. Despite being up all night, her hazel eyes sparkled. And against Annie's advice, she'd bought a tooth-whitening kit off the back of Ray's van with admittedly dazzling effects.

Lauren scratched her chin, said casually, 'You really enjoy looking after Keziah, don't you?'

'Yes, I do. She is a lovely little girl.'

'And you're really good with her. Reading her stories and singing songs and that kind of thing. She loves you, you can tell.'

She fell silent, but it was a silence that seemed loaded with something important.

'Is there something wrong?' Annie said into the quiet.

'No, everything's great. Better than great. Amazing because' – She leaned her elbows back on the wall. The morning sun lit her. Haloed in the light, her hard prettiness blossomed into beauty – 'Omar's got a residency in Ibiza over the summer and he asked me to go with him for a few weeks.'

The pit of Annie's stomach dropped, like she'd just begun the descent on a roller-coaster. She gathered herself, smiled. 'Wow. What did you say?'

Lauren raised her eyebrows. 'What do you reckon?'

'You'll love it. I went there a couple of times with my ex. It's a stunning place.'

'He's got an apartment lined up next to the beach. For free. Which means I can give you my benefits while I'm there.'

'Me?' Annie echoed. 'Why?'

'For Keziah,' Lauren said, with an implied *well, duh*. 'Unless you don't want the money.'

'You're not taking the baby?'

'Ibiza's not the kind of place you take a little kid. Especially when you're with a DJ.'

'Have you asked him?' Annie said. 'I mean, he might be able to find a way to make it work. You could get an au pair, maybe. Or a nanny.'

Stubbing the cigarette out on the balcony wall, Lauren looked away and flicked the butt over the edge. Didn't reply.

'Oh,' Annie said, realisation dawning. 'Oh. You haven't told him you've got a child. Why not?'

That earned her a weary you're-so-naïve glance. 'Those bitches at the club would shove me under a bus to get on that plane. If I tell him I'm bringing a baby, he'll ask one of them instead. It's all right for you, I bet you've been to loads of places. I went to the seaside a few times with foster kid charities and that's it. And it's not like Dev ever took me away.'

Dev. As far as Annie knew, he hadn't shown any interest in the baby. And, the truth was, she hoped he wouldn't. Better an absent father than a bad father.

'Have you told him you're going to Ibiza?'

'He wouldn't care. None of his family, not even his kids know she exists.' She stifled a yawn then changed her tone, wheedling. 'Please say you'll look after her. I don't have anyone else and if you didn't have Keziah to look after, your life would be pointless. You said that.'

'Erm, no I didn't.'

Interruption ignored, she continued, 'And she's really happy

147

with you. You can do those things like read her stories and take her to the park and tell her what the birds are and that. You're a natural.'

Still digesting the request, Annie said, 'Have you asked Donna? I'm sure she'd jump at the chance.'

Lauren rolled her eyes. 'First, she doesn't even know Keziah. She's still pissed off about the whole Dev thing. Second, she'd just go on about how selfish I am and responsibilities and how she tried to get me to have an abortion because I would lose all my freedom.' She finished with the mimicking bossy sister voice. '*You've made your bed. I told you so.* Ugh.' She shuddered.

Annie took a baby-grow from the rail over the radiator and folded it into the basket. 'I'm sure she thinks differently now the baby's here.'

'You're joking, aren't you? She'd call Social Services on me. Have me arrested for baby abandonment. You're the only person I can trust her with. Hang on.' She rummaged through her bag. 'He gave me a picture of where we'll be staying. Look.'

She smoothed a crease from the corner of the photo. It showed a spacious flat, with tiled floors and minimalist furniture. A bank of records dominated one wall, behind a huge DJ deck. Wide glass doors looked out to where palm trees framed the sparkling blue Med.

'Nice,' she said, passing it back.

A series of staccato cries came from the nursery, the warm-up to a full-scale tantrum.

'And this is the club Omar's going to be working at.' She followed Annie into the bedroom, waving another photo. 'It's not some sweaty shithole like round here. It's fifty euros to get in.'

Keziah flung her limbs out, little face screwed up in misery.

Lauren thrust the photo almost to Annie's nose. 'Look. Posh, eh?'

Potted palms. A turquoise pool in the centre. Moroccan-style lanterns.

'I'll let you in on a secret if you say you'll do it,' Lauren said slyly, going to the front door. 'Back in a minute.'

'Lovely,' Annie murmured, lifting the baby out. 'Oh, sweetie pie, let's get you your breakfast.'

While Lauren banged around next door, doing god-knows-what, Annie warmed a bottle of formula in a sterilised bottle.

Keziah squirmed, mouth frantically searching for the teat.

'There you go,' Annie said. 'That's better, isn't it.'

A minute later, Lauren returned, slightly breathless.

'Look at this,' she said, triumphantly. She held out a roll of twenty-pound notes.

Annie felt her mouth drop open. 'Where the hell did you get that?'

'Bank of Dev,' Lauren said, pointing towards the ceiling. 'Manor roof space branch. And spare keys.' She dangled them in the air. 'You can help yourself when you need to.'

Annie rubbed Keziah's shoulder blades. 'I really think you should put that back before he notices it's missing.'

Lauren shrugged. 'People are coming and going all the time. He doesn't keep an eye on it down to the last penny. If all of it went, then, yeah. But not this. He owes me this anyway. But if you don't want it …'

Keziah's face turned puce and her cheeks puffed out.

'Oh dear,' Annie said. 'Someone needs a change.'

The baby lay on the changing mat bicycling her legs. Mouth open, ready to unleash a roar.

'Please?' Lauren said, clutching the photos like holy relics. 'Please say you'll do it. I'll never get a chance like this again. Please? Keziah, tell Auntie Annie you want to stay with her for a while. Tell her I'll pay her.'

Dirty nappy balled and binned, Annie lifted the baby's squidgy feet in one hand and slid a fresh nappy underneath.

'It's not about money. It's that I'm not sure it's even legal. I need to think about it.'

149

Emotions flickered across Lauren's face. Surprise, irritation, a spike of fury. A fresh howl burst from Keziah, and her mother looked ready to join in.

'Well, *I* need to know today, before one of those other bitches gets her claws in him.' She smiled tightly, knelt by the mat. 'You know what, I've got this.'

And while she didn't exactly barge Annie out of the way, there was a firm nudge as she angled herself to tickle Keziah's tummy. The pointed acrylic nails made an unpleasant dry whisper against the soft skin, like tiny scratching claws.

'Who loves Mummy?' she crooned. 'That's right. Keziah loves Mummy.'

'What about Social Services?' Annie said. 'Won't they want to assess me or something?'

Lauren took a striped baby-grow and stretched the neckline, gently lowering it over the baby's head.

'We don't need to tell them. Who's going to know? Omar doesn't know Keziah exists and Dev doesn't care. And people round here are so used to seeing her with you, I bet they think you're her mum anyway. It'll be easy.' She got up off the floor and passed Annie the baby's leggings. 'Even if anyone does come nosing round, you can tell them I've taken *my* daughter to Spain with me.

'And *your* daughter is on the Manor with you.'

Now, Tuesday

The stairs creaked and feet thudded down.

'Is that Liam going already?' Izzy called from the lounge, still sounding sulky.

'Oh,' Annie said, hastily wiping her sleeve across her eyes. She cleared her throat. 'He's got an early shift, so he went home to get some sleep.'

Izzy grunted something in reply and came into the kitchen.

She had changed out of her uniform into a tracksuit and twisted her hair into a high topknot. Her hazel eyes sparkled. She stood directly under the light, haloed by the warm, white glow that cast a sheen on her complexion. Bleached the colour from her hair, turning it blonde. The light emphasised her fine features and the emotions rapidly flickering across them. Sullenness. Concern. A spike of alarm.

Annie swayed on the spot. Izzy blurred and wobbled.

'Mum, what's happened?'

Annie put her hand to her face, realised tears were streaming down her cheeks.

'What's he done?' Izzy bit her thumb. Hazel eyes wide.

'Not Liam,' she managed between hiccupping sobs. 'Just. Nothing. Me being daft.'

Breathe. Breathe. Breathe.

She grasped Izzy's shoulders. 'Listen. I need you to know that no matter what happens, I'm your mum and I love you. Have you got that?'

Izzy looked terrified. 'What do you mean whatever happens? You're scaring me. Is this about Paris, because if it is, I'm really sorry I kept going on about it.'

'It's not about that. Come here.' Annie squeezed her in a bear hug. 'Honestly, and it's me who should be sorry. I wish I could give you everything you deserve. But I've always tried my best, I hope you know that.'

'Please tell me what's going on,' Izzy said in a small voice. 'You've been really weird since Sunday and now you're really freaking me out. Is it something to do with my dad?'

'Your dad? Why, has something happened you haven't told me about?' Annie tightened her grip on Izzy's shoulders. 'What makes you think it's got something to do with him?'

'What you were saying to Mrs Jackson about our "special circumstances". I was wondering if you'd heard from him. It would explain a lot.'

Annie closed her eyes and let the relief flow like warm water through her. Izzy knew nothing.

Some things were impossible to explain, but Izzy's absent dad wasn't one of them. When she was eight or nine, she had come home from school one day fighting back tears. Their topic that week was Family, but their teacher was off with food poisoning. So to help their French, the idiot supply teacher had them drawing and labelling family trees.

'I said I didn't have anything to put except Ma Mère and she didn't believe me,' Izzy said, curling her fingers up inside her sleeves, like she did when she was nervous. 'She told me to stop being silly and I said I wasn't and she made me go and sit in the thinking corner.'

Within half an hour, Annie was being served tea and a custard cream by a very apologetic headteacher. And it was in the tiny, messy office that the 'special circumstances' were conceived.

For a few years after that, Izzy occasionally brought up the man whose DNA made up fifty per cent of hers. And every time she did, Annie kicked herself for not inventing a better cover story on the day of the French lesson. A drunken one-night stand. An anonymous fling. Puritan sensibilities, that's what stopped her. The Father line was blank on the birth certificate, so Izzy would never have known any different.

The title of their cover story was 'The Very Bad Man' and the gist, they fled London because of an abusive relationship. Cut all ties with the past. Moved to another town. Avoided social media so he wouldn't come looking.

And it was the truth. Partly.

'No,' she said, releasing her grasp on Izzy's shoulders. 'I promise it's got absolutely nothing to do with your dad.'

She boiled the kettle and put a camomile teabag in a cup. Frowned. Sod it.

Liam's beers clinked against each other when she opened the fridge door. She extracted one, flipped the cap and swigged directly from the bottle. She switched the kitchen light off and sat on the sofa, staring at the wall.

Izzy, looking slightly reassured by Annie's promises, had taken Smudge up to bed with her and was, hopefully, calm enough now to sleep.

What was crystal clear was they couldn't carry on like this indefinitely. She shuddered, assailed by a glimpse of an unwelcome future where the more she cocooned Izzy, the more she would find herself pushed away. Her fingernails plinked against the glass as she picked at the silver label. Take Paris, for example. There were so many opportunities for discovery, from filling in the passport application, submitting Izzy's birth certificate, to passport control. All of which shrank next to the fear mother lode: letting her out of her sight.

'For god's sake,' she said to the blank TV screen.

She got up and stood in front of the picture of her parents. Lifted it carefully off the wall and propped it against the skirting board.

She'd discovered the old bread oven the first time she decorated the house. Nothing elaborate, just a soot-stained gap where a couple of bricks were missing next to the fireplace. At some point, it would have had an iron door, but that had long gone. Probably discarded by the previous owner who covered it – and the rest of the house – in wood chip.

Annie had been set to do the same when she realised how useful it would be to someone who wanted to keep certain things safely hidden from prying eyes. And that if she hung a picture over it, no one would ever know it was there.

A purple velvet pouch contained her mum's rings and a pair of diamond earrings. Under it, the brown envelope containing two pieces of paper. The first said 'The UK Deed Poll Office' under a fancy coat of arms and confirmed that Annabel Joyce Naughton-Smith was now officially Annie Smith. The second, the one she slid out now, was a birth certificate in the name of Isabel Smith. Mother: Annie Smith. Father: Blank. And her birthdate 2 July.

Her own passport expired years ago. It must all be online, nowadays, surely. Or did you still have to go to the post office? Would she have to send the birth certificate off or would they scan a copy.

Her phone vibrated, the friction against the coffee table's surface creating a sonorous buzz. She put the envelope back and returned the picture to the hook.

It was a message from Liam.

Good to see you tonight. Hope you're feeling better soon. Take care. x

You too, she typed. Hesitated before adding an x.

She tipped the bottle, felt the cold liquid slide down.

Here was a man. A good, kind, solvent man. A man who could be described as 'almost too good to be true'. A man who entered her life recently. From London. And was a police officer.

Her mind spooled back, unpicking each conversation. All those questions he'd asked about her life before she got to Uppermoss. Hidden as innocent getting-to-know-each-other questions. Had she left a trail of breadcrumbs for him to follow?

These things happened. Officers went deep undercover, infiltrating different groups or hooking up with a suspect. Sometimes these cases hit the headlines. Undercover cops so immersed in their double life they blurred the lines. Started relationships. Even had children with some poor woman.

She turned the phone over and over. The home screen lit up with an image of Smudge's long, pink tongue caught in the act of licking Izzy's nose.

But if Liam had been deployed to investigate her, would he really be so upfront about being a detective?

A sudden pain made her wince. Without realising, she had chewed her nail down to the quick and ripped into the nail bed. A bead of blood oozed out and she sucked at it.

She wouldn't have tripped up. She wore the cover story like a pair of old trainers, moulded to her shape through use. In fact, there were long stretches when she forgot that there was a different truth. The actual truth.

No. Liam turning up and then this starting had to be a coincidence.

Which was great. Except she didn't trust coincidences.

She downed the last of the beer and levered herself off the sofa. Put the bottle in the recycling bin by the back door.

It was after ten and she had work in the morning. She should at least try to sleep. The ritual of checking the locks and windows took longer tonight. Double, triple checking. Making sure the alarm was correctly armed. She altered the settings on the security lights so they remained permanently lit. Izzy would have a fit tomorrow, no doubt. Artificial light disturbing the wildlife was another of her personal crusades. But tonight, Annie needed all the comfort she could get.

She went upstairs and peeked in Izzy's bedroom. A wedge of light from the landing crept across the floor, up on to the bed and over the pillow, illuminating Izzy's sleeping form.

The love was visceral. She would do anything to keep this beautiful child safe. Anything. Her heart contracted painfully.

And now they had been found, this helplessness was the flip-side of love.

She didn't know *how* to keep her safe.

Disturbed by the light, Izzy murmured, but didn't wake.

The eyes, the hair, the cheekbones. Even the way she slept, one arm flung above her head. She looked nothing like Annie.

And everything like Lauren.

Then

'Annie, Annie, Annie,' Lauren slurred down the phone.

Annie looked at her bedside clock. 2.55am.

Even with the window open, the air in the flat was stifling. She shuffled upright against the headboard, clutching the phone to her ear. 'Is something wrong?'

'Nothing's wrong!' Lauren said with a laugh in her voice. 'My life is amazing.'

Music played in the background. People talked and laughed.

'Do you know what time it is?'

'Time doesn't matter. Only love matters. You know I love you, right?'

'Are you drunk?' The mattress creaked, she froze, but no sound came from the nursery.

Lauren giggled. 'Cheeky. You know Omar doesn't let me drink.'

'Why don't you have a glass of water and go home and sleep it off, eh?' Annie said through a yawn. 'Ring me in the morning.'

Lauren continued as though she hadn't spoken. 'No one else would have done what you're doing for me, you know? And there isn't anyone else I would trust with my girl. I really miss her, but she's happy with you. She is happy with you, isn't she?'

Annie tiptoed across the landing to the nursery where Keziah slept. The gentle whirring of the electric fan soothed her, camouflaging the night-time sirens and shouts that insinuated themselves through the open window.

'She's absolutely fine.'

'If she's happy and I'm happy and you're happy, then I'm not a bad mum.'

'Course not. Look, shall we have this conversation tomorrow? I was asleep and—'

'And you love her and she loves you. And I love Omar and he loves Ibiza and I love Ibiza,' Lauren finished.

Annie sighed. 'Good, I'm happy for you. But it's three o'clock in the morning. I'm going to put the phone down now. See you on Tuesday.'

And it must have been her imagination, but she could have sworn Lauren murmured, *no, you won't* right before she said, 'You love her like she was actually yours, don't you?'

'Go to bed,' Annie said and put the phone down.

Keziah slumbered peacefully in her cot, dreaming of whatever babies dreamed of, moving her head gently from side to side, as if listening to relaxing music. The corners of her lips twitched in a contented smile, and Annie, also smiling, quietly returned to bed.

She turned the pillow over, searching for a cool spot. Sweat dampened her back, sticking it to the sheet. A plane roared overhead, jetting to an exciting, distant location. After a year on the Manor, she only noticed the proximity of the airport on nights like this, when the still air hung hot and heavy.

She had begun to drift off when a subdued thump came from next door. No one was staying there, or at least if they were, they didn't move around during the day. The thuds and bangs were exclusively nocturnal, and often accompanied by murmured voices and the scraping that seemed to come from inside the walls.

The warning echoed in her mind: *Not your flat. Not your business.*

Over the past three weeks, she had weaned herself off the sleeping pills. Almost. It wasn't easy: her mind and her heart raced for hours at night until exhaustion finally tipped her over the edge. But she had no choice. Suppose Keziah fell ill in the night? Or there was a fire? She couldn't take that risk.

She slept fitfully, dreaming of pale Gollum-like monsters crawling in the roof space above her, until light seeped in around the edges of the curtains. Sipping from a strong black coffee, she went out onto the balcony. The early morning mist gave a romantic outlook to the rosy landscape. Like this, the city looked beautiful.

Keziah gurgled and Annie's heart pulsed with bittersweet love.

'Mummy will be home soon,' she said, buzzing her lips against the soft spot where the bones had yet to fuse. Breathed in the milky lavender scent. 'I'm going to miss you so much.'

The routine of feeding and changing came naturally now, as did putting one hand under the pudgy bottom, rubbing shoulder blades in small circles. Waiting for the thunderclap belch that never failed to startle the baby and amuse Annie.

When Keziah yawned, and her pouty mouth smacked then slackened, Annie dialled Lauren's number. She answered on the second ring.

'Omar's still here,' she hissed. 'Wait.'

Whatever sparked the loved-up phone call last night had clearly left the building. Bare feet slapped on tiles. A door clicked shut. A moment later, the toilet flushed.

'Are you there?' Annie said.

'God, I feel rough. Just let me …'

Water ran. Loud glugging came down the phone.

'Listen,' Lauren said through a gasp. 'I've got to tell you something, and I was going to do it, you know, properly. But I feel

159

like total shit, so I'm just going to come straight out with it. You can say yes or no.'

Keziah grizzled, pumping her arms and legs. Annie picked her up, sniffed at nappy level. Not pleasant.

'So, they've asked Omar to stay on until the end of the summer season, which will be the end of September. Maybe mid-October.'

'Right.' Waited. 'Lauren?'

'And he can get me a job in the club. It's proper cocktails and Champagne, not pints of lager and WKD. The tips are really good. I'll be able to save up, you know, find somewhere to rent off the Manor with a garden for Keziah. So, I was thinking she could stay with you till then. It's only another few weeks.'

Keep Keziah longer? Her heart leapt, then immediately sank. Caring for someone else's child while they went on holiday sounded reasonable, but longer term definitely meant the authorities getting involved.

Lauren coughed.

'I thought you stopped smoking?'

'I have. Nearly. It's so annoying: Omar's got a nose like a dog, he can smell it on me. Same with alcohol. I've got a bad throat because it's boiling in the sun then freezing in the air conditioning.'

'Well, I hope you're enjoying all that lovely Spanish food.'

Lauren laughed again, a raucous sound that ended in a bout of fierce coughing. 'I can't eat. You should see the uniform I'm going to have to wear in the club. There's nothing to it. So, can she stay with you a bit longer?'

'I would love that,' Annie said, cautiously. 'But you won't have seen her for such a long time. And someone is bound to tell Social Services sooner or later and that will cause problems.'

Because I've got a criminal record.

There was the sound of footsteps on tiled floors. A muffled conversation took place. Lauren, her hand over the phone, talked to whoever had just entered the room.

The footsteps retreated and she returned, speaking in a whisper. The persuasive tone replaced by something much harder.

'Listen, Omar's here so I'm going to have to go. All I can say is don't think about it for too long. Because I *am* staying here and if you can't take care of her, I'll have to find someone else who can.' She kept the delivery neutral, but there was no mistaking the threat. 'And then you won't get to see her at all.'

Now, Wednesday

Annie had gone to bed in despair and woken this morning filled with hope.

She hadn't been particularly surprised when she hadn't been able to sleep. Although her body craved a respite from the stress, her head refused to cooperate.

But she must have nodded off eventually, because five minutes before the alarm was due to go off, her eyelids sprang open. At some point, the neurons working the night shift had sifted through her jumble of woes and discovered a solution.

It was a long shot, admittedly. But it was her best shot.

The morning routine went smoothly and the drive to school was subdued, but at least it wasn't silent. When they arrived, Izzy leaned across and drew her into a hug.

'I love you and I'm sorry I've been such a bitch about the Paris thing.'

'I love you too,' Annie said. 'And don't give up on it, I'm still trying to figure something out.'

She watched her stride towards school, a spring in her step, and catch up with Lucy, chattering excitedly. She watched until the two of them and the blazered crowd entering the school, swallowed up by the gates.

And the whole time, she fizzed with not exactly excitement, but a desire to put her plan into action as soon as possible. If it worked, everything would go back to normal. And if it didn't …

Well, she would have to think of something else.

There was a police car parked in front of the surgery door.

Annie's pulse boomed in her ears. She pulled into her reserved space and sat for a moment, quelling the panic. It wouldn't be anything to do with her. It would be about the Maguires.

Or about Liam, whispered Paranoia.

She took a deep breath and pushed open the surgery door.

'Sorry I'm late,' she said, slipping her bag off her shoulder. 'I …'

Two uniformed police officers stood in the waiting room. They turned in unison as she walked in. Their faces expressionless masks.

A cold trickle of dread ran down Annie's spine. The blackmailer knew the money wasn't coming and had told the police. This was it, then. The moment she had been waiting for since she left the Manor.

'I've just downloaded it,' Samara said, coming out of her office. 'Oh hi, Annie. Officers, this is my practice manager, Annie Smith.'

'Hello,' Annie said uncertainly. Her head went light and for a second she thought she might be about to faint. 'Has something happened?'

'We'll need to take a statement from you as well,' one of the men said. 'Have you noticed anything unusual? Strangers hanging around? That kind of thing?'

'What's happened?' she said.

Samara blew out her cheeks, exhaled. She looked at the police officer. 'Can I show her please?'

'Of course,' the officer said. 'We'll need statements from both of you.'

163

'I didn't spot it at first, because they'd slipped it under the shutter,' Sam continued, picking a white square off the desk. It was packaged in plastic. A police evidence bag.

It was a sheet of plain white photocopy paper that someone had written on in black marker pen. Each letter was composed of multiple lines giving it a frenzied, angry appearance.

Dead Bitch.

Annie felt the blood drain from her face. Her hand came up to cover her mouth. 'Oh god.'

'I know,' Samara said, pulling her coat tight across her chest. 'They've gone too far this time. At least we've got the bastard on camera.'

She held out her phone, scissoring her fingers to zoom in. 'Here you go.'

Annie peered at the screen.

'View out front, two this morning. Give it a second.'

The image was grey, but Annie could clearly make out the familiar car park lined with a tall hedge. The white lines glowed under the security light.

'Wait for it,' Samara said. 'There. Can you see?'

A figure emerged from the bushes that separated the car park from the main road. The man or woman strolled towards the surgery. As they neared, the image grew clearer. Dressed in the familiar uniform of black trousers, black hoodie, black gloves and a balaclava. Only the whites of their eyes showing.

'Do you recognise him?'

Samara snorted very softly down her nose. And she had a point: what was there to recognise? But the police had to ask these questions.

The other officer spoke for the first time. 'Could be a woman.'

She looked up, sharply. He was looking directly at her.

'A woman?' the other one said. 'Maybe.'

'Or a teenager,' Samara said. 'Cain Maguire is only seventeen. I really hope it's not him.'

And yes, she saw it now. How it could easily be a teenage boy and not a woman.

'Are you okay?' Samara said, suddenly concerned.

Annie nodded, her mouth too dry to speak, and watched the figure slide the paper under the shutter. And then look at the camera, no shame whatsoever, and stroll off nonchalantly, with his hands in his pockets. Or her hands.

Panic made her tremble.

'Sorry, it's just such a shock.'

'It's me they're after,' Samara said, stroking Annie's hair back from her eyes. 'You didn't do anything. There's the trolling as well.'

'Trolling?' The officer made a note in his notebook. 'What sort of things have they been saying?'

'I think Annie's taken screenshots,' Samara said. 'You can see for yourself.'

The porridge she'd had for breakfast lurched alarmingly. For a moment, she really thought she might be sick. She felt the blood run from the surface of her skin.

'I think,' she swallowed. 'I think I might have to sit down.'

Not sure how she got there, she found herself sitting behind the desk with a glass of water in her hand. Had she fainted?

Samara was bending over her, expression full of concern and worry.

'I'm so sorry for putting you through this,' she said. 'I feel terrible.'

She turned to the police officer. 'Annie had nothing to do with me reporting the Maguires.'

The officer nodded. 'Just to get back to that trolling. Are they on the Facebook page?'

A high-pitched ringing filled her ears. She hadn't deleted Lauren Taylor's comments or banned the profile from accessing the page. It wouldn't take Sherlock Holmes to find out all about Lauren Taylor.

'Yes, but I deleted all the comments and reported the profiles. There won't be anything there.'

The officer nodded. 'Well, if we could still take a look, that would be very helpful.'

The other police officer stepped forward. 'And you haven't seen anything at all? No one hanging about here or at home?'

'I would have reported it straightaway. I've got a thirteen-year-old daughter, you see.'

'And last night, you didn't come back to the surgery at any point?'

A jolt ran through her. Wait. Did he think she had something to with this?

'I wasn't here all day. I don't work Tuesdays,' she said.

When the policemen had finally left, Annie fled for the toilet and locked herself in the cubicle. She sat on the closed lid and stuffed her index finger knuckle in her mouth and bit down. Her shoulders shook with the effort. Tears leaked from her eyes.

'Give me a second.'

'I'll make a cup of tea,' Samara said. 'I've rescheduled the first three appointments, so don't rush.'

Annie looked at herself in the mirror and smoothed her hair back. She blew her nose and splashed cold water on her face. Not great, but better.

'I feel terrible about this,' Samara said, looking genuinely distraught. 'I don't mean to pry and you know I would never ask, but I can imagine this is triggering some difficult memories for you.'

Annie held the mug in both hands and nodded mutely in acknowledgement of the 'special circumstances'.

'I am so sorry. I promise we will put a stop to this.'

As Samara spoke, Annie watched the surface of the tea tremble. It was no coincidence Samara had become a vet. She was one of the most compassionate, caring people Annie had ever met.

Even now, with the trauma of what was happening to her, she was thinking of Annie.

Tears welled up and this time, she couldn't check them. They flowed down her cheek in rivers, dripping off her chin.

'Oh god,' Samara moaned, passing Annie the jumbo box of tissues they kept on the desk for grieving owners. 'I am sorry, Annie.'

Her apology only made Annie cry harder. Samara stood in front of her wringing her hands. But Samara had got it wrong. Annie wasn't crying because she was afraid or because what was happening had stirred up emotions from the past.

She was crying with relief. She was crying with guilt.

'Please go home,' Samara said gently, when the tears had slowed into shuddering gasps.

Annie went to protest, but Samara shook her head decisively. 'No. You're in no fit state to be here while all this is going on. And to be honest, if you can help me to get Helen away from bankrupting us through online shopping, you'll be doing me a massive favour. Have tomorrow off, too.'

Samara's exhaustion was evident in the heavy bags under her eyes. And it was all Annie's fault. Because the note that came under the door, the note that had terrified Samara, *Dead Bitch*, wasn't meant for Samara.

It was meant for her.

Then

Screaming. Someone was screaming.

It wasn't unusual to hear arguments late at night. Shouts penetrated walls, reverberated off concrete, entered through open windows. Petty family rows that had spiralled into violent disputes. Eventually chorusing complaints would join in: *keep it down, some of us have work in the morning.*

But occasionally, there would be sirens and flashing lights. And the following day, tealights in jam jars and petrol station flowers piled under a tree. Taped to the trunk, A4 photos in plastic wallets of grinning boys who would be teenagers forever.

The scream vibrated on a high note of disbelief, interspersed with a name repeated over and over.

'Lindon! Oh my god. Lindon!'

Annie quickly pulled a cardigan over her pyjamas. She checked on Keziah, grabbed her keys and ran down the stairs to the floor below.

Several other people had come out now and in the distance was the sound of approaching sirens.

Lindon.

His pyjamaed body lay across the threshold to his grand-mother's flat. Sylvia cradled his head in her hands and *keened*.

There was no other word for the animalistic wail that chilled the hot, humid night. A man knelt beside them, pressing a cloth to Lindon's side. A saturated cloth that glistened in the light spilling from the hallway.

'What happened?' Annie said.

'Stabbed,' came the nasal reply.

Ray stood behind her. In vest and shorts, his compact boxer's body was a mass of blurred tattoos.

'Has anyone called the police?' she said.

He scratched where a few greying hairs poked from the neckline. 'They'll be here soon enough.'

The man holding the cloth released the pressure slightly and blood pumped out.

'Oh my god, oh my god,' Sylvia chanted, cradling Lindon's head.

Duelling sirens grew closer.

'Why would anyone stab a twelve-year-old?'

But Ray had already melted back into the shadows.

The police car and ambulance headlights lit up the car park. The kind neighbour leaned over the balcony and waved to the paramedic who had just opened the door.

'You'd better bring a stretcher, mate,' he called.

There was quite a crowd now on the landing and people huddled over the wall, watching paramedics wheel the trolley up the ambulance ramp. The last thing she saw was Sylvia, holding Lindon's limp hand. Her work uniform red with blood.

The next day, the beautiful weather still held. She plastered Keziah in sun cream and headed to the park. Green spaces always soothed her. The swish of the breeze through the leaves and the smell of roses transported her to day trips when she was a child. Feeding the ducks. Drinking warm orange squash on a blanket in the shade. Licking drips of ice cream from the side of the cone. Mum and Dad pushing her higher and higher on the swing until she could touch the cotton wool clouds. *That* was childhood.

She felt her buoyant mood deflate the moment the concrete façade of the Manor loomed into view. Surely the architect aspired to more than this ugly block? Something that at least *attempted* to fulfil the basic human desire for beauty and nature. Even the seeds Sylvia had sown had given up, smothered by a carpet of weeds and plastic bottles.

She bumped the pram across the rutted car park, past a man fixing a laminated poster to a tree. Block capitals: *DID YOU WITNESS A SERIOUS INCIDENT?* next to the police logo. Peeling off a strip of duct tape, the man moved, blocking Annie's view. But she had seen enough. Stabbing … twelve-year-old boy … any information … call Crimestoppers … anonymous. Seriously injured.

Thank god he had survived.

The dark stairwell stank of weed. The lift was out of order. When she reached the first floor, she heard splashing.

Sylvia, hair tied up in a scarf, sluiced a bucket of foamy water by her front door. A long-handled scrubbing brush leaned against the wall, and the unpleasant tang of bleach hung in the air. Bleach mixed with something worse. Something that tinged the swill of water pink.

And how had she not noticed last night? A single word sprayed across the boarded-up window.

Grass.

'Hello, Sylvia,' she called, putting the brake on the pram. 'How is Lindon?'

The other woman looked up, eyes dulled with defeat. Deep lines bracketed her mouth and corrugated her forehead. And she seemed to have shrunk, diminished as though she had aged twenty years overnight.

'Thank you for asking.' Every word oozed exhaustion. 'The knife missed his vital organs and he should make a full recovery. He's been very lucky, apparently. He lost a lot of blood.'

She pushed the brush, the stiff bristles harshly scraping across

170

the rust-coloured stains. 'Lucky, they call it,' she muttered, half to herself. 'Lucky.'

'Do the police know what happened?'

The brush moved rhythmically, hard as Sylvia replied, mechanically, 'I was out at work. Someone knocked. He opened the door. He didn't realise he'd been stabbed until he felt the blood. The police say they'll investigate, but it's calling the police that started this.'

'Is there anything I can do to help?'

Sylvia leaned on the brush. 'You can do what I did. You can go to the police and say they're forcing children to sell drugs. You can try to make things better for everyone, and nothing changes. Except they smash your windows. Call you names. Threaten you. They stab your only grandchild.' Her voice cracked. 'And the police can't prove anything because the CCTV is always out of order and everyone else is too scared to speak out. And so the only thing we can do now is leave.'

'Have you got somewhere to go?' Annie said.

'My sister lives near Birmingham, and we're going to move in with her for a while, until Lindon is better. Then we'll have to see.' She glanced towards the pram. 'And when is that little one's mother coming back?'

'Oh,' Annie replied, clasping and unclasping her fingers. 'Soon. Quite soon.'

Sylvia met her gaze with a level stare. Held it for one, two, three. When she spoke, her voice was steady and low.

'The Manor used to be a good place to live, with decent people, but it is no place to bring up children now. It sucks them in and spits them out and no matter how hard we fight, people like you and me are no match for villains like Elliott Devlin.

'I should have left five years ago when my daughter died and I took Lindon in. Put as many miles between my grandson and this place as I could. Well, I almost left it too late to get out.' She

171

nodded once, quickly, at the pram and her tired eyes conveyed the implication behind the words. 'So if you think that poor baby deserves a chance at a better life than either of her parents can offer her, I suggest you do the same.'

Now, Wednesday

Dead Bitch.

After the shock of the note, there should have been Tim Burton storm clouds and a chill breeze stirring the trees into sinister susurration. Swathes of fog shrouding the woods.

Instead, half an hour after Samara sent her home, Annie unbolted the back gate and stepped into Pixar perfect woods. Birds flitted between the trees in cheery song under storybook skies. A warm breeze ruffled her hair. And on their gatepost perched a squirrel, delicately nibbling a nut.

Sunshine filtered through fresh spring leaves, dappling the ground in patches of light and shadow. It was a day for strolling with your dog or enjoying a countryside picnic with your daughter. It was definitely not the sort of day for demanding money from your ex-husband. Yet as she closed the gate behind her, that was exactly what she planned to do.

She tugged her sock where it had slipped down her welly. 'Come on, Smudge. Let's go for a nice, long walk.'

But the dog ignored her, too engrossed in pressing her nose to the base of the fence on the trail of a long-gone squirrel or fox.

The solution had been in plain sight the whole time. How had she not realised? Someone owed her. Someone wealthy.

She had the Vinum Bonum page open on her phone already. She pressed the 'Contact' tab, slid her finger over the number. All she had to do was press 'phone'.

Press it now.

She swallowed, her mouth temporarily dry. A week ago, the idea of speaking to Oliver would have been absurd. On the rare occasions he did cross her mind, she invariably pictured him on the morning of her arrest standing barefoot in the tiled hallway. Sunday morning stubble on his chin, hair flattened on one side by the pillow. Those ridiculous old man pyjamas he insisted on wearing with the fake handkerchief in the breast pocket. Mainly, though, she recalled his parting words. Not to her, but to the two detectives taking her to the waiting car:

I had nothing to do with any of it.

Behind her, the rustling and snapping twigs told her Smudge was on the prowl, panting loudly, pawing at the ground here and there to investigate buried treasure.

She flexed and straightened her fingers, poised to call. This was the right thing to do. If the past had finally come full circle for her, then surely Oliver deserved the same. Let him make amends for letting her down in the past. After all, it was his fault she was in this position, his responsibility to get her out of it.

Clearing her throat, she pressed the call icon. The line rang twice, then a crisp female voice perfectly adapted to short, precise exchanges answered.

'Vinum Bonum, how may I help you?'

'I'd like to speak to Oliver Naughton, please.'

'May I ask who's calling?'

'It's Annabel. And it's a personal matter.'

'I'm afraid Mr Naughton is in a meeting.'

It was like conversing with a robot.

Annie added a stern note. 'If you could tell him it's Annabel *Naughton*-Smith calling about a family emergency, I guarantee he'll step out.'

The woman paused. Then said, 'Please hold.'

Something operatic played down the phone.

Up ahead, a squirrel raced up the huge horse chestnut tree with the forked trunk Izzy loved to climb. Used to, before the teenage years put paid to such pursuits. The leaves shook as the squirrel hid in the canopy. But Smudge remained engrossed in the ground, zigzagging backwards and forward in front of the fence, snuffling through dense leaf litter.

The opera cut off mid-crescendo.

'Hello, Annabel,' Oliver said. 'This is a surprise.'

Instantly, memories whirled like the white flakes in a snow globe. She saw their fingers interlocked across a restaurant table. Their winter wedding in Central Park. The sonographer's sympathetic expression. And the closed front door, viewed from a police car window.

'Hello,' she said. Stopped.

When she'd mentally rehearsed the call, she had phrased the next part as a 'favour'. But on hearing his voice, the carefully planned speech died on her lips.

'My PA tells me we have a family emergency,' he prompted.

She breathed in sharply.

'Yes. Kind of. That's why I'm calling. I need …' She exhaled. 'I need you to give me twenty-three thousand pounds.'

A heavy silence fell over the line.

'Is this a joke?' he said, eventually.

'No. I need money and I need it today. And you're going to give it to me, Oliver. You owe me for what you did.'

She heard footsteps over the phone and the shush of a door shutting on a carpet. She could picture him clearly, in some swanky London office, eyes darting left and right in case of eavesdroppers. When he finally spoke, it was little more than a whisper.

'What is this? Be aware my legal team would take a very dim view of any attempts to discredit me. So whatever you're threatening me with, it's not going to work.'

175

Smudge brushed past her legs, nose still glued to the ground. Annie reached down, stroked the warm fur.

'I'm not threatening you at all. I just want what I'm owed from the sale of the house. *My* house.'

'Whoa,' he said. 'We settled that in the divorce agreement.'

Her planned cool delivery flew out of the window.

'Oh come off it. We both know that wasn't fair, I was a non-functioning mess and in no fit state to be signing anything.'

'You agreed to the settlement. And as for unfair, well, you brought it all on yourself.'

Resentment winded her with a force that took her by surprise.

'You defaulted on a loan against the house I inherited from my parents. I lost everything because of you.'

He tutted, like telling off a naughty child. 'We were married, my name was on the deeds. *Our* loan, *our* house. *Your* choice to sign the loan application form. *Your* decision to steal from your employers. I can't be held accountable for your bad choices, especially not after … I don't even know how long it's been. Fifteen years?'

She wedged the phone between her shoulder and chin. Shrugged off her jacket and knotted the sleeves too tightly around her waist.

'Listen, I need twenty-three thousand and I need it now. That's nothing to you and you owe me.'

He didn't reply straightaway and when he did, he spoke softly. 'Have you got yourself into trouble again?'

She scuffed at a deep drift of gently decomposing leaves at the base of the horse chestnut tree, a few feet from the gate. Dug the toe of her boot right in, kicking the soggy mass into the air.

'Even if I wanted to,' Oliver continued, 'it's out of the question. For a start, what would I tell my wife?'

'The truth,' Annie said. 'That the capital for your business came from your first wife and that you're repaying the investment.'

He laughed. 'You don't know Giovanna. Look, I can transfer

a couple of thousand this weekend, for old times' sake. But that really is all.'

'It's not enough. And I need it today,' she said and to her dismay, her voice broke on the final syllable. Smudge pawed frantically at the heap of dead leaves at her feet.

'You must know I can't do that,' he said. 'I hope you manage to find a solution. Good luck.'

And he hung up.

She hit redial immediately but cancelled before it even rang out. Pointless. The gatekeeper would just block her.

A fly strafed her ear and she swatted the air. Using the back of her hand, she wiped a film of sweat from her forehead. How could she have forgotten how arrogant, how pompous he could be?

Smudge yelped. Above their heads, the palmate leaves of the chestnut waved frenetically, tracking the squirrel's desperate attempts to flee. But the dog had caught the scent and jumped up at the tree, gouging the bark with her claws.

'What is it, girl?' Annie asked.

Something in the scattered leaves caught her eye. Using the edge of her welly, she scuffed the ground. Cigarette ends, burnt down not stubbed out, dotted the ground. Strange.

Come to think of it, the pile of leaves was strange. Usually, the wind worked like a snowplough, scooping leafy, twiggy debris to deposit the length of the fence. A heap seemed more ... intentional. Like someone was trying to cover their tracks.

Cigarette ends. Five, she nudged the leaves with her toe ... six. Seven of them. Right by her fence.

Seven cigarettes. Could it be kids? Occasionally, there were traces of late-night parties in the woods. Empty bottles. The ashy remains of a fire. But never this close to the house. Anyway, Smudge would have let her know.

But a single human could hide, undetected in the shadows.

Even for a dedicated chain-smoker, seven cigarettes equated

to at least an hour. She flicked imaginary butts to the ground. Scanned left, right, down. Up.

The chestnut wasn't huge, but it was easy to climb. In autumn, there were conkers. In the summer, its lobed leaves provided shade for reading.

Whimpering with excitement, Smudge scrabbled against the trunk, her nails scraping the rough bark.

And every spring, new leaves as big as dinosaur footprints concealed the perfect vantage point for surveying their house.

Anyone could smoke seven cigarettes in the natural seat of the easily accessible forked trunk, directly opposite Annie's bedroom window.

Watching. Waiting.

And she wouldn't even know they were there.

Then

Rain poured miserably, dripping off the balcony above. The air was filled with the sound of car tyres splashing through puddles and even the pigeons huddled miserably on the roof of the flats opposite. Typical August bank holiday weather.

No wonder Lauren was so keen to stay in Spain.

'Good girl!' Annie said encouragingly as Keziah goggled at the star from the shape sorter. 'Aren't you clever.'

Someone knocked on the front door. Not Sylvia, she'd seen her leave for the hospital earlier.

'Let's go and see who it is,' she whispered, lifting Keziah to her chest.

Please not Oliver again.

It wasn't. The spyhole in the door showed a woman on the walkway. Neatly dressed, vaguely familiar, but Annie couldn't place her. Jehovah's Witness? Someone from the council?

Her black hair was neatly and sensibly cut short. She wore a navy blazer over a white T-shirt with straight-leg jeans and bright white trainers.

Plainclothes officer conducting door to door after Lindon's stabbing?

'Hi,' the woman on the doorstep said through the narrow

179

opening allowed by the chain. 'Annie, is it? I'm Lauren's foster sister, Donna. We have met.'

Shit. How could she not have recognised her?

'You've changed your hair,' she said.

Donna laughed, taken aback. 'That's right. More professional, for work.'

She waited. Annie didn't say anything.

'Please can I come in?'

A whooshing started in Annie's ears. Her racing heart pumped blood in a furious rhythm. *Oh shit. Oh shit. Oh shit.* Was this what a heart attack felt like?

'Of course,' she said and took the chain off.

Donna smiled down at Keziah. 'I didn't realise you had a baby too.'

'Yes,' Annie said. 'This is my little girl. My lovely daughter.'

'Well, I'm sorry about flying off the handle the last time we met,' Donna said. 'I was worried about Lauren and angry that she wouldn't press charges.'

She glanced at the picture hanging by the door. Patted her cap of hair in front of the mirror. Peered into the spotless kitchen.

What had Lauren said? Donna wasn't in the police, but she worked for the police. She carried that in her observing gaze, neurons busily filing away snippets of information. Storing them like puzzle pieces to be assembled later.

Shit!

The plastic wallet tacked to the nursery. Most people's eyes skated over details, but not Donna's. She would see the nameplate. Wonder why it said Keziah. Put two and two together. *Definitely* make four.

Nipping past, Annie pressed her spine against the door. The plastic wallet crackled at the pressure.

'Do you want to go through to the lounge?'

'Sure,' Donna said, already assessing the shabby furniture and worn carpet. Balancing it against the vase of freesias and scent of polish.

Annie snatched the nameplate, and hastily slid it, facedown, under the cot.

There were framed photos of Keziah propped on the portable TV and hung on the walls. Keziah newborn to five months. Donna scanned the collection.

'Your little girl is very photogenic,' she said, then sighed in a getting-down-to-business way. 'Anyway, I wanted to ask you a few questions about Lauren if that's okay.'

Annie nodded mutely, smoothing Keziah's wispy hair.

'I haven't spoken to her for such a long time,' Donna said. 'Not since that day I saw you when Elliott Devlin attacked her. I've tried calling a few times recently, but the number doesn't work. You know, I've never even seen her daughter.'

Annie frowned sympathetically and pressed her lips to Keziah's fuzzy scalp to stifle the panic swirling inside her.

'I resigned myself to taking them both on, you know,' Donna continued. 'But she has never asked for anything. Not even money, which is really not like her. And I'm embarrassed to say, I was so angry with her about getting involved with Devlin that I decided I was going to cut my ties with her once and for all. I've got kids of my own, I work full time. She was quite happy to put my job at risk by associating with that slippery scumbag. My life is hectic, you know? And she can be so *rude*.' She shrugged, looked sad. 'So I left it. And then I bumped into Alannah, her friend. Ex-friend, I should say. Fuming because Lauren stole her man and went to live in Spain with him. Which would explain why her number isn't in use.'

From the outside, it would appear Annie listened carefully to Donna's impassioned monologue. On the inside, she was deliberately not looking at a photo of Lauren and Keziah on the dining table. If Donna glanced down, she'd see it. And put the two faces side by side and the family resemblance was unmistakable.

She would know.

She would ring Social Services. They would take the baby away from her.

'Anything?' Donna prompted, seeking out Annie's eyes.

'I've just remembered,' Annie said, pointing at a small, neat pile of envelopes on the TV stand. 'Lauren sent me a postcard, I might still have it.'

Donna took the bait, and while she glanced over, Annie shoved the photo into the pages of a book.

'Let me see,' she said, going over and making a show of rifling through the pile of bills. 'Sorry, I must have thrown it out. Marbella. Malaga? And Alannah hasn't heard anything except she took the baby and went to Spain?'

Quirking her glossy beige lips into a wry smile, Donna said, 'Unless she didn't want to tell me, which seems unlikely, given she couldn't *wait* to tell me what a backstabbing two-timing bitch Lauren is. I wondered if she mentioned to you when she was coming back.'

'We weren't close,' Annie said, her own voice sounding fake in her ears but she ploughed on. 'I was surprised she sent me a postcard, to be honest. We fell out over Dev as well. He had a go at me once when I went round and we avoided each other after that.'

Donna bought the lie. She nodded and sighed.

'I don't know. My husband thinks I'm mad for bothering. He hates her, thinks she's a selfish, self-centred cow. And I can't deny it. But she had a terrible start in life. You know her mum abandoned her with a neighbour? Asked her to babysit and never came back, that's how she ended up in care with me. And I've always looked out for her, since we were kids because she can't hold on to friends and I'm the nearest thing to family she's got. Was, at least. Maybe she'll grow up now she's got a child of her own.'

Annie felt a pang of guilt at the other woman's genuine emotion.

'I'm sure she'll be in touch soon,' she said.

Unzipping her bag, Donna said, 'If I give you my number, will you call if you hear anything?'

'Of course,' Annie lied, taking the business card and moving towards the hall.

The other woman rezipped her bag, hesitated and studied the baby.

'Pretty little girl,' she said, thoughtfully. Scrutinising. Slotting puzzle pieces together.

Go now! Jaw clenched in a fixed smile, Annie jogged the baby to disguise the tremor in her limbs.

'It's a shame Lauren went away. It would have been lovely for Keziah to have a friend next door.'

Brushing the nape of the baby's neck with a fingertip, Donna said, 'You never told me her name.'

'Isabel,' Annie said without missing a beat. 'She's called Isabel.'

Saliva filled her mouth like she was going to be sick. Was Donna going around interrogating all the neighbours? Her investigative intellect piecing together clues about Lauren's absent baby and the new baby with the neighbour?

But Donna didn't hang around. And a moment later, Annie watched her enter the car park.

It was like watching a nature documentary with the volume off. Dev's lackeys circled, pulling lazy wheelies. Ramrod straight, Donna strode through them towards a silver hatchback. Halted. Shouted something Annie couldn't hear, but even from this distance she could make out the wing mirror dangling on wires like a dislocated limb.

Donna was fearless. In their ubiquitous black and concealing their individual identities behind a collection of hoods and scarves, the boys were an imposing sight. That didn't stop her. She marched up to them, left hand on hip, right wagging a finger under their noses. Suddenly, she gestured angrily at the flats and said something, *I work for the police?* that struck home because they pedalled, as one, away from the car and towards the row of bins.

Donna flipped the wing mirror once in evident disgust, then, tyres spinning on the pockmarked surface, drove away.

Annie leaned against the sink, dabbing tiny kisses on Keziah. 'Thank you for being a good girl,' she said, fingers splayed across the soft skull. 'And I'm sorry I had to lie about you.'

She turned the tap on with her elbow, picked up the kettle with her free hand and filled it under the stream of running water.

A shadow darkened the window. She raised her head instinctively.

The kettle clattered into the sink. Shrinking back, both arms tightened around the baby and a scream lodged in her throat.

The boy with the bad teeth banged his gloved fist against the glass. Not hard, but slowly and deliberately.

Then he lifted his two fingers and put them to his temple, like a gun barrel, and clicked his thumb.

Now, Wednesday

Bang!

Annie startled upright, like a deer hearing gunshots. She'd been dreaming she was back in her old flat on the Manor. But this was Uppermoss. And she was wide awake.

Smudge hurtled in and launched her front paws at the window-sill, nosing frantically under the curtains. A low growl emitted from her throat.

'What is it, girl?' Annie said, fumbling for her glasses. She grabbed the phone. 4.28am.

Izzy stumbled through the door, rubbing her eyes with the heel of one hand. Her hair spiralled out on messy corkscrews.

She switched the main light on, said sleepily, 'Mum, what's that noise?'

'Go back to bed. Now!'

'All right.' She reached down to scratch her ankle. 'Keep your hair on.'

'It's just the bin blowing over,' Annie said more softly.

Bang! Nearer. Louder.

Dancing her paws along the windowsill, Smudge unleashed a barrage of barks and frantic whines.

'That doesn't sound like the bin, Mum,' Izzy said, slowly. 'And it's not actually windy.'

That was true. On windy nights, the cottage creaked and groaned like an ancient ship in a squall. Trees whooshed like the sea.

'Foxes then,' she improvised.

A beat of silence hung like the interval between claps of thunder. One … two …

Bang!

Eyes glassy with fear, Izzy said, 'That is so not a fox.'

Annie jumped out of bed and pulled her dressing gown on. Grabbed Smudge's collar, dragging her away from the window. She pulled the curtains tight with her left hand, ensuring no chinks or gaps remained.

'Switch the light off,' Annie said in a low voice. 'Go in the bathroom.'

Izzy moaned. 'I'm ringing the police.'

'No!'

Smudge strained against the grip on her collar, throat rasping. Annie let go and she sprang forward, thundered down the stairs. A second later, there was a thump as, howling now, she threw herself at the back door.

'I mean it, Iz,' Annie said, gently pushing her towards the bathroom. 'Don't. They'll think you're a kid messing about. Stay there. And whatever you do, don't look out of the window.'

Someone was outside.

The security light shone around the edges of the kitchen blind, leavening the gloom enough to check the windows and doors were still secure.

Although sweat drenched her entire back, Annie's palms were dry. Her brain had flipped a switch, activating its crisis protocol. Fear hid in a distant corner. Calm descended, bringing with it the resources necessary to protect Izzy. Not freeze. Not flight.

Fight.

Every sound was amplified. The steady flow of air in her nostrils. Smudge's claws scratching on the back door. The knife sliding from the wooden block, its steel handle ice in her palm. The slamming back of the bolts. Smudge shooting past, grunting as she raced around the perimeter of the garden.

Knife raised, she scanned the garden. Shed. Path. Bins, still upright. Back gate locked. Up to the chestnut tree. Everything was still and silent, apart from Smudge snuffling the base of the fence.

The moon was a bone-white disc against the cloudless black sky. The glare of the security light turned the woods beyond into a single motionless shadow.

Annie lowered the knife slightly. Stepped off the doorstep.

Bang!

She jumped. Smudge howled and sprinted across the garden. More like cannon fire than gun shots, a series of blows travelled rapidly from the left, juddering every fence panel. There was a moment's pause, as if taking a run up, then powerful kicks rained against the gate. The dog stood in front, fur spiking down her back, tail stiff, and barking furiously.

The force shook the entire fence. The hinges held, but for how long?

'I've called the police,' Annie shouted over the clamour. 'They're on their way.'

The banging stopped abruptly.

Nothing. No reply, no rustling. Just Smudge, pink tongue flopped to one side, ropes of saliva hanging from her jaws.

'In,' Annie hissed. 'Now.'

She turned the key, slammed the bolts home. Light glinted off the knife blade as it slid in the wooden block next to her phone.

'What did the police say?'

Izzy stood in the kitchen doorway, steepled hands pressed to her lips. Fear radiated from her tense shoulders, her rounded eyes.

'It's okay.' Annie pulled her into a hug and stroking her tangled hair. 'Nothing to be scared of.'

'Did you call Liam?'

'No need, the police were already in the woods,' she said smoothly. 'Chasing some stupid kids on motorbikes.'

Izzy nodded. And it *did* sound credible. Scrambler bikers often used the woods as a racetrack.

'The police have probably got them already,' Annie continued. 'Let's hope they've confiscated their bikes. Idiots, scaring us like that. Now, come on. Back to bed.'

'Can I have Smudge?' Izzy said in a small voice.

'Of course. Now, go on up. I'll be there in a minute.'

But she wasn't.

She listened for the creak of Izzy's bedsprings. Smudge circling the rug, flattening down the fibres in an instinctive ritual before she lay down.

The useful calm began to fray a little at the edges now the crisis was over. She poured a glass of tap water and sat at the kitchen table. She opened the security app on her phone. Live view came on: the still back garden. The security light had timed out and it was dark. She scrolled the timeline back to when the security light came on. But whoever had kicked the gate remained frustratingly out of the camera's range. She rewound, swiping her finger to zoom in on the gate and Smudge silently barking. Still no sign.

Whoever it was, they had gone.

She slipped her hand in her dressing-gown pocket and crept towards the hall. The last thing poor Izzy needed now was another early wake-up. She reached the bottom of the stairs.

Two things happened at once. The security app chirped a notification. And the front outside light came on.

Holding her breath, Annie turned round. She crept back into the lounge and very gently moved the curtain aside.

A figure stood at the end of the drive, black hood pulled tight around an anonymous face. The baggy sportswear could be hiding an average male or a tall female form, it was impossible to tell.

And then it was gone.

The floor rushed towards her and she stumbled to the sofa, put her head between her knees, and willed herself not to pass out.

When the wave of dizziness subsided, she slipped quietly into the kitchen and retrieved the carving knife from the block and placed it on the coffee table. Then she wrapped herself in the sofa throw and laid her head on a cushion, gulping down the acid that surged from her guts.

Then

'Night, night, beautiful,' Annie said, lowering the freshly bathed baby into the cot. 'Sweet dreams.'

She switched on the nightlight and slotted a disc into the player. The soothing melodies of the lullaby disc helped Keziah to fall asleep, but they also took Annie back to her own mum, singing softly. Happy memories.

The new chair by the window looked good. She had spotted it in a skip near the park and carried it home balanced precariously on the side of the pram. An afternoon spent ripping off the stained Dralon and stapling a cheerful floral print to the frame gave her an excellent chair for next to nothing. Moving to the Manor had taught her to be resourceful.

Oliver held strong views about anything that smacked of DIY or, even worse, arts and crafts. Planning the décor yourself was borderline acceptable, but the actual decorating was definitely best left to the professionals.

He'd be horrified to find her rummaging around the local charity shops. Finding bits for the nursery, like the Beatrix Potter prints and a nightlight in the shape of a cloud. A shelf hand-painted with daisies and filled with teddies and books.

A car horn blared in the car park and Annie got up to close

the window. She had almost saved enough for new curtains now, and she was already planning a revamp of her own bedroom next.

After the rain, the August night was warm. Too warm to have all the windows closed. She opened the balcony door a little and let the slight breeze drift in.

As the ending notes of 'Greensleeves' segued into 'Lavender's Blue', and she waited for Keziah's breath to slow and her limbs to relax into peaceful slumber, she settled into the new chair. Comfy. The stiffness in her limbs softened as the stress of the day began to melt.

Donna hadn't suspected a thing. And if she and Lauren ever kissed and made up, well, she'd deal with explaining the lies then. And as for the boy banging on the window, they were just looking for someone new to pick on now Sylvia had gone. Lie low for a while, don't give them any ammunition and they would tire of her quickly enough.

She yawned. After the unexpected twists and turns of the last few years, she knew you could never predict what was around the corner.

It was the scent of woody aftershave that woke her. Only a split second before the hand clamped over her mouth and a muscled arm pinned her to the bed.

She couldn't scream. Couldn't move.

'We need to talk,' a man said. Garlic on his breath. Mint and cigarettes.

Dev.

The arm lifted. Something smooth and cold pressed against the centre of her throat, indenting the thin skin. Metal. A shout stayed trapped behind her teeth, smothered by the hard, flat palm and excruciating grip on her jawbone. She bucked, kicked, clawed her fingers at the broad forearm.

Was Keziah safe?

Dev leaned his elbow into her breastbone. The pressure crushed her lungs. Blood inflated the veins in her forehead and she felt her eyeballs bulge. The darkness of the room turned darker. Redder. She was going to die. Right here. Suffocated in her own bed.

Some ancient instinct surged in her brain. *Don't fight, survive*, it ordered. And battling every conscious urge, she willed herself limp.

'That's better,' he said, conversationally. 'Now, I am going to take my hand from your mouth. But if you make a single sound, I will put a bullet in you. Do you understand?'

Sparks flashed in the periphery of her vision. She managed a mangled grunt of assent. The weight lifted. Wonderful, pure air rushed to inflate her lungs and she gulped it down.

'Now,' he said. 'I need you to listen to me very, very carefully. I hear you've been talking to the police.'

'No, I—'

The gun struck her temple. Fireworks exploded behind her eyes. Warm wetness trickled down her cheekbone.

'What did I say?' Dev hissed, tapping the barrel on her cheek. 'I said. Not. A. Sound. Can I have your full, *silent* attention?'

Annie breathed in tiny, tight gasps.

He clicked the bedside light on. She winced, blinked against the glare. Waited for the shadowy bulk to snap into focus.

It remained shadowy. He was dressed in black and wearing a neoprene balaclava. Holes for eyes, slit for lips even though there was no mistaking that voice. Or the gym-pumped bulk of him. He wore black leather gloves. Not the padded biker or skier kind, but thin. Flexible. And in the right one, he held a gun. She'd never seen one in real life before, but it certainly looked authentic.

She swivelled her gaze to the right. Her phone, on the bedside table. Only a few inches away. Could she …?

'Let's try again,' he said. 'I am going to be very, very clear. I have been told you have been talking to the police. Don't deny it. You were seen letting a woman into your flat today. She stayed for about ten minutes, then left. So what I want to know is, why did you ask her around today and what did you say to her about me. And I am expecting this verbatim with *specific details.*'

He emphasised the final two words with tiny pulses of the gun.

'Honestly,' she swallowed, trying to moisten her dry throat enough to speak. 'She came to see me. All she wanted to know was if I had Lauren's contact details because she couldn't get hold of her. That's it. I swear.'

He didn't say anything. Did he believe her? All she could see were his lips and his eyes, and they were impossible to read. His grip loosened. He reached the hand without the gun over to the bedside table and picked up her phone. Switched it on.

'Pin,' he said.

She didn't reply.

'Pin.' He pressed his arm down.

'0101.'

He began scrolling through her calls and messages. 'Are you telling the truth? Who else have you been talking to?'

'No one,' she whispered.

He laughed, his thumb rapidly clicking the keypad.

'Jesus. Lauren said you were a freak, but I thought she must be exaggerating.' He turned the phone round. 'Look. Call log. Messages. Lauren, Lauren, Lauren. Literally no one else. You're obsessed, you sad bitch. No wonder she wanted to get away.'

She opened her mouth to speak, but he shoved her back down on the bed effortlessly.

'Don't.' He got up off the mattress, towering over her. Put the phone on the table. 'Count yourself lucky you're getting a warning. Oh, before I forget. Don't talk to that old woman downstairs again, either. The one whose grandson got himself stabbed. If you do, I will know. And if you even think about speaking to the police, I will come back here. And I will know, because I have spies everywhere, including in the Met. You got that?'

He moved towards the window, his back towards her.

She moved on impulse, grabbed her phone and jumped off the bed.

She didn't even make it to the door.

Fingers biting into her shoulder, he threw her down. Her head whiplashed off the mattress.

'Now I can't trust you,' he said. 'Now I—'

She drew her knees in and pushed as hard as she could, driving her feet into his hard muscled stomach. He barely swayed.

The fist came out of nowhere. Pain detonated inside her skull. Wetness streamed from her nose. His hand slapped over her mouth and pinched her nostrils shut, forcing the blood down the back of her throat. Couldn't breathe, couldn't swallow, couldn't cough.

Everything shimmered.

And then the hand lifted. She could breathe. Not through the sucking, wet mess of her nose. But through her mouth. She coughed, drowning in her own blood.

'Now look what you made me do,' he said.

A buckle clicked and she heard a leather belt slither through denim loops.

'Fucking bitch,' he murmured, climbing on the bed. He straddled her, using his thick thighs as a vice. She heard the sharp buzz of a zip, and her mind pulsed with horror as she realised what was about to happen.

And then, from the next room, came a sudden cry. Not a gentle whimper, but a scream like breaking glass.

Dev paused.

Keziah's cry soared to a single screeching pitch.

Then the weight pinning Annie on the bed lifted. She turned her head to one side. Raw lungs fought for air, but even racked by coughs, she heard the belt buckle clink closed.

Then he yanked her upright by the hair. Whole chunks ripped from the roots. Pain beyond pain.

'If you say one word about me to anyone, I will know.'

And then he was gone.

Then

She couldn't explain how she got through the hours after Dev left. Survival instinct. An ancient, internal self that dragged the horror into a hidden recess and instructed the conscious Annie to hold a wadded towel to her nose while she soothed Keziah back to sleep. To close and lock the balcony door. To shove the bloodstained clothes and bedding in the washing machine. To wrap a bag of frozen peas in a pillowcase in an attempt to ease the agony of her scalp.

And finally, when the first glimmers of daylight appeared, to place the largest, sharpest knife from the kitchen drawer under her pillow and collapse. At least, until the persistent shrill of the phone woke her.

'What the fuck are you playing at?' Lauren demanded.

'What?' Annie said, in a croak.

'Guess who just called me, fucking raging because you have been shooting your mouth off?'

A violent tremor rolled up from her feet, fanning to encompass every part of her. She clutched the coverless duvet, stiffened with dried blood. Her blood. Cold. So cold. Her teeth chattered, pain drove splinters through her nose, her cheekbones, her scalp.

Delayed shock. The detached part of her whispered soothingly. *It's okay. Deep breaths.*

'So he calls me, while I'm in the apartment,' Lauren continued. 'So I go out on the balcony. But I don't realise Omar is standing by the bedroom window. And then he's got the hump because he hears a man's voice coming out of the phone. So that's grief from Dev and grief from Omar and it is all your fucking fault. Are you *trying* to ruin my life?'

Her tongue felt two sizes too big, mangling the reply. 'Did Dev tell you he came here?'

'He said you'd been talking to the *police*.'

Talking was effortful. Everything hurt. 'Only Donna. She came here, but I never said anything about him.'

Wary now, Lauren said, 'You didn't let her see Keziah, did you?'

'She thought she was mine. Alannah told her you'd taken the baby to Spain.'

'Right,' Lauren said, slowly. 'Well, that's one thing you haven't fucked up at least. But you need to learn to keep your mouth shut. You have no idea what Dev is like.'

Tears leaked, dripping onto the pillow. His hand over her mouth. The arm pinning her down. The darkness swallowing her sight like an eclipse. The click-clack of the belt buckle.

Yes, she did.

She spoke in harsh rasps.

'I have to tell you something. Last night, Dev broke into my home and he attacked me in my bed. He had a gun. I thought he was going to rape me. Kill me.'

There was a short pause.

'Well, he didn't,' Lauren said, flatly. 'But if you go to the police about it, then he definitely will.'

Her brain had hit overload. She couldn't process what Lauren meant.

'Do you understand what I'm saying? He tried to rape me. He hurt me,' she said. 'I need to take Keziah away from the Manor, somewhere far away from here, somewhere safe. You need to come home. I can pay for your flight.'

There wasn't much to pack. Clothes and teddies of Keziah's. Lauren could fit her life in a suitcase. She had a bit of money put away, not much. Enough for a train ticket and a night or two in a hotel while they planned the next step. Norfolk? Lauren said she liked the seaside.

But Lauren, when she finally answered, was incredulous. 'Are you out of your fucking mind? What will I say to Omar? He'll think I've come back because of Dev. I've got a great apartment, friends. I'll lose my job if I come home now. No way am I coming back to the Manor when for once in my whole shit life I'm *happy*.'

Annie shuffled up the bed and the pain shifted and spread, like hot ball bearings rolling around her skull.

'He assaulted me,' she said again. 'And Lindon, Sylvia's grandson, twelve years old and he nearly died. He needs to be stopped.'

Lauren screeched in frustration. 'Don't be so fucking stupid. You go to the police and they will be all over that flat. They'll find everything and Dev will know I told you what goes on there. He will absolutely kill me. You hear me? You call the police and I am dead.'

'He hurts women,' Annie said. 'He needs to be stopped.'

There was another long pause. When Lauren spoke, her voice was low.

'There are no witnesses, no evidence. It'll be your word against his and trust me, Dev won't have any problems finding an alibi. He won't even be charged. And he will take Keziah and she will go and live with him and Megan. And then he will find me, he will kill me, and you will never see Keziah again. Do I make myself clear?'

In the days that followed, the teenagers on their bikes followed her everywhere. Even with Keziah in the pram, they swept in too close, jostling her, trying to knock the shopping out of her hand.

So she made sure her hasty forays to the minimart happened before nine in the morning. The boys had to sleep sometime.

At night, they patrolled the walkway, banging on the kitchen window, on Keziah's bedroom window. In the end, she moved the cot next to her own bed.

Not that she slept, just dozed now and then. Enough to keep her from tipping into the abyss. Every creak, every thud appalled her. When she heard them come and go next door, she curled up in a ball and rocked herself to sleep. One night, a few days after the attack, someone shoved a lit firework through the letterbox. She sealed the flap with tape after that.

Whatever made her Annie separated from her body and floated up to the ceiling, like a balloon, to watch dispassionately the cringing, fearful thing she'd become.

Was this what having a nervous breakdown felt like?

Even though it had been over ten years, she missed her parents. And in the days following the attack, it grew acute. She remembered a bank holiday weekend at the little guesthouse in Wells with the rabbits in the garden. Mum and Dad spreading the checked picnic blanket on a dune under the brightest blue sky. The crackle of greaseproof paper as they unwrapped ham sandwiches and slices of Jamaican ginger cake. Their soft voices as they told her the story of her adoption.

And she remembered thinking they didn't need to tell her she was special, or that they chose her, or that they loved her. Because she already knew.

One night, she sat with the old medication in front of her. The sleeping pills and the anti-depressants she once again depended on to function.

Despite upping the dose, she lived in a twilight haze where nothing made sense. Even Keziah only lit a flickering happiness, like a guttering candle.

The boys rode their bikes up and down, up and down. Banging on her windows. Every time she looked out, they were there. Even in snatched moments of sleep, they were there. People came and went next door. Thuds and scrapes and bangs.

She popped two pills and chased them down with a swig of water. They gave her a headache, so she shook the last two paracetamol from the plastic tub and took those as well.

Then she pinched the pills into a heap in the middle of the table.

Do it. Let go.

She could take it all away. End the worry, the sadness, the fear, the guilt, the pain. No one would miss her. No one would care.

She sat for a long time, staring at the table. Then Keziah cried. Annie scooped the tablets up in her hand and dropped them in the empty plastic tub.

'I'm here, love,' she said.

Now, Thursday

'Mum!' Izzy shouted from downstairs.

'I'm here, love,' she said.

Annie splashed icy water over her face, barely glanced at her reflection as the rough towel dried her cheeks. Didn't need to. She knew what was there: skin the texture of old porridge. Dark smudges under her eyes like old make-up no amount of cleanser could erase. Wild hair resembling something you'd wash floors with. She gargled with mouthwash, but the sour taste at the back of her throat remained.

The thudding in her temples echoed the banging on the fence last night.

She hadn't gone back to sleep. Every time she drifted to the fringes of sleep, Dev loomed over her, unbuckling his belt. His weightlifter's body pinned her to the mattress. In the end, she gave up and when the grey glimmers of dawn appeared, she put the knife back in the block, went upstairs and tried to come up with ways to make this nightmare go away.

The banging in her head merged with the knocking at the bathroom door. She dipped her mouth under the tap and drank in great, gasping mouthfuls.

'I need a shower.'

'All yours, love.'

Izzy stood on the landing, shaking her hair out from the top knot.

'Did they catch them?' she said.

'Catch who?'

Izzy threw her an exasperated glance. 'The kids on the motorbikes? The ones who kicked the fence last night? Honestly, Mum, sometimes I think you've got dementia or something.' Pause. '*Joking.*'

'They didn't come back, so I assume so,' Annie said. 'Have your shower, I'll make some breakfast.'

When she heard the water thud against the tiles, she hurried downstairs and into the lounge. She lifted the picture of her parents up without taking it from the hook and felt inside the space. Her fingers closed around the small velvet pouch containing her mum's jewellery.

'Sorry,' she whispered to their portrait. 'I promise this will be the last time.'

While the kettle boiled, she texted Samara.

Sure you don't need me today?

Samara rang immediately.

'Firstly, totally do not come in today,' she said. 'Helen is itching to get out of the house. And secondly … well, I would have called you earlier, but I didn't want to disturb you. I've got some very good news.'

'Go on,' Annie said, scraping the last of the marmalade onto Izzy's toast.

Samara's voice was gleeful. 'Someone reported Cain Maguire for boasting about harassing us on Snapchat. The police took him in for questioning and he confessed straightaway to harassing us. Like, instantly. Apparently he's not the hard case he makes himself out to be. What do you say to that?'

'Er, I say that's great news,' Annie said. 'Fantastic news.'

'I know!' Samara said. 'Honestly, it's such a weight off my mind. That 'Dead Bitch' note really freaked me out. Anyway, I'll let you enjoy your day off. See you tomorrow.'

'See you tomorrow,' Annie repeated and put the phone down. Cain Maguire? It didn't make sense.

'Who's that?' Izzy said, wafting in on a cloud of coconut shower gel. She crunched the slice of toast.

'Samara,' Annie said, slowly. 'I'm not going to work today. So I'm going to drop you off and come straight back home.'

'How come?' Izzy said, spraying crumbs over the kitchen table.

Annie passed her the side plate. 'Use that, please. All that stuff with the Maguires, you know the people who had the puppy farm? It all got a bit much yesterday. She's got Helen in to cover. And Samara was ringing to tell me they're questioning the Maguire's son. Anyway, hurry up, we're going to be late.'

'Ah,' Izzy said, and Annie could almost hear the cogs in her mind working. '*Ah*. So that's why you've been so weird all week. Well, that explains a lot.'

But it didn't. It didn't explain anything.

'What are you doing?' Izzy said suspiciously as Annie undid her seatbelt.

'Since I'm not going to work,' she replied, opening the driver door, 'I thought I'd walk you in to school. After what happened last night, I thought you might be a bit nervous.'

The threat of further rain hung in the air and there was a brisk breeze.

Izzy didn't budge. She had her bag clamped to her chest. Seatbelt still on.

'Er, no. I'm fine.'

Annie stood on the pavement. 'It's okay. I think I'd like to. I just want to make sure you get in okay. Especially as you've turned the Family Safe app off.'

'I can switch it back on,' she said, getting her phone out. 'I told you, I only turned it off because it drains my battery.'

In reply, Annie closed the driver's side, walked round and opened the passenger door.

'You can't be serious,' Izzy said. 'Tell me you don't mean it.'

'Out. Now, please,' Annie said.

A pair of girls stopped behind her.

'Hi, Izzy,' one of them said, peering into the car.

Annie stepped aside. 'After you, ladies,' she said.

The girls squeezed through and one of them turned round, whispered something and they both giggled.

'For god's sake, Mum,' Izzy said, getting out of the car. Her jaw was set in a miserable line and a stain of colour flushed her cheeks. 'You are so embarrassing.'

'Don't forget your hockey kit,' Annie said brightly, locking the door.

Izzy picked up the hockey bag and flowery pump bag.

'I can literally see school from here,' Izzy said, pointing between the trees to where a sliver of tiled roof was visible. 'Please don't come in with me.'

Up ahead, kids in blazers headed towards the school gates. Ambling, laughing, hurrying, talking. Singly, in pairs, in groups spilling onto the road. Dozens and dozens of them. And not one accompanied by a parent.

Next to her, Izzy walked slowly, clutching her bag to her chest like a shield. Her head down so low her chin rested on top of the rucksack.

'Mum, please,' she said quietly. 'Let me go.'

Annie stopped.

'Okay,' she said. 'Go quickly. But text me the minute you're inside. Okay? And wait in the playground for me after hockey practice. Don't come out of the gate.'

She leaned in to quickly kiss her daughter on the cheek, but Izzy stepped out of the way. Without a single word or a backward glance, she began to jog towards the other kids.

Izzy moved gracefully, her athletic frame built for sport and movement whereas Annie, short and wide-hipped, struggled to pick a tea towel off the floor. Izzy had hazel eyes and hair that sprang from her head in a cloud of natural soft spirals. She had a dimple in one cheek and double-jointed thumbs. She was good at art and dance but struggled with maths.

None of these traits came from Annie, because biologically, Izzy wasn't hers.

But she was hers in every way that counted.

She used to think that by removing her from the Manor, she had saved Izzy. But the truth was, Izzy had saved her.

Then

Ray had parked by the bins, forcing Annie into the narrow channel between the side of his transit van and the communal skips. The stench of rotten meat was overpowering, and a couple of times loud rustling suggested their clandestine meeting had a rodent audience.

'I can do it,' Ray, the man who sourced Lauren's fake driving licence, said. 'But it won't be cheap.'

Annie pulled the hood lower over her eyes and the scarf up until they almost met. The swelling had improved, but the bruises remained. Deep aubergine around her eyes and where the gun hit her, fading to lilac and yellow towards her jaw. Parts of her scalp itched, the new hair poking through was coarse as straw. But there were a couple of raw pink patches where the hair would never return.

'How much?'

He snapped his chewing gum a couple of times, folded his arms across his chest. The old tattoos blurred into one blue mass.

'Two grand. Upfront.'

Two thousand pounds? The divorce had gone through now, the settlement agreed. Her part had gone to solicitor's fees, court costs and paying off debts. But she had a tiny amount left over. Not enough, though.

'Depends what you want,' he continued. 'I can do it cheaper, but it won't stand up to scrutiny. Two grand and you get everything legit, rubber-stamped official. You got anything you can sell or pawn?'

Annie pictured the sock containing her mum's jewellery. 'Maybe.'

He nodded. 'Kwik Kash, next to Aldi. My brother's place. Tell him I sent you.'

'How do I know you won't tell anyone?'

He snorted. 'You don't, but it works both ways, see. You don't tell anyone and I don't tell anyone. That's how this operates.'

Nothing about this man was trustworthy. But what choice did she have? She was desperate.

'I'll need a couple of days to get the cash together,' she said. 'When will you have it?'

'Give me the money first,' he said, turning away. 'And then we'll talk.'

Two days later, a note had dropped through her door.

2k. 11pm tonight.

She had managed to scrape it together and still had enough left for two train tickets north. Just. The pawnbroker's ticket was safe in her bedside drawer. She knew Mum would understand, but she still felt a pang of guilt.

At half past ten, she put on her disguise of black joggers and hoodie. They hung loose from her newly skinny frame. Since *that* night, she had no appetite and when she did manage to eat a spoonful of cereal or a slice of bread, she struggled to keep it down.

At five to eleven, she leaned over the cot to kiss Keziah.

'I won't be long, love,' she said. 'Everything is going to be okay, soon. I promise.'

She wrapped her black scarf around the lower portion of her face and, after checking the walkway was clear, slipped out the front door.

Ray had parked in the same place as before.

'Have you got it?' he said.

She nodded and handed him the roll of notes secured with an elastic band. He licked his thumb and finger then counted each one.

'When will it be ready?' she said.

He grunted. 'A couple of days. Did you write the details?'

She handed him the slip of paper. He angled it towards the orange glow of the streetlight.

'Name Isabel Smith,' he muttered. 'Mother Annie Smith ... no father. Date of birth second July, place Islington ...' He tapped the paper. 'This address here, is it traceable?'

Annie shook her head. 'Stuck a pin in a map. Look, I need you to promise you'll do this. Please. I'm desperate.'

'You need me to promise, do you?' he said with a sudden flash of yellowing teeth, rimmed with black at the gum margin. He laughed then, a phlegmy unpleasant squawk. 'I don't make promises.'

Annie had a very bad feeling, a very bad feeling indeed about Ray. And as she walked towards the stairwell, the panic oozed through her veins. She had just given virtually every penny to an archetypal petty criminal in league with the man who assaulted her and had as good as admitted she was kidnapping his child. Desperation had made her reckless. She moaned inside the scarf and gripped the banister, legs weak as water. Rapid footsteps pounded down the stairs. One of Dev's teen runners. She dropped her head, but he didn't see her. On the Manor, black sportswear made you invisible.

For the next few days, she holed up in the flat, unable to eat or sleep. And then when she had given up all hope. An envelope dropped through her door late at night. And when she opened it, and saw Isabel Smith's perfect birth certificate, she sat down on the hall floor and cried and cried until every part of her ached from it.

Now, Thursday

Annie shook the contents of the padded envelope onto the black velvet tray the jeweller had placed on the display case.

'Two rings and a pair of earrings.' She placed them neatly in a row. 'Diamonds in both. Not to sell, just for a temporary loan.'

'No problem,' the jeweller said, taking a small piece of linen and a magnifying glass from a case. 'Let me just have a look.'

It would have been easy to cry at that moment, picturing Mum's hand holding her small, sticky one, feeling the cold metal against her own skin. And later, sliding the rings off Mum's fingers in the hospice when she had been so thin, her knuckles stood out like huge knots in string. And the diamond hoops, Annie remembered glinting in Mum's ears on special occasions. In her own ears, too, on the day she married Oliver.

'I can offer you six hundred today,' the jeweller said.

'For which one?'

The lady folded the magnifying glass into the case and snapped it shut. 'For all three pieces, as collateral against an instant loan.'

The bell jangled, another customer came in.

'I thought they'd be worth more,' Annie said.

'I'm sorry that's the best I can do. Would you like me to print off the paperwork?' The woman took her glasses off, then addressed the man who was staring at a display of vintage cigarette lighters. 'Won't be a moment.'

What else could she do?

She nodded, not trusting herself to speak, and five minutes later zipped a contract covered in minuscule font into her bag, alongside an envelope containing twelve fifty-pound notes.

Outside the shop, she clutched the bag tightly across her chest. Despair welled up from the pit of her stomach. She remembered Dad coming home exhausted from twelve-hour shifts and weekend after weekend of overtime and she never heard him complain, not once, because he did it for his family. For her and Mum. If only the monetary value of the jewellery reflected the emotional value, the sweat and sacrifice the original purchase required. For six hundred pounds, she may as well have kept them.

By tomorrow, she needed fifty thousand pounds and she had less than half of that. And she was out of options.

She parked by the library, and while hopelessness settled on her mind like thick, grey fog, her legs carried her halfway there, before her knees weakened. She needed to sit down before she fell down.

The war memorial had benches and flowerbeds around a central pillar with a brass plate detailing the names of the long-forgotten young men of Uppermoss who sacrificed everything for future generations. She sat down heavily.

A family came out of the library opposite, the three kids clutched picture books. Dad hoisted the smallest child on his shoulders and pure joy infused the boy's delighted giggle. One girl, slightly older, flicked through a picture book and chattered excitedly to her mum and skipped alongside.

A sob caught in Annie's throat. Every building in the village, every inch of the pavements contained a memory of her life with Izzy. And there were memories still yet to be made everywhere. The restaurant she'd planned to book for Izzy's fourteenth birthday in July. The shop where all the girls at Uppermoss High bought their prom dresses – and the row that already waited in the future. *Plastic cups and disposable plates, Mum! Shoes I'll never wear again! It's so wasteful!* and Annie gently persuading her not to miss this landmark night with her friends.

A sudden gust of wind fluttered the banner outside the church. The brightly painted egg with a smiley face and little arms and legs invited families to the 'Eggstravaganza' and Annie remembered an experiment Izzy's class did in Year Four.

Some poor TA had been tasked with blowing thirty eggs until only the fragile shell remained. Each child had been given one along with instructions to carry it everywhere and return it to school, three days later, unscathed. Izzy took her responsibility seriously, and Egg Sheeran was nestled safely in his cotton wool bed for two and half days. Until Smudge knocked him off the kitchen table.

That was motherhood. You wrapped your fragile charge in cotton wool to shield them from the dangers of the world. So afraid, so careful. And then one day, the world broke in anyway and smashed everything beyond repair.

A wood pigeon flew down and pecked hopefully among the daffodils at the base of the war memorial.

It was impossible to imagine Lauren making packed lunches and ironing uniforms. Helping a teenage Keziah with homework. Keeping her safe on the Manor.

Izzy had a good life in Uppermoss. A happy life and a happy future, filled with love and opportunities. No matter what happened tomorrow, no one could deny Annie had been a good mum.

She took out her phone. Took a deep breath and dialled the number of the text. It went straight to voicemail.

'I've tried,' she said quietly, even though the fat wood pigeon was the only eavesdropper. 'I've tried everything, but I can't get all the money. I've got just under twenty-four and that's it. I've got nothing left to try.' A lump began to form in the back of her throat. 'Please don't do this to her. She knows nothing about any of this and she's got a great life. I've taken care of her, loved her all these years and to have all that ripped away from her … You'll be punishing me, but it'll be so much worse for her. It's going to destroy her. Please, please don't do this to her. You can gladly have the money I've got. Gladly. Just please …' her voice faltered. 'Please keep her out of this. She doesn't deserve it.'

She ended the call, keeping the phone in her hand and closed her eyes. Her throat ached and her nose stung, but she didn't cry. She was hollowed out. A shell, with nothing left inside.

The phone vibrated with a message.

Don't you think Keziah deserves to know the truth?

There was another buzz and another photo of Lauren, another familiar image appeared. The last bed on the maternity ward of a hospital that had long since been demolished. A pink 'It's a Girl' balloon bobbed next to a single New Baby card. Lauren, tired and impossibly young, smiling shyly down at the bundle in her arms.

Time spooled back to the overheated hospital and the miracle of tiny limbs, those first mewing cries. Fists curled like a miniature fighter, Keziah's determination, stubbornness, her zest for life pierced Annie's heart. It was love at first sight.

And in the last fourteen years, that love had grown every day.

She had taken that photo on her old digital camera and printed it out at Boots the day before Lauren flew to Ibiza. Stuffed the glossy paper in a carboard wallet and slipped in the front pocket of a pink suitcase when the taxi arrived to take her to the airport.

The only person who could be sending those photos was Lauren.

But it couldn't be her.

Because Lauren was dead.

Then

Lauren seemed to have entirely forgotten she had a daughter. Or, at least, she hadn't contacted Annie to check on her welfare. And with Sylvia gone from the Manor and Donna and Alannah believing the baby was in Spain, it was as if Keziah Taylor ceased to exist.

Annie had bought a plain black rucksack at the Army and Navy stores near the pawnshop and packed it with clothes, a few teddies. The photo of her mum and dad, slipped out of the frame and sandwiched between the pages of a book, went in too. As did photos of Keziah, the precious paperwork – birth certificates, her deed poll certificate, divorce papers. The pawnbroker's ticket.

Everything else she could carry was swept into bin bags. She waited until she heard the reversing beeps of the refuse truck as it entered the car park. Raced down and threw them in the communal skip seconds before it tipped into the back of the truck.

She had a train timetable, but she hadn't booked the tickets. The plan was to wait until they were at the station to see how far north the money would take them. Somewhere she and her daughter could start a new life.

She dressed Keziah in an anonymous blue vest and leggings. Clothes to blend into the crowd.

The difficult part was going to be getting in to next door.

Over the last couple of weeks, she'd been noting the comings and goings. There wasn't a precise timetable, but the hours between six and ten in the evening were the quietest. Presumably, it was their peak street time. A couple of the boys had come and gone, but not many drug deals happened on Tuesdays.

When she was sure Keziah had settled down for a nap, she put her ear to the wall and listened.

Silence.

The idea of being back in that flat, Dev's flat, filled her with dread. He had the key, could walk in at any moment. And this time, she knew she wouldn't escape with two black eyes and a handful of bald patches.

She pulled on the uniform of hoodie and joggers. Sat with the spare keys to Lauren's flat in one gloved hand, a pocket torch in the other.

Listened again: still silent.

She peeped in on Keziah, peacefully sleeping. A contented smile curling her lip. The shadow of her unfeasibly long eyelashes lay on her pink cheek.

And something shifted inside her. She *had* to do this. The dread remained, a knotted ball in her guts. But she wasn't doing it for herself, it was for her daughter.

She lifted the partition between the two balconies. Next door was in darkness. She put Lauren's spare key in the lock, turned it and carefully slid the door on the track. Once in, her socked feet whispered across the carpet.

The air smelled of stale food and there were empty takeaway cartons on the marble-topped coffee table. Rice clung to the tinfoil sides, congealed but not rotten. A mug half-filled with tea felt stone cold when she touched the side.

Bedroom next. Crumpled bedsheets suggested sometimes visitors stayed over, but nothing else to indicate permanent inhabitants. No toothbrush in the bathroom. No clothes or shoes. Even Lauren's TV had gone.

Male voices came from outside on the walkway. Footsteps too, heading towards the door. Dev?

She slipped back out onto the balcony and pulled the door and lifted the partition, painfully scraping her shin against the rough concrete. Shockwaves of pure agony shot up her leg. She bit her lip hard to prevent a cry of pain escaping.

Inside her own flat, she hurried towards the kitchen, doubled over out of sight. Listened as the men went past. Heard the echoes of their laughter ring around the stairwell.

Almost sick with nerves, she leaned against the worktop. Just a pair of unknown neighbours on their way out. Nothing to do with Lauren's flat.

Ignoring the fearful voice that whispered, *don't go back, don't do it*, she retraced her steps.

This time, she worked swiftly.

She pulled the chair under the ceiling tile with a grey smudge in one corner. Pressed her palm flat and lifted it up and across, like a waiter carrying a pizza. The small pocket torch lit the black cavity, snaked with wires and thick pipes furred with dust, and glinted on the plastic-wrapped bundles. Drugs. Money. A gun wrapped in a piece of old towel.

She had an unwelcome flashback to that night. Cold metal pressed against her skin. The molten agony of the handle striking her temple.

Her mind presented a tempting scenario. Lying in wait for Dev. Holding the gun to *his* temple. Avenging every woman he had ever hurt with a curl of her trigger finger.

She rejected it. Money. That was all she came for.

She grabbed as many as she could and stuffed them inside the hoodie. Returned the ceiling tile and chair.

Back inside the flat, she delved inside the plastic bags and drew out bundles of tens, twenties and fifties. Her heart soared. She'd been worried they might be fresh-minted forgeries that would be next to useless to her. Who knew what areas of business Dev might be in? But they were used notes. The kind of cash you could take into any bank or any shop and no one would bat an eyelid.

She scanned the bundles, making quick calculations. Not enough to buy a private island, but more than enough to kick-start a quiet new life.

She stuffed the packages of cash inside the rucksack.

It was time.

'We're going on holiday, little one,' she said, lifting Keziah out of the cot and putting her in the pram. 'It's exciting.'

Luck was on her side.

There was a flash of lightning. A low rumble of thunder and sudden rain lashed against the kitchen window. Annie slipped her trainers on and put her thin waterproof over the hoodie.

She fixed the rain cover over the pram, put the rucksack on her back and, leaving the keys on the hall floor, pulled the door until the Yale clicked.

She hurried across the wet walkway, head down as the pram splashed through puddles. She had to stifle a bubble of laughter. Even the boys who circled on their bikes had run for cover. There was no one around. Just an anonymous figure pushing a pram towards a waiting bus.

The bus driver barely glanced at her. The bus was half empty. She parked the pram and set the wet rucksack on the floor next to her seat.

And as the bus pulled away from the Manor, she didn't look back.

Now, Thursday

She hadn't done this for years.

Search histories were a minefield. Every online news report about someone being arrested for an unsavoury crime featured the phrase 'had recently been searching for'. So she never risked using her own devices or the PC at the surgery. Internet cafés used to be good, but they were a thing of the past now. And that's why, when the shock of the photo receded enough for her to trust her legs, she crossed the road from the war memorial and entered the dusty hush of the library.

A bank of PCs lined the wall, each booth partitioned off with a screen made of that fuzzy stuff they put on noticeboards. There were two free PCs right in the middle, but the issue was that she couldn't use the PCs anonymously. Every user had to key in their library code. She picked a book from the crime fiction section and pretended to read the blurb.

An elderly gentleman wearing a grey bodywarmer pushed his chair back and shuffled towards the desk, leaving his glasses case and folded *Daily Mail* behind. Annie shoved the book on the shelf and slid into the warm seat. *Yes.* Still logged in.

A quick glance confirmed the man had reached the queue at the front desk.

Annie's pulse thrummed in her ears as her fingers typed, *Keziah Taylor.*

For reasons only they knew, the library staff kept the toilet key tethered to a chunk of wood. The man took it. Good. A couple of minutes, which was all she needed. The search results appeared and even though she expected it, the entry on the missing-person site jolted her.

Missing: Keziah Taylor. Last known whereabouts: Spain, possibly Malaga. Current age: 14. There was a blank grey oval in lieu of a photo and a generic message: *Keziah we are here for you if you want to talk.*

Izzy had just started school the first time Annie found the page, and for the next few weeks, Annie barely ate or slept. But nothing ever came of it. The age automatically updated every year on 28 March, but nothing else: no news stories, no police investigations, no comments. Keziah Taylor remained a footnote on the internet, one of the many children who vanish without trace every year.

It could only have been Donna. No one else knew or cared enough.

She glanced over her shoulder. No sign of the man. But she had to hurry. She wasn't here for the missing-person page.

Typing *Elliot Devlin* made her guts squirm, but her hand stayed steady. Not many results, a few unconnected LinkedIn and Facebook pages. But *this*, she sat straighter in the chair, this was new. An online news story dated a few weeks ago with his name buried somewhere inside.

The library's old pipes rattled and rushed with water. She glanced in the direction of the toilet. The door opened. She took her phone out and quickly snapped a photo of the screen. Scrolled down the page to the end of the article, clicked the camera again.

'Excuse me,' the man said, crossly. 'That's my computer.'

'Oh.' She half-stood, hunched to block the screen, and tapped the keyboard. The library homepage loaded. 'I've logged you off. Sorry.'

She pushed the wheeled chair back, grabbed her bag off the desk. She dipped her head so her hair fell in a concealing curtain across her face. Pointless really: the library had CCTV. Ignoring the man's irritated 'obvious … left my glasses … just gone to the toilet', she hurried across towards the exit.

Fat drops of rain were falling from the April sky. Holding her phone tightly, she put her hood up as she half-jogged to the car park. The rain pattered quicker now, and when she got inside the VW, it rattled against the roof.

She caught her breath, opened the photo of the screen. Zoomed in. Felt all the breath whoosh out of her.

For a second, she thought the image accompanying the story was Izzy. She blinked, looked again. The image showed a young woman in sportswear, crouching down with one leg extended in front of her. She had giant sunglasses on and her dark hair curled in long spirals.

Internet sensation JayDee opens up about her difficult childhood

Not Izzy, the girl was a few years older, but the similarity was unmistakable. Something clicked in the back of Annie's mind. A piece of the puzzle slotting into place. She put her trembling fist to her mouth, eyes devouring the fuzzy writing on her phone screen.

The TikTok star talks about the dad she doesn't know and how she feels about his possible release from prison. 'I don't know if I'm ready to forgive him,' she says.

For those of you unfamiliar with the term 'influencer', JayDee has an explanation. 'We're like a big brother or sister,' she says. 'Someone who can give tips about clothes or make-up or love or life in general.' What she doesn't mention is how lucrative this role can be. Although only twenty-one, JayDee has an agent. She is coy about how much she earned in the previous year from her work as a brand ambassador for several online retailers, but it's enough money to fund a lavish lifestyle. She's also about to launch a clothing and make-up range and is being touted as a contestant in the year's Strictly.

But JayDee (real name Jessica Devlin) is at pains to point out that her life hasn't always been easy.

Until the age of seven, JayDee lived with her mother, Megan, baby sister Cara and her father, Elliot Devlin, on a quiet, leafy street. Her life changed forever when her father was convicted of drug offences and received a prison sentence. During his time in prison, he was charged with attempted murder of a fellow inmate and his term was extended as a result.

But it is his arrest for the manslaughter of his former mistress, Lauren Taylor, who was only twenty years old when she died from a head injury in a squalid flat, that causes JayDee the most pain.

'The charges were dropped due to lack of evidence,' she says. 'But he had a track record of violence against her and even my mum was convinced he was guilty. Until his arrest, I had no idea that my dad's legitimate property business was just a front.' She shrugs and examines her perfectly manicured fingernails. 'In fact, he was a major drug dealer who exploited kids, dragging them into a life of crime.'

And she really had no inkling about her dad's double life?

'One of my earliest memories was Mum having a huge fight with a woman who I now know was Lauren. And the weird thing was, they could have been sisters, they looked so alike,' she says. 'He was furious with Mum over that. But the drugs, guns, the grooming – no. He kept all that well away from home.'

He was also implicated in the stabbing of a twelve-year-old boy, but due to a lack of evidence, the case never came to court. Why does she think that is?

'No witnesses. People were scared to come forward,' JayDee says. 'From everything I've heard, he was terrifying.'

So, how does JayDee feel about him now?

'It's difficult,' she says, weighing her words carefully. 'I remember being very close to him before he went to prison. I don't think it *would be an exaggeration to say I idolised him. But my younger sister, Cara, was only eighteen months old when he was arrested, and she has no memories of him at all. We lost the house, the cars and everything. We had to move away to start again.*

'*My mum remarried very quickly, and we both grew up calling our stepfather Dad. She wanted to completely erase our real dad from our lives and for years I thought he'd left us to go and work abroad. I think I was twelve or thirteen before she told me the truth. I went off the rails for a while then. I was so angry with him, her, the world. But now I understand why she did it and we've got a great relationship. She and Cara are my two best friends.*'

Has she got a message for anyone currently living in a dysfunctional household? She nods ardently.

'*Whoever needs to hear this, listen. You are not alone. Know that this will not define you. You don't have to live the life your parents did making all the same mistakes. You can break free of the cycle and make a success out of your life. Don't let the bad experiences hold you back. The past is the past, it's the future that counts. The future is amazing.*'

And one last question. Elliot Devlin is due to be released this year. Does JayDee think she will see him?

'*I don't know,*' *she says simply, and for a moment, the air of confidence wavers and she is a little girl.*

JayDee has donated her fee for this article to the Safe Space Women's Refuge.

Annie put the phone facedown on the passenger seat. Emotions bubbled through her. Fear, despair, anger.

Realisation.

Dev was out of prison.

Then

It had been six months since they left the Manor and still, several times a week, she woke drenched in sweat, still with the feel of Dev's breath on her cheek. His heavy arm flattening her lungs.

He would know now, of course, that she had stolen his money. And that featured in her dreams too. Sometimes she listened to him breaking in downstairs. Smashing the windows. Kicking in the door. Tramping up the stairs like an ogre in one of Izzy's storybooks. *Fee fi fo fum.*

During the daylight hours, she focused on building a new life for herself and her daughter. She found a job as a receptionist at a vet's surgery and, using Dev's money to pay the deposit, bought the tiny labourer's cottage. She pushed the memory of what happened at the Manor to a deep place in her mind and got on with the business of raising her daughter.

And then a number she didn't recognise rang on her mobile. And her world spun on its axis yet again.

'It's me,' Lauren said, hoarsely. 'I'm back.'

Now, Thursday

Annie was halfway home when the phone rang. The road ahead tilted and shifted. Panic swept through her. *It's him. It's Dev.*

But it wasn't. It was Caro Fraser.

She pulled up on the kerb.

'Have you read the email?' Caro said, against a backdrop of outdoor sounds. Rain falling, a dog barking close by.

'No. What email?'

'From school. About the man.'

'Man?' she said, suddenly alert. 'What man?'

'Oh,' Caro said, and Annie heard a gate bang shut like a gunshot. 'A couple of the girls reported a man hanging around outside school after netball practice last night. He followed them, trying to take photos of them. They had to run into the newsagents.'

'Oh my god,' Annie replied, her mouth completely dry.

'They sent it this morning, but I've been out with the horses so I've only just seen it.'

'Does it say what he looked like?'

'Very vague. Black jacket with a hood up. Nothing identifying. It's probably nothing, but better to be safe than sorry.'

'Of course,' she said faintly.

'So,' Caro continued, 'I'm going to pick Lucy up tonight. Would you like me to give Izzy a lift home too? I don't really want them catching the bus until this is sorted.'

'Yes, please, to the lift. And thanks for letting me know, Caro.'

She clicked open her email and there it was, from the school. She scanned the screen, diaphragm tightening with each sentence.

'Last night … two Year Eleven girls reported a man loitering around the gates … he tried to speak to them, but they walked away and raised the alarm … police have been informed … recommend caution … no need for alarm …'

Her whole body filled with shock. He was here. He knew where she worked, he knew where she lived. He knew where Izzy went to school. He could be there, now, peering through the railings. Waiting for her to come out for lunch.

Without looking, she pulled out. There was a sharp blast on a horn and a car swerved around her, missing an oncoming van by millimetres. The van driver blurred past, but the driver in front waved his arms, blaring the horn intermittently until he turned up a side street.

Realising that Dev was behind everything opened the door to a locked room in her memory. A series of images, like stills from a horror film, flitted through her consciousness. Dev's hand over her mouth. The click of the belt buckle. The muscular arm pinioning her. On the brink of a panic attack, she gulped in air. No time to panic. She had to stay calm, for Izzy's sake.

A speed camera flashed, but instead of slowing down, she pressed her foot to the accelerator. More horns blared, more furious drivers gesticulated as she weaved in and out of the traffic. None of it mattered. Nothing mattered, except getting to Izzy before he did.

Glancing between her phone and the windscreen, she tapped her thumb on the school app. Found Izzy's timetable. Geography. Room G27. G was … ground floor? Okay.

Up ahead, a man in a hi-vis leaned on a spade. Temporary traffic lights.

'Stay green, stay green,' she murmured, bracing her foot on the accelerator.

Dev. Her stomach twisted into knots. He couldn't tell Izzy the truth. He couldn't be anywhere near her.

Oh god, oh god. Her mind spun off in hideous directions. If he did a DNA test, proved he was her father … would he claim her? Offer her a home?

And, once she knew the truth about Annie, would Izzy want to go?

There was still enough time. If she got to her now, they would have enough time to get the dog, pack a few things and run. She'd got the loan money in her bank account. It wouldn't last, but it would be a start for a new life.

School was just up ahead. The gates were closed, so she parked on the yellow zigzags outside, not caring that she was now blocking half the narrow side street.

She pressed the external buzzer. No reply. Pressed again and kept her thumb on the buzzer, until it was finally answered by a school secretary who manged to pull off sounding simultaneously bored and angry.

'Can I help you?' she said.

'I need to speak to my daughter urgently. Isabel Smith, Year Nine.'

'Can I ask what about?' the secretary replied.

A wave of hysteria swamped her. Annie clamped her hand over her mouth to turn the inappropriate, insane laughter into a cough. *Pull yourself together.*

She cleared her throat. 'It's a personal matter, but it's very important.'

The gate buzzed and Annie jogged through on legs that felt as though they would give way at any moment. When she reached the front office, the secretary buzzed her in. Everything shimmered round the edges, unreal.

'Is everything okay?' the secretary said through the partition.

The vestibule was lined with artwork from the students and one of them was a mirror mosaic. Annie caught sight of herself, splintered into a hundred pieces. Her hair was half in, half out of its ponytail. Grey smudges under her eyes spoke of no sleep; her face was pinched and drawn. And – she looked down to confirm – yes, her fleece was on inside out trailing a white washing instructions label on her hip.

'The app says she's in Geography, so if you could just get her, that'd be great,' Annie said, bouncing on the balls of her feet, eyes scanning the corridor and the glass window in the double doors that led into the main building. It was very quiet.

'Years Nine, Ten and Eleven are in a special assembly at the moment, so if you'd like to wait, they should be finished in about' – the secretary looked up at the big silver wall clock – 'twenty minutes. You can have a seat there.'

Stifling a scream of frustration – what was *wrong* with this woman? – she replied, 'It's a family emergency. A private one.'

'Well, I'm afraid—'

A teacher swiped through the double doors that led into the corridor. Without stopping to think, Annie ran in behind her.

'Ms Smith!' the secretary called, alarmed.

But Annie was jogging down the corridors now. She'd only been in the hall last week for Izzy's parents' evening, so she knew exactly where it was. Turn left, down a bit. There. Big double doors.

The secretary's heels tapped briskly along the tiled corridor.

'Ms Smith, you're not allowed in there!'

Annie burst through the doors, almost tumbling in her haste. The auditorium had a stage at her end in front of tiered seating. There were rows of plastic chairs clipped, every one of them filled with a pupil. Every one of them with a shocked expression. Every one of them staring at her.

'Izzy,' Annie shouted. 'Izzy.'

On stage, Mrs Jackson froze mid-sentence. The screen to her

left showed a PowerPoint slide with the caption: *Stranger Safety: practical tips for teenagers.*

The secretary's tapping heels caught up with her. 'Mrs Smith!' she said. 'Please come back to reception.'

Subdued giggles and whispering erupted into peals of scandalised laughter.

'Be quiet, please!' Mrs Jackson said, hurrying down the steps. 'Mrs Smith, can I help you?'

But Annie was occupied scanning the sea of open-mouthed faces. A group of them craned their necks, whispering and almost climbing over the backs of the chairs to look at Izzy, who had hunched her shoulders up around her neck and was staring fixedly at her knees. Panic and embarrassment flamed her cheeks.

Several flustered teachers milled around now, tasked with the impossible job of herding the students back to their seats. Loud voices submerged by the gleeful uproar.

'Come on,' Annie called, making her way up the aisle. 'We're going home.'

But Izzy slumped in her seat, chin resting on her collar clearly praying for invisibility.

A hand patted Annie's arm. Mrs Jackson.

'Why don't you and Izzy come to my office,' she said quietly. 'We can have a chat.'

She gestured at Izzy, who peeled herself off the chair and clenching her hand inside her blazer sleeves, scuttled to the door under the gleeful stares of more than half the school.

'Iz …' Annie started, grasping her forearm.

Izzy shook her off and once she had got out of the seating, ran to the door without a word. Annie jogged after her. Caught up as they reached Mrs Jackson's office.

'Iz, I'm sorry,' she said. 'I know that wasn't great but—'

'Do. Not. Speak. To. Me.' Voice thick with held-in tears, Izzy wrapped her arms tightly around herself.

'Hey,' Annie said, reaching for a hug.

227

Izzy flinched and shrank against the wall.

Realisation jolted through her like electricity. This simply wasn't going to work.

'Shall we sit down?' Mrs Jackson smiled expectantly, gesturing in her office. 'And we can get to the bottom of this.'

As though a plug had been pulled, the fight suddenly drained out of Annie.

No way would Izzy agree to leaving. And no matter how she framed it, nothing would sound credible. Because the only credible reason was the truth.

'I am so sorry,' she said, slowly taking a seat. 'I think that the email about the man following the girls panicked me, for various reasons. And I was worried about Izzy's safety and I thought if I could have her at home with me, I could protect her. But ...' She leaned forward and Izzy jerked away, bony knees knocking together. 'I'm sorry. I didn't mean to embarrass you. I just panicked. I know you're safer at school.'

Mrs Jackson nodded sympathetically. 'It's perfectly understandable that you're concerned. I'm sure all the parents are. But please rest assured that Izzy is completely safe here.'

Annie stood. 'Thank you. I'll pick you up at the gate when you finish hockey practice. And I'm sorry. I love you.'

Izzy picked at a thread on her skirt hem. She didn't reply.

Then

Two days after Lauren's call, Annie stood in the foyer of an anonymous chain hotel and listened to the uniformed receptionist reassure her that their babysitting service would take excellent care of her daughter.

'Look.' The woman turned the screen around. Baby Izzy filled it, the picture as clear as if she were in the room with her. Next to her sat Monica, a qualified nursery nurse with an enhanced DBS check and a paediatric first aid certificate.

'Honestly,' she continued, 'I'd bring my own kids here every night if they'd let me.'

'Any problems at all and you'll call straightaway?' Annie said, clutching her carrier bag tightly.

'Absolutely. Please, go and enjoy your night. Your daughter will be absolutely fine.'

It was the sort of place that attracted an eclectic clientele: city break sightseers, people on business, backpackers. All sorts. Anywhere else, the receptionist might have wondered at a woman in unflattering joggers and a hoodie leaving her baby in a hotel. Not here. The rush and swell of guests swept Annie out of sight and out of mind.

And on her way back to the Manor.

She stared from the bus window as it travelled from the pleasant location of the hotel through less affluent areas, where bags of rubbish piled up on the pavements and people walked with their heads down.

The bus stopped. A man got on, sat next to Annie and proceeded to unwrap a kebab. Shreds of cabbage fell from his lips as he ate, sloppily and noisily, and the stink of meat churned her already swirling guts.

She almost dropped the phone when Lauren's voice came down the other end, talking of splitting up with Omar, coming back to the Manor flat to find strangers living next door.

Annie's instinct had to been to hang up. Lauren didn't know about Uppermoss, she thought they were in another part of London. She didn't know about the birth certificate either. Or that Keziah Taylor was now Izzy Smith.

Apart from Annie, the only person who knew the truth was Ray. Ray who had lived on the Manor his whole life. Ray who could not be trusted.

And that was why, on this unseasonably cold night, Annie pulled her hood down over her face, and her scarf up so not a recognisable inch of flesh showed. The icy drizzle kept trying to turn to snow and few people braved the streets around the Manor and those who did kept their heads down and their feet moving quickly.

Seeing the Manor again jolted her more than expected. So many memories jostled to come to the fore.

But it was Lauren who came as the biggest shock.

She opened the door without a word. Her hair was lank and greasy. She was pitifully thin. No light in her eyes, dull skin and she had a cold sore at the corner of her lip. Her left cheekbone was bright red with a graze and a green-yellow old bruise ringed her eye.

No vestige of the glowing girl about to jet off to Ibiza remained.

The flat was worse than ever. The air was thick with stale

smoke and there were food wrappers and makeshift ashtrays littering every surface.

'Who did that to you?' Annie said, waving at her face.

'Who do you think? Where's Keziah?'

'Not far,' Annie said carefully.

'You shouldn't have taken her.'

'I didn't take her. You left her behind.'

Whatever Lauren was about to say was lost in a paroxysm of coughing.

'Do you want me to get you a glass of water?'

Lauren shook her head and poured herself a glass of vodka. She didn't offer Annie one. She lifted the glass clumsily to her lips and clear liquid spilled down her chin. She wiped it with the back of her hand and then licked the drops.

'What happened to Omar?' Annie said.

'We split up,' she said shortly.

'I'm sorry to hear that,' Annie said, meaning it. 'I know you liked him.'

For a fleeting moment, Lauren looked like the young girl she had been when Annie met her. Vulnerable and alone. Then the shutters came down.

'Well, I'm back now,' she said, crossing to the cluttered coffee table. She picked up a tiny plastic bag and dipped her finger in it then quickly wiped her finger around her gums.

'Oh, Lauren,' Annie said sadly.

'Don't you *oh Lauren* me,' she said. 'When it's your fault.'

'How do you work that out?'

Lauren sniffed hard and rubbed her nose with the heel of her hand.

'Who do you think Dev blamed when his money went missing? How do you think I've got this?' She pointed at a fresh bruise on her cheekbone. 'He said I must have told someone where it was hidden. He said no one could have just found it.'

Oh god. Her heart pounded. This was a set-up. She glanced at the door in terror. Any minute now he was going to—

231

Lauren read her panic. 'He's not coming here, if that's what you're worried about. He was here this afternoon, but I didn't get you here to grass you up. You're no good to me if Dev gets you first. I want my daughter back.'

Annie's throat tightened.

'Lauren,' she said carefully. 'She has got a really good life. She's happy. Do you think it's fair to bring her to live somewhere like this?'

'I'm her mother. She is best off with me.'

'You haven't seen her for so long. She won't remember you.'

'You took her away from me!'

'You abandoned her,' Annie said. 'You went off to Spain and then Dubai and you just left her. You didn't even call to see how she was. You can't come back now and pretend you're her mother. If you genuinely cared about her, you wouldn't have left her in the first place.'

Lauren topped up her glass.

'I agree,' she said simply.

Taken aback, Annie stared.

'I do,' Lauren continued. 'You'll be a far better mum than I am. But if you want to keep her, then you have to do something for me.'

She should have known there would be a catch. There was always a catch with Lauren.

'What do you want?'

'Money,' Lauren replied. 'I want you to give me the money you stole from Dev so I can get on with my life.'

'Let me get this straight. You want to sell me your daughter?' Annie said.

At least Lauren had the grace to look embarrassed. 'It's not like that. I want her to be happy, but I've ended up with nothing. Look at me, back in this place.'

She picked compulsively at a scab on her arm.

'Can't you just get some more?' Annie said, gesturing at the ceiling.

Lauren threw her a withering glance. 'Don't be stupid. Do you think Dev would let me get away with that?'

'Well, I can't give you the money,' Annie said. 'Because I bought a house with it.'

When she thought about what happened next, the memories were jerky like old video footage.

She saw Lauren fly at her, brandishing the vodka bottle like a club.

She saw herself stepping out of the way.

She saw horror in Lauren's eyes. Her arms windmilling. The glass flying out of her hand and smashing. Then the sickening crack as the back of Lauren's skull collided with the marble-topped coffee table.

Lauren crumpling and sliding to the floor.

Annie remembered panting, waiting for her to get back up. To shout. Fight back.

And when she didn't, walking over.

Thick dark blood oozed from the back of Lauren's head. Her face wasn't the same shape anymore. Her eyelids fluttered and small gasping sounds issued from her slack lips. As Annie watched, her limbs twitched.

'Jesus, Lauren,' Annie whispered, taking out her phone.

She was about to dial the third 9, when her finger froze above the button. Lauren's eyes had rolled upwards in their sockets. White stuff leaked from the side of her mouth. Yellow fluid dripped from her nostrils.

And suddenly, everything was crystal clear.

No matter how soon the ambulance got here, she wasn't going to make it. And when they arrived and found Annie here, the only witness, what then? Question after question unravelling the cocoon she had spun around Izzy.

So, instead of calling an ambulance, Annie put the phone back in her pocket. Then she picked Lauren's cheap pay-as-you-go handset up between her finger and thumb and put that alongside. Next, she walked across to the loose ceiling tile and pushed it up and out of the way.

And waited.

After a few minutes, Lauren spasmed, like a thousand volts ran through her. Her throat rattled wetly.

And then she lay still.

Head down, hands in pockets, she walked briskly but not quickly enough to draw attention to herself. The fluorescent lights of a bus station were up ahead, a cleaner wearing headphones swilled foamy water over the concourse.

Annie went up to him and mimed taking off headphones.

The cleaner raised his eyebrows in a question.

'I need a payphone,' she said desperately, her voice muffled through the scarf. 'Please can you tell me where there's a phone?'

He pointed at a bank of phones on the furthest wall and she hurried towards them, holding her hood tight over her forehead.

The phones had silver keypads and black receivers. She picked one up and this time, she pressed 999. It was answered in two rings.

'Emergency. What service do you require?'

She kept the scarf between her and the mouthpiece.

'Police please. It's urgent.'

'Putting you through now,' the operator said.

So much adrenalin pumped through her that she didn't need to fake the emotion in her. 'Hello, I'm worried about my friend, Lauren Taylor. She rang me just now to say that she thinks her boyfriend is attacking her. His name is Elliot Devlin. It's Manor Park, Flat 2a. Please hurry. He's done it before, but this time, I really think he's going to kill her.'

'What's your name, please?' the operator said.

The cleaner continued mopping the floor. Annie felt the eyes of the CCTV on her.

'Please help her,' she said and hung up.

If the police ever reviewed this footage, they would see an anonymous black figure – hood up, scarf to her chin – replace the receiver and wipe her eyes with the back of her gloved hand, clearly upset. She turns her head nervously, as you would if your friend was in danger. Then the anonymous caller would merge into the crowds.

Annie wove down side streets and back streets until she found a Tube station to take her back to the hotel.

The neighbours must have heard Lauren and Dev arguing earlier in the day. After all, those walls were paper thin. His fingerprints would be all over everything, including whatever was inside the roof space. The flat was in his name. He had a history of domestic abuse. Hopefully, they could link him to the attack on Lindon. And then there was Donna, and no doubt she would have a lot to say.

And Elliott Devlin would finally get what he deserved.

Because, after all, everyone knew what he was like.

Now, Thursday

Annie parked outside the school gates five minutes before the end of hockey practice. She got out of the car and went to the railings. The bright red bibs of the players darted across the grass, vivid splashes against the green. From this distance, it was impossible to single Izzy out.

She paced up and down in front of the gate. Back and forth. Back and forth.

All afternoon, her insides had fizzed with trepidation. She couldn't catch her breath properly and the shallow gasps hurt her chest, like a weight pressing down on her.

A whistle carried on the wind, the double note signalling the end of the match.

Like the whistling on the Manor, summoning the boys on their bikes, signalling a collection or a delivery. More of Dev's victims. Like Lauren. Like her.

She'd saved Izzy from him. That was the important thing.

She checked her phone, but there had been no further messages. Not since the one of Lauren in the hospital. She had gone to delete it countless times.

So tender, holding her baby for the first time.

So different from the Lauren in her head, with her cheekbones jutting at the wrong angles. Dying while Annie watched and did nothing. Not a prayer. Not even a kind word.

She moaned, doubled over from the visceral anguish of remembering.

Two girls, hair in ponytails and carrying hockey sticks, stopped and giggled. Annie couldn't hear what they were whispering, but she didn't need to. The blanks required little imagination.

That's Izzy Smith's crazy mum. The one who ran into assembly. God, can you imagine? I would totally die of embarrassment if my mum did that.

Everything fragmented, whirling and reconfiguring like the coloured glass shard in a kaleidoscope.

Dev was in Uppermoss.

The last stragglers exited the school gates. But there was no sign of Izzy.

'Excuse me.' She jogged to a girl carrying a hockey stick across her shoulders. 'Is Izzy Smith still on the field?'

'Izzy?' the girl said with a frown. 'I think she went home after school.'

A chill enveloped Annie's entire body.

'Sorry, what was that?' she said faintly.

'Izzy wasn't at practice tonight. She isn't here.'

The girl walked away.

Annie slipped in through the open school gate, tapping quickly on her phone.

It went straight to voicemail.

'Iz, it's me. I came to pick you up from hockey, but I can't see you. Can you give me a call when you get this?'

She scanned the sports fields. Some boys practised penalties on the football pitch and some girls a foot smaller than Izzy played netball on the court by Mrs Jackson's office window.

The Family Safe app showed Izzy was at school. She had to be here somewhere.

'Nice to see you again, Mrs Smith,' the receptionist said, her facial expression strongly implying the opposite.

'Do you know where Izzy is? I thought she was at hockey, but maybe there's another club on.'

The receptionist shook her head. 'Not today, I'm afraid. We've got staff safeguarding training in the hall and the teachers are tied up in that.'

'But she's here,' Annie said, thrusting the phone under her screen. 'Look. That's the Family Safe app. It says she's here.'

The receptionist scrutinised the screen. 'Ah. It only says until 2.55. You can see it's been switched off. They all do it.'

'Well, where is she then?' she said, unable to hide her alarm.

'I'm afraid I don't know. Have you tried calling her?'

Of course I fucking have!

Annie swallowed down the words and instead nodded quickly. 'Voicemail.'

'Have you tried Lucy Fraser?'

'Not yet,' she said, dialling Caro's number before the sentence was out.

Caro got as far as 'Hel—' before Annie interrupted.

'Have you seen Izzy?' she said, going back into the yard. 'She's not answering her phone and the app says she's still at school. I'm here now, picking her up, but I can't find her. Please tell me she's with Lucy.'

The pause that followed stretched on and on. Annie's heart plummeted.

'Lucy went to the Trafford Centre after school with some friends,' Caro said. 'But Izzy wasn't one of them.'

Annie sat on the edge of the kerb. 'Where is she?'

'Don't panic. I'm texting Lucy now to ask her if she knows where she is. There, sent. What about home, do you think she might have gone straight there?'

'I can see on our alarm app if anyone has opened the door,' she said dully. 'She's not there.'

'Hang on. Incoming,' Caro said. 'Oh. Okay. Well, Lucy says Izzy definitely isn't at the Trafford Centre with them.'

'Right,' Annie said. Calm and measured. 'Well, I'll have to keep looking, I guess.'

'Keep me posted,' Caro replied.

And it wasn't until she ended the call that she realised she was crying.

She opened the last text message, the letters wobbled behind the film of tears.

Don't you think Keziah deserves to know the truth?

She pressed the number. Straight to voicemail.

'Please, Dev,' she said. 'If you have to tell her the truth, then do it. I'll take whatever is coming but please don't hurt her. None of this is her fault. She doesn't deserve to get dragged into things that happened to her when she was a baby. Wherever you've taken her, let her go back home. Or at least let her call me so I know she's safe. I'll still get you your money, I promise. Tomorrow. Just tell me when and where. I'll be there. Please let her go. She's a great kid. Please.'

The end of the message came out as a whisper, strangled by grief. All she ever wanted to do was protect Izzy and whatever happened now wouldn't alter the fact she had failed.

A text alert.

A snatched photo, fringed at the edges where the photographer had caught the edge of a bush, unfolded on the screen. Izzy outside school, carrying the hockey stick and flowery pump bag she had this morning.

She is a great kid, the message read. *A real chip off the old block.*

She stared at the letters until they became meaningless squiggles and dots.

This was it, then. The end of the line. One of those pivotal moments when her life would spin off in an unexpected direction.

She scrolled down her contacts. Found L for Liam. He didn't always have his personal phone switched on at work, but she knew he would pick up his voicemail as soon as he could.

'Hi, it's me. I need to speak to you urgently about something. Please can you call me as soon as you get this?'

She got up off the kerb and rolled her shoulders back.

That was it then. The awful, sordid truth about who she really was waited for Izzy with the inevitability of nightfall.

And there was nothing Annie could do.

Then

Bland pop played over the speakers in the hotel foyer. The reek of overcooked eggs drifted from the breakfast room and the two scalding coffees she'd downed sloshed around her guts like water on a spin cycle.

Don't you dare be sick.

Annie reeled away from the counter, jerking Izzy back so hard she tripped backwards over the rucksack. The printer whirred.

'Did you enjoy your stay?' the receptionist said. She ripped the receipt and placed it on the fake wood counter.

'Oh, yes. Thank you. Very nice.'

'Thank you,' the receptionist said. 'Hope to see you again. Have a good day.'

What must this neat young woman with perfect teeth and neat beige nails think of Annie?

'Thanks,' she replied. 'You too.'

But outside the revolving doors, the world exploded in a cacophony of traffic and people. The rucksack bit her shoulders and Izzy, snotty and miserable, whinged.

'One more thing,' she said brightly. 'Then we'll go home. I promise.'

But Izzy had chosen today to exercise her tantrum muscles.

When she was in the pram, she kicked and screamed as rushing pedestrians, clutching takeaway coffees, surged around them. A woman wearing a beige suit and bright white trainers leapt back, almost tripping over them. She scowled at Annie and continued striding on.

Through all of this, Annie felt like she was watching the world through a pane of glass. Inside her bubble, last night's events were what was real. What was going on around her now seemed like something she was watching on TV.

'Upsy-daisy,' she said, scooping Izzy into her arms.

With the rucksack on her back, her daughter clinging to her chest like a primate and one hand gripping the pram handle, she continued awkwardly along the pavement.

'Look, darling, a bus,' Annie said, breaking into a slow jog. 'And we're going to get it.'

The black coat, scarves and gloves nestled in the bottom of the rucksack. The woman standing with the baby on the bus, hopefully, did not resemble the anonymous black-clad figure who had travelled the same route last night. Even so, she carefully angled herself away from the bus CCTV during the journey, burying her face in her daughter's fuzzy curls.

Images flashed in her mind as the bus bounced along. Lauren's slurred accusations. Her demands for money. How she'd fallen. The crack of her head against the marble corner of the coffee table.

Annie screwed her eyes tight shut and swayed, clinging to the pole on the bus. Barely registering the crowded bus.

The woman behind her tutted and gave the rucksack a gentle shove.

She'd protected Izzy. What else could she have done? Let Izzy be swallowed up by the care system? Let the future she deserved, the future only Annie could give her, dissolve into nothing?

She set her shoulders and turned suddenly, swinging the rucksack into the woman behind her.

'Sorry,' she said and pressed the buzzer. 'We're getting off here.'

It was awkward to unload pram and baby and rucksack off the bus, but she was past caring if other passengers glared or drivers caught behind the bus grew impatient. She lowered Izzy, thankfully calmer now, into the pram. She bent down to tug her coat straight where it had ridden up.

'Nearly finished,' she said soothingly. 'Home soon.'

This wouldn't take long. She unwound her scarf and looped it over her hair, tugging the fabric forward so it shaded her face. An ordinary woman, pushing a pram down an ordinary high street. That's all anyone would see. As long as she held her nerve. One more thing and they would be back on the train. Back home. Safe.

Her heartbeat quickened as she remembered the last time she'd taken this route, with her mum's rings burning a guilty hole in her pocket. Now she had cash to redeem them.

She neared the shop, the crowds were thinner here. Not as many people rushing to work. Up ahead, the three golden balls hung from the sign and she quickened her pace. As she did, she noticed a man coming towards her. The flattened boxer's nose and squat physique. He was unmistakable. Ray, the man who could get anything from the Manor. The man who only six months earlier had got her a fake identity for the child she was pushing in the buggy.

She dropped to her knees and started fussing with a stuffed giraffe dangling from the toy bar. Shaking her head slightly, she let the scarf obscure more of her face. When he'd passed, she stayed there, trembling for a few seconds before she straightened. Her lower back winced under the weight of the rucksack and she twisted round to relieve the pressure. And in that same moment, he turned and looked directly at her. A woman and a baby.

Oh god. Was that recognition in his eyes? She grabbed the pram handle and jerked it forward, but the wheel caught at an awkward angle on the edge of a paving slab and Izzy let out a squawk of protest.

She didn't dare look back. She moved quickly, swallowing

down the bile that now flooded her throat. Fear gave her energy to move briskly towards the shop. Was that where he had been? Of course. He was Ray's brother.

She hesitated then risked a quick look behind her. He had gone.

She leaned against the shutters of a takeaway and forced herself to take a deep breath. Bands of steel squeezed her ribcage, forcing the breath from her lungs. Black dots swarmed around the edges of her vision. Was she having a heart attack? God, the irony if she dropped dead in the street now, leaving Izzy alone after everything she had done to keep her safe. *Breathe. Breathe.*

After a few seconds, her vision cleared. She could not fall to pieces here. Not now.

She pushed the pram towards the shop. The bell jangled as she opened it.

A Perspex partition separated the counter from the shop. The man behind it looked at her.

'I've come to collect these,' Annie said, handing over the ticket.

'ID?' The man tickled the mouse of an ancient PC.

Annie took out her purse and handed over a bank card in the name of Annie Smith.

The man shook his head and tapped the back of a handwritten notice: *No photo ID, no business.*

Shit.

She was tempted to bail then. The only photo ID she had was her driving licence and it had her Uppermoss address on it. It wouldn't take much to link the dots on the paper trail and tie her back to Lauren. The police would have found her body hours ago. What if they started investigating the woman behind the frantic 999 call?

The pawnbroker scratched his nose. Annie pictured her mum, and suddenly missed her with a fierce pang of longing that brought tears to her eyes. If she didn't collect the jewellery now, she would never see it again. The precious memories would be broken up, the gold melted, stones dispersed.

'Here.' She slid the licence across the desk.

The man took forever typing on the screen. Because it was angled away from her, she couldn't see his notes. An electric fan heater blasted hot air directly down her neck and she felt sweat prickle along her upper lip.

She desperately, desperately needed to be out of there.

He took the licence and opened the lid on the photocopier. It clanked and whirred to life.

'With the interest, that's seven hundred pounds,' he said, taking the copy from the tray.

She reached in her pocket and took out a bundle of notes fastened with an elastic band. Peeled off twenties and lay them on the counter.

'Six eighty, seven hundred.'

The man flicked through the pile with his red thimble, counting again.

'Sign at the bottom,' he said, passing her a sheet of A4 before disappearing into the back.

He was probably only gone for a few minutes, but it felt like an eternity to Annie. She kept her hat pulled down low over her face and cast frequent glances through the dirty window.

'Here you are,' he said, eventually, passing her a small velvet bag tied with a drawstring. 'Two rings and a pair of diamond hoops.'

She shook the contents of the bag out into the palm of her hand and examined them. A lump rose to her throat as she pictured the rings on her mum's finger. The earrings in her ears.

'Thank you,' she said, turning to leave.

But the man had his head down, stapling the copy of her driving licence to the receipt and didn't acknowledge her.

She pulled her scarf up as high as it would go and with her head down, nudged the door open. Looked up and down the street. The coast was clear.

There was no sign of Ray.

There was a taxi rank up ahead. She pushed the buggy over

the uneven pavement. Just one more hurdle to overcome: the journey back to Uppermoss. There were always police at the station. She'd have to be careful to keep her nerve. They would have found Lauren by now, surely.

She got in the first taxi.

'Where to?' he said through the partition.

'Euston, please.'

'Mama, mama,' Izzy cried out in alarm as the taxi jerked forward to join the stream of traffic.

'Don't worry,' Annie said, clasping her tightly on her lap. 'I've got you. And I won't let anything bad happen to you.'

Now, Thursday

Caro Fraser flashed on the screen.

Annie answered immediately. 'Caro, hi. Has Lucy said anything? Have you heard from her?'

'Mum?' Izzy said hesitantly.

'Oh thank god,' Annie murmured. 'Are you okay? Did he hurt you? What did he say to you?'

There was a brief silence. Then:

'What man? What are you on about? I've been at the Trafford Centre with Lucy. But don't blame her. I told her not to say anything because I didn't want you to know.'

The words came out in a rush, like they had been building up inside her and now they had to burst out in an unstoppable deluge.

'And I switched that stupid app off because I hate feeling like you're spying on me all the time. Like you don't trust me at all. And then what you did today in assembly, Mum. I wanted the ground to swallow me up. And then everyone was laughing at me and sniggering about how my mum is mental and I'd just had enough. I needed some space. So I didn't go to hockey practice because I knew the team would make a big joke of it. And don't have a go at Lucy. I made her lie.'

She finished with a deep shuddery breath.

'It's fine,' Annie said. 'I'm just glad you're okay.'

That took the wind out of Izzy's sails.

'Oh. Thanks.'

'And just ignore that stupid stuff I said about a man,' Annie continued smoothly. 'I've had this paranoid thing buzzing round my head ever since I read the email about the man hanging around outside school. But I'm all right about it now. I can see I was being silly over nothing. Listen, do you want to ask Caro if it's okay for you to stay over tonight?'

It was. And Izzy was touchingly pleased.

Annie's relief, however, was smothered by a fiery wall of rage. She picked up the phone. Pressed Dev's number again.

'You bastard,' she said after the message beep, unable to conceal her trembling rage. 'You total, fucking bastard.'

She ended the call and her phone vibrated in her hand. Liam. Oh god, the bizarre, out-of-context message. She let it go to voicemail. Picked it up straightway.

He sounded worried. 'Hi, I'll try you again later. Hope everything's okay. I'll leave my phone on so you can call me anytime. Take care.'

She didn't have the emotional resources left to invent a convincing lie. Not one she could deliver with any degree of conviction, anyway.

Nothing major, she texted. *I just felt incredibly guilty about being so off with you the other night. Wanted to apologise again. Ignore me! A xx*

Not great, but it was the best she could do. Especially as the first glimmerings of a plan gleamed around the edges of her mind. An idea that if she ironed out the details might – *might* – work.

She'd been having the nightmare again. Back on the Manor, Dev creeping in to her bedroom. The belt slithering to the ground. And

248

then Lauren, next door, her head smashed to a bloody pulp. But this wasn't part of the dream. This was Smudge, who'd jumped off the bed and was scrabbling and whining at the door.

'What is it, girl?' Annie said. She patted the bed. 'Come on. Back to sleep.'

But Smudge was having none of it. Her claws scraped frantically, gouging at the wood.

The house was freezing. There was no moon and her bedroom was pitch-dark. She fumbled for the bedside light and groggily pulled on a cardi and picked up her phone. *3.04.*

'What is wrong with you?' she muttered and released the latch on her bedroom door.

Smudge shot down the stairs, and her whine became a howl as she flung herself at the back door. Annie followed her and switched the burglar alarm off. The security light was on, flooding the front garden. Although that in itself meant nothing because foxes and badgers, even owls flying by, could trigger the sensor, a ripple of apprehension ran up her spine.

Still.

There was something about Smudge's behaviour. Howling, scraping.

She tugged at the collar. 'Enough,' she said sharply, fumbling for the security app on the phone. Click. The camera showed the deserted front garden lit like a football pitch. There was no one there. Her phone clattered to the floor as Smudge shook her off and battered at the door, howling in a strange, high-pitched way, dragging her nails down the wood.

She slowly drew the bolts back. Smudge hurled herself through the door and immediately began to nose furiously at a wet bundle on the step with a frantic yelping Annie had never heard before.

She put her hand to her mouth to quell a rising surge of nausea.

It was a tiny rabbit. A wild one.

And it was very, very dead.

It had the perfect cotton wool tail and soft tawny fur of its many siblings, but the resemblance to the sweet things that came to nibble on the front lawn ended there. This was the mutilated corpse of a rabbit. The fragile skull bones had been splintered. Obliterated until the button eyes and velvety soft ears were indistinguishable in the reddened, pulpy mass.

Annie closed her eyes. Forced the revulsion into a corner and her brain focused on what needed to be done.

The cold lino chilled through her thick fleece pyjamas. A defenceless wild rabbit with a bloodied splintered mess where its head should be. The symbolism could not be clearer:

Lauren.

And there was something poking out from under its tiny paw. A piece of paper.

She pulled on her boots and her work fleece. Moving on autopilot, she opened the under-sink cupboard and took out the rubber gloves she used when she occasionally dyed her own hair. The pink rubber was streaked with black dye build-up. She pulled them on and gingerly tugged the corner of the paper, trying to tease it out. She could see there was writing and an image, bluey green. A map?

It was a map. It showed a place she and Liam had walked the dogs together only a couple of weeks ago. A reservoir, high up on the moors that spanned the M62. There was a slip road off the eastbound carriageway that joined a winding unlit lane. A track really. And at the end of it was an old pumphouse.

This had been circled on the map in thick black pen, alongside block capitals spelling the terse message: *12AM. £50K.*

Every creak, every breath of wind outside released fresh cortisol flooding through her veins. Leaves rustled, shadows raced. The moon peered through the clouds. Beyond the end of the garden, the woods whispered. Annie pulled the shed door open and picked up the spade and snapped a thick rubble sack from the roll.

Imagine you're at work.

Dealing with injured and dead animals was part of the routine at the surgery and slipping into that pragmatic frame of mind helped Annie to manoeuvre the blade of the shovel under the mangled corpse like a chef taking a grotesque pizza from the oven. The limbs shimmied with the movement. The skin sack remains of its head lolled.

She opened the rubble sack and carefully chucked the poor creature inside. Blood and scraps of fur clung to the blade in a long, glistening smear.

Fragments of bone and blood remained in a sticky ooze over the step. But she would have to deal with that later. She locked the kitchen door and pocketed the key then carried the bag and its hideous cargo up to the end of the garden and through the gate into the field in front of the house.

Her red pyjamas were the only splash of colour in the monochrome world of the night-time woods. Leaves and twigs crunched underfoot. She gently tossed the poor creature under a bush. There was no way she was digging a grave at this time. And anyway, foxes and badgers needed to eat.

As she got back into bed, the adrenalin rush that had propelled her into the woods with the rabbit's mangled corpse drained away, leaving her shaking. It felt as though the cold night air had penetrated her bones. She shook like she had a fever, but she was cold.

She heard the dog whine and scratch next door and let her into her own bedroom. The alarm system was armed but Smudge was better than any burglar alarm. Her nose and ears a thousand times more sensitive than Annie's own.

And right now, Annie needed all the help she could get.

Now, Friday

A nasty metallic taste coated her tongue and her teeth and she woke to eyeballs full of grit. But with a clear plan of how to deal with today.

Smudge followed her downstairs and pawed at the front door. Annie unlocked it, bracing herself against the frame as she pulled the dog off the bloodstained step. She shut the dog in the lounge with a dish of kibble and frozen peas. Ruled by her stomach as usual, Smudge set to eating while Annie boiled the kettle.

'Good girl,' Annie called.

The dark stone was stained darker in places by the blood. Annie boiled the kettle and took the scrubbing brush and squirted washing-up liquid and scrubbed.

Step one of her plan involved calling Izzy. The line rang and rang until she was about to hang up and call Caro instead when Izzy answered, her voice cross and sleepy.

'Mum? It's like six o'clock,' she said. 'Why are you ringing so early?' A note of panic crept in. 'Has something happened? Is Smudge okay?'

'Smudge is fine,' she said hastily. 'And I'm fine. There's nothing wrong.'

There was a thud and a creak of bedsprings. Even though she

couldn't see her, she knew Izzy had just flung herself on her back on the twin bed in Lucy's bedroom. She could see the room in her mind's eye. The gymkhana rosettes around the mirror. Posters and photos all over the walls. The overflowing bookcase. Headboard adorned with the same LED lights that Izzy had.

'I just wanted to check you're okay,' she said.

An exasperated grunt came down the phone. 'Of course I'm all right, Mum. Why wouldn't I be?'

'No reason,' she said lightly.

Tears clogged her throat and she coughed to disguise them. *I love you, Izzy. Everything has been for you. I've always done my best. And if after today you never want to talk to me again, then I will understand and I want you to know how sorry I am and how I only ever wanted the best for you.*

'Is that it?' Izzy said, yawning. 'Can I go back to sleep now?'

'One last thing,' Annie said. 'Can you ask Caro if you can sleepover tonight as well?'

'Sure.' She sounded surprised. 'Thanks, Mum.'

Now, Friday

Step two of the plan involved arriving at the surgery early. And, crucially, before Samara. At seven o'clock, she pulled into the deserted car park. Disarmed the alarm. She hung her coat up on the peg in the staffroom and turned her PC on. Then she opened the safe.

By the time the Land Rover pulled up outside the surgery, step two was complete.

'You're here bright and early,' Samara said as she changed into her white surgery clogs. 'Couldn't sleep?'

'I thought I'd catch up on the paperwork and everything,' Annie said, smiling. 'And check the accounts. There are a few advance payments going out for building materials that I wanted to look at. Make sure everything's in place. No hiccups.'

'And is it?'

'All in order,' Annie said, closing the page on her monitor. 'There are a few big bills going out today, so brace yourself for a bit of a shock if you look at the balance.'

'I promise I won't look,' Samara said. 'All this nonsense with Cain Maguire, who incidentally, is now backtracking on his full confession now he's realised writing *Dead Bitch* counts as making death threats and is actually quite serious.'

'He's denying it then?'

'Not everything.' Sam walked into the staff kitchen and put a carton of milk in the fridge. 'Just the more serious aspects. Anyway, on a happier note, some of our friends have just opened a B&B near Ulverston and Helen and I thought we could treat you and Liam to a weekend if you'd like to go. As a thank you.'

The concern engraved on Samara's face made Annie want to cry. In fact, she wanted nothing more than to let the truth out. The everything truth. Her criminal past. The attack. Lauren's accidental death. Izzy's real identity.

The date with Dev tonight.

How what she thought she knew about Annie was a lie, worn smooth by years of practice.

Despite everything, she thought Samara would be on her side.

And that made her unwitting role in Annie's plan even more painful.

'That's so kind of you, but you don't need to apologise for anything,' she said, feeling the guilt like molten lava swirling in her stomach. 'None of this is your fault. And it's all been so hard on you and Helen. You're the ones who should be planning a weekend away.'

Samara smiled wanly. 'Soon. Once the baby comes along, I guess we won't have time. Or the money.'

The final part of the plan had to be completed at the cottage.

She opened the loft hatch and flicked the catch to release the ladder, which rattled noisily down. The old black rucksack from the army surplus store was up there somewhere. And, rolled up inside, the baggy black joggers and plain black hoodie she'd brought from the Manor all those years ago.

The fabric smelled overpoweringly of mildew, but the nylon rucksack had kept them dry. The trousers were a tighter fit than the last time she wore them, but that was no bad thing. She'd been slim to the point of weakness back then. Now she felt more able to stand up for herself.

She packed the rucksack with the packages of notes, a mix of tens, twenties and fifties.

The rucksack bulged, and when she lifted it in one hand, it was like lifting a dumbbell. Fifty thousand pounds was a significant amount.

Around her the cottage was quiet. Smudge curled up in the basket under the kitchen table. And when everything was prepared, Annie sat in the dark, and prepared herself.

Dev.

The thought of seeing him again in only a couple of hours made her stomach heave. Hot, sour vomit raced up her throat and splattered the kitchen sink. She leaned shakily against the draining board until the nausea subsided.

The woody aftershave. The unyielding palm over her mouth. The pain. The fear.

She splashed water over her face, realised her teeth were chattering.

The canvas portrait of her and Izzy stared down from the wall. Their identical curls entwined so you couldn't tell where one of them began and the other ended.

Shared DNA didn't make successful families. Shared love, values, experiences did. These were what really counted.

Izzy was the person she was in spite of her DNA, not because of it.

She dialled Izzy's number. She picked up straightaway.

'Hi, Mum,' she said cheerily. Music played in the background.

'Are you having fun?' Annie said and all she could think was *If my plan doesn't work tonight, this is the last time we will ever speak to each other.*

She dug her fingernails into the soft skin of her forearm, leaving little crescent-shaped marks.

Do. Not. Cry.

'Yeah, really good,' Izzy said, oblivious. 'We had pizza for tea and now we're just watching Netflix.'

'Okay, well, have a good night. Love you. See you in the morning.'

I hope. I hope. I hope.

'Love you too, Mum.'

Annie held the phone to her heart and blinked away tears. That was one fear she could put aside: Izzy was an open book. If Dev had contacted her already, there was no way she could have hidden it.

When she stood up from the table, Smudge got up and stretched, her claws scratching the old quarry-tiled floor.

'Sorry,' Annie whispered, tickling her under the chin. 'You can't come where I'm going.'

Now, Friday

Annie drove in the slow lane, keeping the speedometer needle fixed on sixty-five miles. Before she left home, she had checked her brakes and headlights. Because being stopped by the police with fifty thousand pounds in used bank notes on the back seat would throw a whole toolbox of spanners in the works.

The normally hectic stretch of road was peaceful at 11.35pm on a Friday and the slip road was entirely deserted.

Moonlight illuminated the road out to the reservoir. There was nothing up here, save the occasional sheep as the car climbed higher up the windy road. From this high point, the city stretched out in a network of streetlights. It looked so small. So far away.

As she neared the place where the road disintegrated into a stony sheep track, Annie cut the headlights. She needed to cover the final mile or so on foot.

She put the rucksack on her back and set off. It wasn't long before sweat slicked down her back and dampness spread out from under her arms. The thick hoodie and gloves were winter clothes and the spring night was warm. She paused to pick a sweaty strand of hair from her forehead.

Which way now?

The water was a huge teardrop set in the side of the hill, gleaming like mercury in the silvery light.

The old pump station stood dark against the water. A car pulled up on the bridge that was the easiest access to the place. She watched a figure get out. Her heartbeat quickened. From this distance, she couldn't make out his features, and in the dark it was hard to be certain. But there was something about that swaggering roll, something years in prison hadn't managed to eradicate.

'Come on then,' he shouted into the darkness.

The voice was unmistakable. A distant sea rushed through her ears.

Now or never.

She walked down the slope towards him.

'There you are,' he said, conversationally. 'I was worried you wouldn't come.'

Close up, he wasn't the same man he had been all those years before. The weightlifter's bulk diminished after years in a prison cell with no access to steroids. His hair had thinned too. And he seemed smaller, more stooped.

'Is it in there?' he said, nodding at the rucksack.

She nodded and hugged it tight to her chest. She didn't speak.

'Well, pass it over,' he said, impatiently. 'I've been waiting a long time for this.'

'How do I know that will be the end of it?' she said. 'I mean, how do I know you won't come back again and ask for more next week or the week after or the week after?'

He laughed. 'You don't. Give it here.'

She stepped back suddenly up the slope, holding the rucksack tightly.

'No. Promise me you'll leave her alone. No matter what you think of me, you can't want her to suffer.'

'Doesn't bother me,' he said.

'But she's your daughter,' Annie continued, retreating up the slope. 'You can't want to destroy her.'

'I only ever had Lauren's word for that. Anyway,' he said, 'just give me the fucking money. I didn't come here for a chat.'

But she retreated further up the hill. 'Wait, I'll get it out.'

She tipped the plastic-wrapped bundles on the ground and threw them one by one in his direction.

He opened the top one and flicked through the notes. His expression turned to disgust.

'What the fuck is this?'

He snatched up the second bundle, tore through the plastic with his clawed fingers. Checked through the notes. Same for a third.

After she had got in from work, Annie had covered the kitchen table with the cash she received from the pawnbroker, two notes on each pile. Then she cut a whole packet of photocopying paper to the rough dimensions of a bank note and sandwiched stacks of them between the real notes before wrapping them in old carrier bags and Sellotape.

'Where did you think I was going to get that sort of money from?' she said. 'I'm a vet nurse.'

'You dragged me all the way out here for a few hundred quid?'

He came towards her, his face contorted with rage. Her mind and body went back to that night in her flat. His hand over her mouth. The fear when he undid his belt. The pain when he hit her.

She scrabbled to get away, but it was too late. He was on her. He pulled her down to the ground.

'I'm going to make you regret that,' he said, kicking her knee. Stars burst behind her eyelids. 'And whatever I do to you …' He grabbed hold of her hair and yanked it. She felt as though her scalp was ripping from her head, she could hear individual strands of hair ripping like Velcro from her scalp. Her face grazed against a rock, jolting her teeth.

'You ruined my life, you fucking bitch. You stole my family

from me, took my girls away. Framed me for something I didn't do. Ray told me what you did, taking the girl. But I'll make sure she knows what a lying, stealing bitch you are. I'll make sure she knows who her slut of a mother was too.'

The pain was excruciating. Black dots swarmed at the edge of her consciousness.

She scrabbled away, but not quickly enough. He grabbed her ankle, dragging her back down to the floor. She banged her head and for a second, her head swam. He straddled her body, his body so heavy it crushed her lungs. He put his hands around her throat.

'I should have done this the first time,' he said, tightening his grip. The pressure on her windpipe made her eyes bulge. Everything went red then grainy like the snow on an old untuned TV.

Wait. Wait.

Now.

With the last of her strength, she pulled her hand out of her pocket, complete with the syringe she had taken from the surgery. She had combined two of the pre-filled syringes with enough of the mixture to fell a stable yard. She plunged it into the hard muscle of his thigh and pressed the plunger down.

Dev yelled in pain, immediately loosening his grip on Annie's neck.

'What the fuck was that?' he shouted, twisting and grabbing hold of his thigh.

Annie tried to wriggle away, but he had her pinioned.

'You bitch,' he said, and his voice came out in a high-pitched yelp. 'What was that?'

He reached his hands back around her throat and began to rhythmically pound her head against the ground. Her teeth banged against each other, her head rattled. His body held her fast now. Everything went grey.

This is it. I'm sorry, Izzy. I only wanted to protect you.

But then Dev slumped back on his haunches. Air rushed into Annie's lungs and she gasped. He stumbled to his feet, swaying.

'What have you ...' but the words were slurred. He staggered a few steps then fell to his knees.

He pitched face forward.

Annie lay gasping for breath for a minute or so. Dev didn't move.

He had landed awkwardly, almost comically. Bent forward with his forehead to the ground.

She planted her foot squarely on his backside and nudged. He fell over. His breath was shallow now. He let out a long, rattling gasp and then there was nothing. It began to rain and the water refreshed her and also stung on the scrapes on her face. She peeled off her gloves. Underneath she wore surgical gloves from work. She touched his cornea. No response.

Don't think. Just act.

For the next ten minutes, her mind retreated while her body worked on autopilot. She breathed out, then got to work.

Dragging his body to the pump station was difficult. Although he was thinner than she remembered, he was still heavy and as the rain fell, it mingled with her sweat.

She took the notes from the rucksack and put them in her pockets, ready to give back to the pawnbroker to retrieve Mum's jewellery She tucked the bags and paper inside the front of her coat. Then she stuffed as many rocks as she could inside the rucksack. It took a while to strap it to his chest and even longer to pull him to the side of the bridge. Then she took a marker pen from her inner pocket and wrote the word GRASS across his forehead.

'That's for Sylvia and Lindon,' she said and, putting her foot in the small of his back, shoved him over the side.

She sat heavily on the ground. The rain fell steadily, shifting up a gear from steady to deluge. It ran down her face in rivulets, running in cold streams down her neck. Her teeth chattered either from the cold or from the shock. Or both.

The car. Somewhere, someone woke up this morning to find

their car missing. She crawled over, checked the number plate carefully. Two number plates, one screwed over the other. No way Dev would have come here in his own car. Joyriders, that's what the police would think.

And as she sat there, trying to get her breath, a message alert beeped in the darkness.

She took out her phone, aware she was shaking. Stared. Blinked. Put her hand over her mouth to stifle the hysteria welling up inside her.

Hello Annabel, the message said. *After our telephone conversation, I have decided that I should return my share of the proceeds of the sale of our house to you. If you could send me your bank details, I will arrange for my accountant to deposit fifty thousand pounds with you as soon as possible. I hope this will enable you to move on with your life.*

Regards, Oliver.

Three months later

Annie draws Izzy into an enormous hug. With the weight of the rucksack on her back, she almost topples over.

'Have you …' Annie starts. It's on the tip of her tongue to check again that Izzy has her phone, her purse, her passport, but she swallows it down. 'Caro will be here in a minute,' she says.

The summer sunshine dusts the cluttered workshops with gold. Outside, Smudge gives a single commanding bark and Annie opens the door to let her in. It's a beautiful day. She lifts her face up to the cloudless blue sky and lets the warmth caress her skin.

A car approaches. 'They're here!' Izzy says, rushing to the front door, almost toppling over again.

Annie goes to bolt the back door. She checks herself and leaves it open, so the smell of warm grass floats in.

The gate creaks as Caro and Lucy approach the house.

'Bring me something lovely back from Paris,' Annie says, tugging Izzy's rucksack straps so she can give her a kiss. 'You know, I haven't been there for years. Maybe we could go together, now you've got your passport. Or maybe we could go somewhere else.'

'Yeah, I'd love that – Luce!'

The two girls embrace awkwardly around the bags. The delight on their faces makes Annie, and Caro who is behind Lucy, smile.

'I've told her she has to phone every day,' Caro says. 'And to do exactly what the teachers tell you to. No messing about. No wandering off.'

Lucy rolls her eyes and Annie suppresses a smile.

'I love you, Mum,' Izzy says and squeezes Annie as tightly as the bag will allow. 'Look after Smudge for me.'

'Will do,' Annie replies. 'And I love you too. Enjoy yourself.'

'I'm going to miss her,' Caro says with a sigh as the girls go to the car. 'I hope they'll be okay.' She packs Smudge in the car because she's going to look after her for the weekend. Poor Smudge is still not well enough for the long journey.

'They're very sensible girls,' Annie says. 'I know they'll be fine.'

And then the Range Rover is gone.

As she goes back inside, Annie prods her consciousness, looking for the panic she feels when Izzy is away from her. It stirs a little, lifts its head and then curls back into a sleepy ball. Even the tremor of panic over the passport passes quickly. It's a genuine passport, issued by the passport office without a single qualm or question. Another document to prove that Isabel Smith is Isabel Smith. Paid for, like the Paris trip and the remainder of their mortgage, by the money Oliver deposited in her account.

And as for Dev? Those nightmarish last few moments stalk her dreams, she can't deny it. She wakes sometimes, sweating and tangled in the duvet. Nightmares where he is once again pinning her to the ground. Making her powerless. Thriving on the fear. Although sometimes a man rises out of the water in her dreams, she knows there is nothing to worry about.

She keeps an eye on the local news, but the abandoned car has never been mentioned. But she knows when they find his body, and it is inevitable that will happen, she will just need to hold her nerve. Ride the storm.

No, there is nothing to connect this quiet middle-aged woman with a violent prisoner like Elliott Devlin. Dev has spent his life

265

accruing enemies, and even if he is found she is sure the finger will never be pointed at her. There is no one to point that finger, no one to link the two of them.

The last connection between Lauren and Izzy is gone. But, sometimes Annie sees flashes of Dev and Lauren when she sees Izzy in a certain light. Or a certain facial expression. And then a cold chill consumes her and she has to remind herself that even though she has killed, she has killed to protect Izzy. And nothing matters more than keeping her safe.

'Safe,' she says it out loud as she heads upstairs. 'We are safe.'

Annie picks up her new pyjamas and shakes them out. Cream silk with a hummingbird motif. Expensive, but so beautiful. She folds them carefully into the almost full suitcase. She gets her washbag from the bathroom and puts it in the elasticated pocket at the side. What else? She mentally ticks the list as she carefully looks through the case. Clothes for dinner. Clothes for walking. Boots. An anorak because, although the weather forecast promises a fine week, the Lake District is notoriously unpredictable. Liam is in charge of the dog food, so all she needs to pack for Smudge is a blanket for the car. Since she exorcised the demons of her past, things have been going well with Liam. *Very* well.

She zips the suitcase then opens her jewellery box. The earrings that belonged to her mum twinkle in the light as she slides them in, pulling a strand of hair that gets caught in the butterfly fastening.

There is a muffled beep. Somewhere, under the pile of clothes, her phone is buried. She rummages through. It's probably Izzy, telling her she loves her. Or maybe Liam, reminding her to pack something or other.

It's not.

The number on the screen belongs to a dead man.

Hello Annabel, the message says.

She moans and drops the phone as though it has scalded her fingers.

How—?

A car pulls up outside. She looks out. A white hatchback is parked in the lane.

A moment later the doorbell rings. She looks on the app on her phone. Standing on her doorstep is a man with a shaved head. His nose is flattened, off to one side like it's been broken a few times. There is no warmth in the smile that shows yellowed teeth, blackened around the margins. A few more wrinkles, but he hasn't changed much since the last time she saw him, outside the pawnbrokers on the day after Lauren's death.

Missing pieces of the puzzle drop rapidly into place. How Dev knew where she lived. How he knew her name. How he knew where his daughter was. *Who* his daughter was.

Her mind works quickly, sending her into the lounge where she lifts the picture of her parents up and feels around. Her fingertips close on a syringe. The backup she prepared for Dev in case of breakages. She slides it inside her sleeve, behind the scrunchie around her wrist.

She opens the door.

'Hello, Annabel.'

'Ray,' she says, surprised at the steadiness of her voice.

His tone is friendly, but his eyes are as sharp as steel. They bore into her head, reading her mind.

'I'm looking for Dev,' Ray explains. 'Maybe you can tell me where he is.'

He's holding a mobile in one hand, the most basic kind, not a smartphone. Car keys dangle from the other. The car behind him is a large hatchback. From the outside, it looks as though the boot must be quite spacious.

'You tell me. You've just texted me on his number.'

'This number?' He holds it up. 'Oh, this isn't his phone, it's mine. Not my usual one, obviously. A special one just for you.'

'You sent the messages?' she says slowly, her mind racing. 'The photos?'

He nods, looks pleased with himself.

'What do you want?' she says.

She can tell from the way he looks at her that he considers her weak. The way she used to be. He doesn't know that she is a different person now. But she will use it to her advantage. She draws her shoulders in, rounding her posture, allows a little fear to creep into her eyes.

'Well' – he uses a fingernail to pick between his teeth. His knuckles look a little swollen. Arthritis, maybe? – 'Dev owes me money. Favours I did for him while he was in prison. And when I tell him he needs to pay it back, he says he can get it, but he needs to find Annie who used to live next door to Lauren. Only problem is, he doesn't know where she is. And I tell him I can help him with that. So, I visit my brother and do a bit of Sherlock Holmes, you know. Had your address so finding out your workplace and your phone number and that. And then I drop you a quick text.'

A flash of memory. She sees herself back in London, the day after Lauren's death. Sliding a copy of her driving licence under the glass partition in the pawnshop.

In three hours, Liam is going to pull up outside her house. Liam the policeman. And here is this man who is clearly not from around here. And who knows everything about who she was, who she is and what she's done.

'So, the last time I spoke to Dev, he was on his way here to get my money for me. But the funny thing is,' Ray continues, 'no one has seen him since. He never came back.'

He pauses, examining whatever he has just dislodged from between his teeth.

'Well, he's obviously taken the money and done a runner,' she says. 'He's probably in Spain right now.'

He laughs, and the car keys jangle in his hand. Her mind's eye moves further up the lane, the disused barn filled with rusted farm equipment and old tarpaulins. There is space in the barn for a white hatchback. And there is space in the white hatchback for a man.

'Nah. I took insurance out against that happening. He knows if he tried anything like that, his girls would have to pay. Jess and the little one. Not so little now, though, is she? Same age as your girl, right?'

Out of sight, Izzy travels along country roads to school, excited for her trip to Paris. Liam packs his case for their trip to the Lakes. Fish nibble at Dev, down in the silt at the bottom of the reservoir.

'I mean, he hasn't seen them in years, but he still cares.' Ray continues. 'He's not a complete bastard.'

She looks at the man on her doorstep. She sees him for what he is: a nasty thug threatening her family. He's lost a lot of weight. He looks diminished. Weak.

'So, Annabel, you going to tell me where my money is?' he says.

The syringe presses behind the scrunchie on her wrist, hidden by the long sleeves.

'Come in, Ray,' she says.

Dear Reader,

Firstly, thank you so much for reading *My Lovely Daughter*. If you're anything like me, I'm sure you have a million books calling to you so I am so grateful you chose to spend your time with mine. And if you've found your way here because you read *The Perfect House* first, then I'm so happy to see you again.

We've all heard people say, 'I'd do anything to protect my child' and that's the idea at the heart of the *My Lovely Daughter*: how far would a mother really be prepared to go? I've always been fascinated by characters who inhabit the hazy space between right and wrong. Characters like Annie, who believes that if the end secures Izzy's happiness, then all means – lies, kidnap, murder – are justified. But how far is too far? Is Annie more selfish than selfless? Does Izzy deserve to know the truth, no matter how painful?

If you've enjoyed reading *My Lovely Daughter* or *The Perfect House* it would be amazing if you could post a review. Writing a book is a solitary pursuit involving many hours hunched over a keyboard. Reading lovely reviews makes all that hard work worth it! I'd love to hear what you think. I'm @rachinthefax over on Twitter talking rescue dogs, environmental issues and books, or on rpbolton.com.

Hope to see you again soon.

Love,
R.P. Bolton x

Acknowledgements

Writing a book is a team effort and I'd like to say a huge 'thank you!' to my agent, Anne Clark, and to Cat Camacho, Abi Fenton, Sarah Goodey, Eldes Tran and everyone at HQ Digital for their invaluable insight and support.

Thank you to the tireless, fantastic, dedicated Team Paws at www.paws2rescue.com. This amazing charity helps those in need, both two and four-legged, and found me the perfect writing companions in Minnie and Lola. Thank you to the staff and students at MMU, particularly Andrew Hurley and the MA Folks. Lots of love as always to Amanda P., Christina K., Eddie K. and to DSRF for patiently answering endless questions. And not forgetting Tim and Christian: you two are the best.

Dear Reader,

We hope you enjoyed reading this book. If you did, we'd be so appreciative if you left a review. It really helps us and the author to bring more books like this to you.

Here at HQ Digital we are dedicated to publishing fiction that will keep you turning the pages into the early hours. Don't want to miss a thing? To find out more about our books, promotions, discover exclusive content and enter competitions you can keep in touch in the following ways:

JOIN OUR COMMUNITY:

Sign up to our new email newsletter:
http://smarturl.it/SignUpHQ

Read our new blog www.hqstories.co.uk

🐦 https://twitter.com/HQStories

f www.facebook.com/HQStories

BUDDING WRITER?

We're also looking for authors to join the HQ Digital family!
Find out more here:

https://www.hqstories.co.uk/want-to-write-for-us/

Thanks for reading, from the HQ Digital team

LM

Praise for the author

'Gripping, well written and genuinely creepy' Cass
Green, *Sunday Times* bestselling author

'*The Perfect House* is a nail-biting deep dive of paranoia and
tension that had me rushing to turn the page! A chilling,
nerve-racking debut that will leave your heart racing! This
novel latches on and refuses to let go' Karin Nordin,
author of *Last One Alive*

'Wow. All the wows . . . I couldn't believe my eyes when I was
reading this book. It's a good novel and I think everyone must
read it. It has larger-than-life characters, wow narration and of
course a terrifying ending' NetGalley reviewer, ★★★★★

'A stunning thrill ride of a novel! Left me speechless and
thinking about it long after I'd finished it. A must read!'
NetGalley reviewer, ★★★★★

'Increasingly tense and creepy' NetGalley reviewer, ★★★★★

'There's a sense of unease that grows as the plot progresses that
is magically done and like nothing I've read before! A fantastic
thriller with intriguing characters, I read it in one sitting. A
must read!' NetGalley reviewer, ★★★★★

'A thrilling story that keeps you reading until you reach the
shocking ending' NetGalley reviewer, ★★★★

'A gripping story that I couldn't put down'
NetGalley reviewer, ★★★★

R.P. BOLTON lives in Manchester with her partner, son and three lively rescue dogs. When she's not reading, writing or walking the dogs, she'll be at the gym, at a concert or indulging in her passion for nature. *The Perfect House* was her debut thriller and published in 2021 and *My Lovely Daughter* is her second novel.

Also by R.P. Bolton

The Perfect House